ANCIENT ARROWHEAD

Jason Hancock

PublishAmerica
Baltimore

Hardcover 978-1-4626-1357-1
Softcover 978-1-4626-1356-4
PUBLISHED BY PUBLISHAMERICA, LLLP
www.publishamerica.com
Baltimore

Printed in the United States of America

This story is dedicated to Amanda, my daughter, for she is the reason for my clarity and focus in my resurrection. May you find the love and happiness that you seek and deserve. Love you always.

—Dad

A very special thanks to Bonnie Donovan for taking the time, at very short notice, to photograph the author picture contained in this book. I am grateful evermore for your kindness and charitable contribution to this work.

CONTENTS

ANCIENT ARROWHEAD

CHAPTER ONE

Jasper and the arrowhead

"Thomas! Thomaaaaaas!" called a distant voice.

The boy heard his mother calling him for dinner of course, but his pup Jasper was sniffing out treasure. Well, not exactly treasure. Not exactly a pup either.

Jasper was a little over ten months old now and he was nothing short of enormous, for a dog his age anyway. In fact, most dogs wouldn't get this big in their lifetime. You see Jasper wasn't ordinary. Thomas knew it the day he found Jasper over ten months ago.

It was an overcast day late in September and Indian summer had come to visit. Ninety-eight degrees is hot, even for June or July, but on the eve of October it was strangely peculiar. Especially since the sun was hidden by cloud cover. Silver colored ones at that.

Not many people notice clouds anymore. They're so busy running through their monotonous daily checklists, that they forget to stop and smell the roses. To listen to the birds singing sweet melodies to each other or to lie in grass and gaze into the sky and cloud surf.

Automation has made us like the drones of a beehive. Seek out what's important to our self -preservation and ambitiously collect needless possessions to lavish our own egos.

Anyway, these silver colored clouds were collecting themselves together over this small town in Massachusetts.

BUT, not all people kept their eyes forward in civilized servitude. Not Jonas Lightbringer. He had been around long enough to know when something extraordinary was about to happen.

TWWWWWWack!!

A crack of blue arch appeared in the sky. There was an incessant buzzing sound like that of a hive. Then as soon as it began, it stopped. The normal chattering of birds and animals was missing from the ambience. The world had fallen into a deafening silence.

It sent shivers down Thomas' spine. He was swinging out on the rope swing at Mossy Pond. Before he decided to let go and cannonball into the water he swung back in. The need to show off in front of his best girl seemed less urgent than his want to avoid being electrocuted.

Suddenly a streak of blue lightning fire broke from the sky and struck ground, down by Old Copper Dam.

"Mary did you she that?" Thomas asked.

"Yeah." Was about all she could manage to squeeze through her awestruck lips.

He took her by the hand and together they ran to the top of the hill overlooking Old Copper Dam. As they were about to reach the summit they could see a dome of white light, where the bolt of lightning had touched down. Then it disappeared. The air around the pair of young loves seemed somehow electric. The hair on Thomas' arms stood up, and his skin tickled with delight.

Thomas began to run toward the dam and noticed Mary was no longer running along side him. He turned back to see what was holding her up.

"I'm afraid Tom." Mary said worriedly. She alone called him

Tom. He liked that. He liked it even more when she called him Tommy. When she did, he would get all giddy and blush.

"Aw'com'on Mary, it'll be okay." Thomas insisted.

He took her hand in his and they both cautiously approached the dam, inching their way down the other side of the hill.

Before they got there Mary said "Look Tom" pointing at where they had seen the white light.

There before the dam, was a crater. The circumference of the bowl was about twelve feet and it was deeper than a tall man. The lightning bolt had thrown dirt and rock for several feet. Some of it landed some distance up the hill and some of the soil material was thrown into the dark murky water adjacent to the hole.

Thomas approached and now noticed the blast created a crater at least eight feet deep. It looked as though a large artillery shell had cleared the earth and created a hole for the imposing force to take shelter in. A common strategy for troops in World War I. Troops had a theory that a shell would never land in the same place twice. The reason for this was due to wind change, the heat of the barrel expanding with every launched mortar round and possibly a slight difference in weight to each round. There are probably several other factors but I'm not an expert on munitions, so I would only be speculating if I continued.

Upon reaching the crater, they heard whimpering, like that of a puppy.

Thomas and Mary ran to the crater to see a small puppy staring up at them, very small indeed. As small as a newborn kitten. Smoke was rising all about the puppy from the lightning strike.

"How ya' suppose he got down there?" Asked Mary. "He should have been burned alive." She added.

But Thomas didn't hear her. His attention and mind were closed to everything peripheral to the senses.

"Hi little one. I'm going to call you Jasper." Thomas whispered to himself.

He picked up the pup and it was shaking like little puppies do at birth. The little thing peed on Thomas. Thomas just laughed.

"You can't possibly keep him." Mary proclaimed.

"Why not." Replied Thomas.

"What if someone lost him?" She asked.

"Who would have lost him down here Mary?" Thomas fired back.

"Your parents will never let you keep him." She said confidently.

"We'll keep him hidden then." Thomas said.

"Where?" Asked Mary.

"I don't know, in the attic maybe. I'll think of something." Thomas said joyfully.

She saw the look in his eyes. The look a child gets when he tastes his favorite ice cream. She loved that look. She loved him. Her mother though, did not.

Her mother, Brenda, had forgotten innocence and laughter. She had forgotten what it was like to run through the hay fields to evade her boyfriend and his adolescent yearnings. She would be giggling, he would be telling jokes and tickling her on the inside of her thighs. The kind of tickling that turns all girls to jelly.

Parents often forget the inner child that walked the miles to get to who they are now. It's a shame really.

So Mary, Thomas and his new- found gift went scurrying on home. Thomas' mind was working overtime, like a steam engine beginning a steep incline over a long ravine. He was trying to formulate a scheme in which he could disguise and conceal his newest member of the family. He wasn't the type of person to mislead his parents, but what would they have him do, leave the shivering puppy and abandon it to its peril. I think not. Even so, it would take some cunning and clever negotiation if his parent's were going to let him keep the dog. He would contemplate these matters later. For now he would be content just to know he had done the right thing. They would understand. Wouldn't they?

If they hadn't been so transfixed on the puppy and the unusual circumstances to which it had been found, they might have seen a man standing watch over them. The man was on the opposing side of the bank to which the dam was connected. He observed this occurrence with great interest.

Then after the youngster's had jaunted off with their new discovery, the man looked up into the heavens with a wry smile.

"What have got for me this time Lord?" He questioned irreverently.

That night while Thomas was about his task of getting the puppy settled in, he went about some undercover recon work. Thomas put Jasper into an old open shoebox. He removed the Chex-Mix from his shirt pocket that he had smuggled from the newly renovated pantry and placed it in a small clean glass ashtray. He put it in the shoebox and the puppy crunched away at the sustenance joyfully. He then placed the milk cap he'd taken from the recycle bin in the box as well and filled it with cream. He was happy and so was the famished puppy.

Then after the puppy had had his fill, Thomas removed the cap and ashtray from the small sleeping quarters he had created for Jasper. He placed them on the nightstand at the head of his bed and then the exhausted young man climbed into bed.

He covered half of the box with shavings left over from his recently deceased hamster, Moe. Thomas had a hell of a time convincing his folks to allow him to keep a hamster, or rodent according to his father. Although, after some time his parent's came to appreciate his responsible concern and caring for his pet. He wondered how they would react to his new project.

He pulled the sheets and blankets up so they covered him and the box. He whispered good night to Jasper. Jasper looked up at him in newfound admiration and his wild eyes gleamed with love.

Thomas smiled.

He slept.

He dreamt.

Thomas was walking with Jasper. Jasper was still only tiny, but he walked without stumbling, like newborn puppies often do. They were walking down a dirt road, which Thomas was not familiar. Suddenly there were flies swarming all about him. They were flying toward him smacking him in the face, getting into his hair, ears and nose. They were becoming a real nuisance. They were everywhere, and Thomas began to panic. They were overwhelming him. Jasper was powerless to help his master. He chomped at the flies and ate the ones he could reach but there were too many of the pests. Jasper whined with worry. Fruitlessly Thomas kept swatting at them and still more came. Then when he thought they would overtake him, they fell dead from the air.

There are so many he thought.

He began walking again and he could hear crunching and squishing beneath his bare feet. He lifted up his left foot to see mashed flies stuck to it. It looked like thick, chunky raspberry jelly, raspberry jelly that had taken a turn for the worst.

While he was looking down he noticed the shoes of someone standing in front of him. The person was very close to him.

Fear set in.

Jasper though still a puppy, began growling. Louder and louder he growled, like a locomotive coming toward you on the tracks. He was barking now. Thomas turned his attention away from Jasper and back to the stranger.

Thomas looked up slowly inching his way up the person's frame, afraid of what he might see.

First he saw the boots, which were black as midnight. Then to the individual's jeans and they too were pitch black. Then came a red shirt and tie that were so dark they were almost black, like the color of blood. Thomas was certain the figure was that of a man. The person's frame and posture was too erect and arrogant to be that of a woman. Still, there was something not manly about this form.

He then met those eyes. Blazing with a light hue of green, so light, as to be mistaken for yellow. The man's hair was pulled back with thick grease. His discarnate smile pierced Thomas' soul.

Thomas was paralyzed with fright.

Thomas noticed they were standing at two intersecting streets. On what was supposed to be a stop sign, was a wooden heart.

"Well son, you're at the crossroads. You're not gonna' cause a row now are you." The figure in black said in a shrill voice, nearly a laugh.

Thomas. Thomas. He heard a distant voice calling to him.

Jasper crouched as if to strike the well-dressed stranger.

"Thomas. Thomas! Wake up." He heard his mother call.

His mother pulled back the blankets and he jumped up with a start.

She looked down and saw the puppy.

"What's this Thomas Joseph?" Thomas' mother asked in that disapproving tone.

And she used his middle name too. She often did this when she was on stage three of anger or disappointment. But she jumped right over stage two. This is the stage where he puts on his sad frown and brown puppy dog eyes and she usually let's up. But what was he to do now that she crossed that place where you can stop someone from engaging in a bad fight.

"You know you can't keep him." She said, reaching for the dog.

"Noooooooooooooooooooooooo!" Thomas yelled.

Then he did it.

He slapped her hand away.

Thwack!

The look on her face of shock gave way to disgust and finally to tears. She ran from the room sobbing. She rushed out into the hall and into the bathroom, which was the next room from Thomas,' and bolted through the doorway. She slammed the bathroom door with a stout violence behind her. She began to cry heartily. She was starting to become infuriated. That little…

Now he had done it he thought. He had never talked back. Never had a cross word with her, he never even cursed aloud to friends or peers. Now he had gone and slapped his mother hard on the hand.

From downstairs he heard his father cursing himself. Up the stairs he came. He cautiously approached the bathroom. He knew to be wary around a crouching tiger. Women were like that when they were emotionally wounded. They were much like a cobra ready to strike anyone who came into their zone, even if that person was not responsible for the injury. Just a defense mechanism, that's all, and an effective one at that.

"Laura honey. What's wrong?" He asked tenderly as he got to the bathroom door.

She was startled, because she thought he was off to work.

"Why aren't you off to work?" She sobbed.

"Well I came back to get my wallet for the lunch truck and I heard the door slam." He explained.

She tried to stop sobbing.

"Are you okay?" He questioned.

He didn't like when she cried. It made him sad and angry. He would put an end to the person who made her this way, but he had to tread lightly just in case it was…

"Yes." She said. "Just having a 'female moment'." She went on.

Thomas, who was peeking out, could hear this standing and listening next to his bedroom door. His room was directly adjacent to the bathroom. She didn't tell him, he thought. He was relieved and then mad at himself. Tears started falling from his face. He ran to his bed and buried his head in his pillow, so no one would hear him cry. He was fourteen now, he wasn't supposed to cry.

He heard his father in the distance.

"Okay honey. I'll leave you be." He said.

His father knew better than to pry into the 'female moment'. This is why he treaded lightly before he blew his top. He couldn't rightly get mad only to find out it was her he was directing his contempt. He had rattled that cage before. You don't want to see a woman turn into a badger. It's like a tornado inside a china shop. Messy. And boy it's hell to recover from.

After he had pried into the 'female moment' he couldn't get near her for a month. She slept on the couch for two weeks. And he had to fix his own meals, until she saw he was eating cereal three times a day.

Men quickly forget how to take care of themselves, after having been spoiled so long by their spouses. They don't want to go back to caring for themselves and purposely fail to recall anything they use to know how to do before meeting their partner's. It's the wives who clean up their husband's. Before that a man cared not for his un-kept hair, crusties in the eyes or his foul body odor. What are these things until a woman points them out? Mere technicalities and not important, until a woman cares for you, then you realize how significant these things really are. A woman can take Darwin's Theory of Evolution and prove it overnight. She can take what use to be her caveman boyfriend, and turn him into an upright citizen very quickly. It's what they do. You know what I mean. That hairy, unclean, salamander of a man that ate last night's pizza for breakfast and brushed his teeth with warm beer. The man you used to see staring back at you in the mirror. Yeah that one.

Thomas' father knew if he wanted any more nights in satin, he had better get, while getting was good. He made off to work with a heavy burden. He hoped that by some miracle when he got home that the 'female moment' had set sail for a foreign port.

When the downstairs door had closed behind his father, the bathroom door flew open.

Thomas' mother ran to his bedroom, for she was boiling with anger. She wanted to inflict the same pain and anguish on him. Then she was upon him. But... she stopped. She saw him balling his little head off and she melted. She always did when he cried, and he was really going on now.

She sat down on the bed and he flew into her arms. He was crying to the point of hyperventilating.

"Okay calm down." It's okay." She reassured him.

"I'm so- so- so- so- sor- sor- rrr- rr- y." he managed to squeeze out in spurts.

Now, Jasper peeked out from his hiding spot.

His features were somewhere between a Wolf and a German Shepard. He had a solid white body with blue eyes. His coat was as white as the driven snow. His eyes were the kind of blue the sky is, when spring kisses winter goodbye.

He let out a yip. Then both ears turned up and he tilted his head sideways. He let out a small whine as if to say sorry for the trouble I've caused you but I had nowhere else to go.

Animals can often sense the tone of human situations and conditions.

"Well he is adorable." His mother finally said.

Jasper yipped his approval.

Thomas broke from her embrace and slowly peered up through his glossy eyes. Now he had turned the tables and gone right to stage four. She was helpless to say no.

" You're going to have to get a paper route or something. We're in a pinch as it is." She said. "You're father…" She broke off.

"Will he let me keep him momma?" Thomas pleaded He called her momma when he was scared. She knew this and she coddled him.

"I'll talk to him." She assured him.

"Can you convince him?" Thomas asked.

A smile broke across his mother's face ear to ear.

"Every woman can convince her man." She said confidently.

Then he smiled. Everything was going to be okay. It's funny how much better you feel after you come back from disaster to find out everything will be all right.

That night, his father smiled most.

Everyday, Thomas would wake up happier than the day before.

He would run home from school with Mary and find that Jasper had torn up an old sneaker, or had gotten into a newspaper or book and destroyed them. He didn't care though; it just made him laugh and wonder what Jasper might do next.

Everyday Jasper got bigger. It seemed to Thomas that the more his affection for the dog grew, so did Jasper. He wasn't the only one to notice either. More than once he was trampled under his father's feet.

"Who ever would have thought a runt would turn into such a beast of a dog." He'd say.

And so things were good.

So after explaining the discovery of Jasper, we find ourselves in the woods across from where the cemetery meets Four Ponds, over ten months later. Between the cemetery and the ponds there is a meadow half the size of a soccer field. On the one side nearest the cemetery is a long rock wall and running perpendicular to the wall is an old wooden fence.

A Polish farmer and his sons had pulled the stones out of the ground and placed them along the cemetery boundary marking the end of their land. This is the only area remaining of the once large farm acreage. The reason for this is a sad story. The farmer had several children and his favorite was the oldest of a set of twins. The reason for this was that this son reminded him most of himself. He was a hard worker. He was unyielding in his beliefs and conviction, even if those were not very popular. He cared not for being popular, as did his siblings. What he cared about was being righteous. His mother adored him for it. One day though, his mother died. Everything began to change. His father met a wicked self absorbed and deeply materialistic woman. She would grow into a cancer in the very spirit of the polish farmer. He married her despite the disapproval of his children. One day the farmer died. He hadn't made a new will before he did so. This treacherous woman now seized the property that was supposed to be transferred to the oldest twin. She removed all the children from the property and remarried. Then she sold the farm in sections to the highest bidder. A sad but all too true story of complication, oversight and bitter betrayal in a small town.

All these years later Thomas and Jasper were hunting for treasure here. Jasper sniffed all around a wooden fence post, like he was about to uncover some bounty. He located something and began a wild yap.

"Ruff! Ruff! Ruff!" Jasper barked.

Jasper was really good at sniffing things out, and he was really in a raucous now. Thomas believed he had found something significant this time.

Jasper started digging. Tearing up dirt with his huge paws. Flying sod passed Thomas' head.

"Go get it boy." "Go get it." Thomas encouraged.

Now the hole was two feet deep. Then three. Then four. Jasper's back feet were still out of the hole on the ledge, but the rest of him was inside. Dark soil and stones were being easily tossed under his legs. Then abruptly he stopped. Jasper began barking frantically.

"Come on boy. Let me see what you've got." Thomas said.

Thomas climbed in after Jasper jumped out and began to probe the ground at his feet. He bent down when he felt something sticking out of the ground. He wiggled it back and forth, till he pried it loose. He looked at the item he had grasped in his hand and was a bit bewildered by it.

" It's an arrowhead, I think." Thomas said in wonder.

He put both hands on the ledge of the hole and boosted himself up. He was still looking at the article when he called out to his dog.

"Jasper." "Jasper?" "Where are you…?" Thomas asked then stopped abruptly after glancing up in search of the whereabouts of his dog.

Standing behind the mound of excavated earth that Jasper displaced, was a man holding a large stick. He was about twenty-five feet from Thomas at this point.

His hair was gray and un-kept, falling upon his back and shoulders. He had an equally un-kept beard, which was silverish-blue. And his clothes were not very familiar, at least to this day and age. Very peculiar he was, very curious indeed.

He wore what appeared to be some sort of overcoat with a hood and pockets. The original color of the coat was anyone's guess. The man, come to think of it, probably couldn't tell you either. It was a gift given to him long ago in the hills of North Dakota. We'll call it dirty yellow for the sake of argument and detail. Out of one of the breast pockets was the top of an old Bible. His brown Indian pants give way to dark work boots.

It was what was in his hand, now that Thomas recognized it was no stick, which caught his immediate attention. It frightened him, and not just a little.

Though not Jasper, Jasper sniffed up and down the man, wagging his tail.

Jasper didn't seem to sense any danger, and Jasper was a great judge of character. His love for his master was no less than Thomas' love for him. Nothing and I mean nothing, would bring the fight to Thomas while Jasper was on watch. Jasper didn't feel the fight coming to his master from this man and it showed.

In the man's hand was an eight -gauge double barrel shotgun.

"Whatcha' got there, young man?" Said the old stranger.

No one had ever called Thomas young man. He liked that. So he let up his guard a bit and approached the man cautiously.

"I think it's an arrowhead." Thomas replied.

"I think it's more than that. I think it's a means to an end." The man returned.

"What?" Thomas asked dumbfounded.

"I'm sorry let me introduce myself." He said.

As he said these words, Thomas could make out the man's teeth. Yellowish brown stains were on what teeth he had left. Thomas shuddered.

"My name is Jonas." The man said. "And YOU, must be Thomas." He went on in a matter of fact fashion.

Thomas hadn't told him his name. He shuddered again.

"How do you know my name?" Thomas asked tentatively.

"I'm in the business of knowing what is and what should never be." Laughed the man.

"And what business is that?" Asked Thomas.

"Your business. And soon enough, my business too." The man said solemnly, pausing between phrases.

Thomas didn't like where this conversation was headed.

He had a good head for things that were about to happen. That's why he was so good at cards and chess. He knew what his opponent was about to do before they did them. Someone once told me that a good chess player was five or more moves ahead of his opponent. The reality is that a great chess player is only one move ahead, this being the right one. And this he thought, was going to be something of a sort to which he did not like.

The man sensed Thomas' uneasiness and decided not to overwhelm him. Lord knows there would be plenty to do so in the future. Confounding Thomas with excessive nervousness at this point would be asinine.

"Remember son. A means to an end." He said.

And with that, the man was off. He placed the shotgun in the holster attached to his back and reached inside his overcoat. He withdrew a brown weathered pouch. From inside the pouch he broke off a black piece of what looked like condensed tea leaves. He placed it in his mouth and started to chew. He spit a large stream of black chaw from his lips and continued his crossing of the meadow.

Thomas watched him as he hopped the wooden fence and made his way down the hill out of sight.

Thomas looked down at the item in his hand and wondered if he had found a treasure or a curse.

"Thomas dammit! Dinnertime!" His father yelled.

It was far enough away but, he could tell by the tone of his father's voice, he meant now.

After dinner that night Thomas lay in bed turning the strange item over in his hands. It came to a rough edge as if it had been eroded down to a blunt tip. It must have been lying there for a long while. Thomas wondered how it had come to be where he found it. He speculated whether or not it had been buried or carried there by natural forces. It was shaped like a pine tree except it had no trunk. At the base of the arrowhead was a hole the size of a dime. It was as deep as half of the stone. That was something bizarre too. The stone. It was unlike any type of rock Thomas had ever encountered. It was a light red. When Thomas had cleaned the arrowhead off of dirt and grit he saw the color of the rock was not of any he had ever seen before. It looked like something you might find on Mars, the red planet.

It wasn't a small arrowhead either it was the size of a large index card. Thomas thought it was rather large for a weapon that a Native American might use and wondered about its intended purpose. Thomas got up from bed and put the unique arrowhead in an old tackle box on his bookshelf. It was a long while before he drifted off to sleep.

CHAPTER TWO

The Cemetery

Through the rest of the summer Thomas, Mary and Jasper were inseparable.

Jasper was very protective of Mary and it often showed. Like most dogs, Jasper was overly protective of woman and children. One day a certain member of the neighborhood boys found this out the hard way.

He had been riding along on his bike and saw Mary with her back turned, smelling the wild flowers in the front of her house. The boy, Johnny Waters, crept up behind Mary and pulled her hair.

"Mary, Mary your arms are hairy. Mary, Mary your arms are hairy." He sang.

She was so shocked by him coming up behind her and pulling her hair she let out a shriek.

"Johnny Waters you better quit it!" Mary screamed.

Jasper heard her alarm.

He and Thomas were coming up to Mary's the back way through the pricker patch because they were going to surprise her. Jasper sprang into action. He would thwart Mary's enemy by force.

Overcome.

Eliminate.

Destroy.

He burst through the pricker bushes, snapping twigs and branches alike. He came around the house full bore. He let out one loud bark and flew into action.

Johnny saw Jasper coming on and could only let out a gasp. Jasper crashed into the boys left knee as he tried to turn and run. The boy toppled up in the air and came crashing down on his back knocking the wind out of him. Jasper knew he had done enough damage. Nothing permanent but enough to warn the boy what would happen if he did it again. Jasper drew back and watched the boy roll around holding his chest. Then the wounded boy got to his feet dazedly and stumbled back to his bike. Jasper stood his ground, always keeping himself between Mary and the boy.

Johnny Water's was too shaken up to cry but not to pee himself.

"Serves you right Johnny Waters." Mary puffed.

Thomas came running up.

"Are you okay Mary?" Thomas asked concernedly.

"Yes, thanks to my hero." She said rubbing behind Jaspers ears.

This is a joy to all dogs and Jasper reveled in it as long as he could.

"Sometimes I think he is more protective of you than me." Thomas remarked.

"Good boy looking out for Mary. Good boy." Thomas rewarded.

They both watched Johnny walk off pushing his bike with one hand and trying with the other to conceal his soiled jeans.

Jasper felt justified in his approach to this situation for he loved Mary but he couldn't help but feel a little remorse for having hurt a youngster. If a dog can feel repentance, that is. Well of course they can. Why do you think they are mans best friend?

The three sometimes spent there free summer days in Goreman's field, chasing one another until they were exhausted.

Jasper was always the one with the most energy. Often he would knock them down and lick their faces, sending them into hysterics. Jasper would oftentimes trot through the stream that divided the field in two and when he chased them down they would get all soak and wet.

Other times they would go off swimming at the rope swing. Thomas would swing off the rope swing and Mary would throw sticks out for Jasper to retrieve. Jasper's head would stick out of water and he would do the doggy paddle all the way back to Mary. Jasper barked at Thomas every time he jumped from the rope, as if to say be careful you goofball.

On a few occasions Henry, Thomas' father, took them all fishing at the reservoir. Henry took a summer vacation every year from the cereal factory and decided to take them fishing when he was free of chores. Jasper wasn't supposed to be on State Recreation and Conservation Land, so they often went early before daybreak. Jasper liked the wide-open spaces to stretch his curiosity and quick legs. He would chase squirrels and chipmunks until they scattered under rocks or fallen limbs. The squirrels would sometimes taunt him from a tree limb. They would drop acorns or fruit down on him and squawk like squirrels do. Their tails would be vibrating in agitation and they would be speaking in their native tongue. The entire woods would be in frenzy.

Jasper liked when one of them would land a fish. He would bolt into the water and try to attack the wriggling captured fish. If he could get a hold of it, he would grasp it in his large jaws and each time he would be astonished at the awful taste. Jasper wondered about this ritual of taking something from its habitat by force and then throwing it back. Sometimes though if it were of a significant size they would take it home and cook it. Jasper noticed it tasted a lot better in this manner.

They laughed and played. It was a joyous time. But as with all things, they must pass.

Henry often remarked to Laura, Thomas' mother, how Thomas would show off in front of Mary and that Mary would just eat it up. This caused both of Thomas' parents to smile. They were pleased to see this relationship blossoming into fruitfulness.

Although not Brenda, Mary's mother, she was loath to watch this. Jealous even. She would in time try to bring this germination to an end, and not just on a few occasions.

When Thomas got home the evening before the first day of school he noticed his father had picked up another model airplane for them to put together. He and his father had quite a collection of models. They had quartered off a section of the small den in which his father watched the ball games, for the model town they were building.

Thomas relished these moments with his father, because Henry was often at work or busy around the house restoring the old place. So when they would be able to spend time doing something constructive together it made Thomas happy.

That night after dinner he and his father worked at putting the model together.

This particular model represented a scaled down version of an actual fighter jet in WWII. This particular model was a P51D Mustang Fighter. They had many models including a train with tracks and depot station, buses with a terminal, planes and cars from all eras. They collectively added to the small town they created for their figurines a little at a time over quite some period. It was really becoming quite a collection.

They had fun putting these replicas together. Sometimes gluing and snapping in of the required pieces, other times painting or applying the appropriate stickers to the particular model. They bought all the necessary accessories for them. They used the quick drying cement suggested by the model company. On occasion they would purchase some items outside the norm to place inside the town. Sometimes using Lego's to help construct the living quarters and create the appearance of a thriving town. They took the Lego figures of people and placed them in the vehicles to drive the automobiles, buses and trains and others to fly the planes.

Thomas and Henry had used this quick drying cement before in building their train depot, and bus terminal. It took many trips to the store to replenish their supply of it. The labor was meticulous and slow. It took a lot of glue product to complete the terminal and station, but it was worth the effort. It showed on both of their faces and Laura was content to knit and watch them while they worked together.

They finished up for the evening, to about halfway complete and Henry told Thomas it was bedtime, he had school in the morning. They put away the utensils and washed the glue and paint from the tiny brushes. Then after tidying up, Thomas went off to brush his teeth and prepare for bed.

Like all kids preparing for the first day off school, Thomas had much on his mind and was a bit anxious. Thomas was getting into bed when his mother came in. She had come in to give him a goodnight kiss. Thomas decided to divert himself from this mundane preoccupation with a barrage of questions for his mother. The best way to avoid bad habits is through distraction.

"Mum, why did you call me Thomas?" Thomas asked.

"Well we thought that's what God would have wanted." She explained.

"I thought you had to go to church, to believe in God." He replied.

"People who go to church only profess to others that they believe in God. Damn do-gooders." Said his father leaning in the doorway.

"Oh Henry." His mother retorted.

"What your father means," as she looked back at Thomas, "Is that it's what's in your heart that matters. You always need to remember that, even those who proclaim not to trust in God, He still has the mercy enough to trust in them." She went on to say.

"So then God is a good guy." Thomas joked.

"Yes I suppose he is. He is the controller of all things. There is one God who watches us all. He is the culmination of all that is and is not." She claimed.

Thomas looked puzzled.

"Then which religion is the right one?" Thomas asked.

"They are all of them right, as long as they welcome another's belief to also be righteous. God is Buddha. God is Mohammed. God is Jesus. God is the Norse Gods, the Native Indian Gods, all that is Greek mythology and so on. If men lived as brothers in arms there would be no need of religion, but that's a topic for another night." She finished.

"So why does he make bad things happen?" Said Thomas.

"So he can test your faith." His mother replied while tucking him.

"Faith in what?" Asked Thomas.

"Hope." She returned kissing him gently on the cheek.

"Okay Laura that's enough for one night." Ordered his father.

"Good night, Thomas." They said in unison.

"Night." Thomas said as he drifted off to sleep.

Thomas had another strange dream that night, one involving the well-dressed stranger.

The hour was late and he was walking through the cemetery. In the distance he heard a wolf howling. He saw the man from the other dream, the one who begets flies, sitting upon a gravestone. Behind him he could see a Mausoleum. The man was peeling an apple. Thomas looked down at the gravestone he was perched on and it sent shivers through him.

Morgan.

His family name.

He ran from the cemetery onto the train tracks, hopped the fence through the warehouse district and jaunted into Xtra-Mart parking lot. He arrived winded and bent down holding his knees with his hands.

He was standing in front of the fuel pumps when a black Town Car pulled up to them. The window came down and Thomas leaned forward to see whom it was.

It was a figure with a hood on. The figure pulled back the hood to reveal itself. It was a skeleton. The skull of this undead creature started chattering it's teeth and began laughing in a demonic chuckle.

"Fill 'er up son. Fill 'er up on fear and doubt." Said the creature from the underworld.

He continued that sinister laugh.

"Let's see if we can find some music." He shouted.

Running through the stations he passed Johnny Cash, Neil Young, Led Zeppelin, The Beatles and the Stones.

"Ah, here we go." The talking skeleton said. The car stereo blared out an old punk tune. The lyrics were burning in his subconscious memory. The Misfits, a long lost great tune.

Thomas couldn't think it was hard to remember what had brought him to this place.

Then a voice broke through the horror punk, death rock. It was a familiar voice at that.

31

Mary.

"Arrow through the heart and hope to die. Faith and love our battle-cry." The sweet voice sang this verse over and over each time getting louder and more melodic.

This seemed to perturb the evil imp and it roared with wrath. He smashed the radio with his bony fist. Fragments of plastic and dashboard flew about.

The skeleton pushed down on the brakes and gas simultaneously. The tires were squealing and the rear end of the car was fish tailing crying to be released. He ended the break stand and burst out of the parking lot. He knocked over the stop sign leading to the street. The stop sign was a wooden heart.

Thomas came out of the dream drenched in sweat.

Oh God he said to himself. No way to start a day, he thought, let alone the first day of school.

He lumbered to the shower, brushed his teeth and put on his new clothes. His mind was burdened by his nightmare and he was sluggish to get his motor going.

He examined himself in the mirror, when he was fully dressed. He pulled at a couple of stubborn nasal hairs. He put a little mouse in his thick, brown and feathered hair. He plucked his eyebrows between the two, so it wouldn't extend across in one line.

Thomas was a handsome young man and he was tall for fourteen. He was six foot one inch and he was thinly built, though not too thin to be considered skinny. His nose was narrow and straight. He had big brown eyes and little acne. He had very little hair on his chest but some around the nipples. He had a treasure trail though from his belly button to his genitalia. Mary often tugged at this patch of hair to get Thomas to chase her. It always worked. He had straight brown- layered hair that he feathered down the middle. His hair almost touched his shoulders. He liked it this way.

So did Mary.

This is where Laura and Mary disagreed. Laura was after Thomas all the time to get it trimmed. Mary would always talk Thomas out of it. If Laura didn't like Mary so much she wouldn't have let Thomas resist.

Thomas ate some oatmeal and kissed his Mom goodbye. He headed out the door with Jasper in tow. The screen door slammed back to its resting place.

They rounded the side of the house and he put Jasper out on his chain.

Thomas thought about how heavy the chain was. This was Jaspers third. Finally his father went down to the Marina and picked up a tow chain.

"This will keep him fixed." His father announced coming through the front door with the heavy linked chain.

Henry wrapped the chain around a metal post beam that he cemented in a sauna tube, four feet in the ground. He had one his friends from the small local airport weld a steel hook fastener onto the chain. He then clipped it onto the dog's leash.

Jasper didn't mind though. Jasper carried it around like it was a clothesline.

And Thomas suspected, that if Jasper wanted to, he could break it.

He left Jasper after a good petting on the belly and rode his bike up to Mary's.

Mary was in her bedroom going through her clothes. All about her queen- sized bed, were several outfits. She had gone through many combinations of apparel.

"Should I wear the green sweater with the beige skirt? What shoes would I wear? No I think I'll wear the white blouse with the tight blue jeans. Thomas will like that." She went on to herself with a devilish grin.

"Hehehee." She laughed when she thought of how Thomas would try to be sly and sneak a peek at her young fit body.

She was au natural. Mary didn't wear makeup, she didn't need to, but she did experiment with perfume.

She remembered Thomas' first reaction to her scented perfume.

Thomas was muttering to himself as he came up the porch to call on her. He was caught up in some secret conversation with himself and she wondered which side was winning the argument. Thomas often talked to himself aloud. He felt he got the best answers, from himself. It's only crazy if you talk to yourself in the third person. Right? Who knows what's crazy? I'm sure psychiatrists would have an educated hypothesis about this but what do they know about an adolescents plight anyway.

On this occasion Mary saw him coming up the road, the front way on the street, and she ran downstairs to greet him. She wanted to gauge his response to her new fragrance.

Thomas rang the bell at the same time Mary opened the door.

"Oh I didn't know"… He trailed off in marvel of the pleasant heady scent.

His mind was aflutter. He couldn't remember what he had been so absorbed in. What was I thinking about? I was on the brink of a discovery. Who cares? Screamed his inner voice. Look at what you are about to discover here.

She giggled and let him in.

So now upon looking in the mirror at her slender body, she closed her eyes and imagined what scent Thomas would like today.

Green apple she thought.

She went to her bureau and searched through her aroma manipulators. She obtained the green apple and stood in front of the mirror. She sprayed some on her neck and on the inside of her wrists. Then she laughed and sprayed some on her small hard breasts.

Mary was gorgeous to all that laid eyes on her. Although this was evident to others, she was very self-conscious, not unlike many young women. She would ask if you thought she was fat. She would be temporarily reassured by the person's rebuttal. She was five foot three and one hundred and two pounds, hardly fat by any stretch. She had strawberry blond hair, which turned to straight blond behind her ears. Her hair was straight, until it got to the last two inches and it twisted into loose curls. She was slender and very shapely. She had small breasts but they were as hard as baseballs. Her butt was small, but round, like a heart shape and you could bounce a quarter off her belly.

As she put on her chosen school clothes, she daydreamed about her and Thomas. Her fantasies and delusions about her and Thomas were becoming more and more frequent. They were also becoming more detailed and lucid. She began to imagine Thomas kissing her neck under an apple tree in autumn when the apples began to fall and the pigment in the tree leaves began to change. She closed her eyes and ran her hand over her breast…

Thomas, who was down below, was looking for a small pebble to throw up at her window, to alert her he was there. He found a perfect sized one and tossed it up and it struck a white window shudder attached to her front window.

Clink.

Mary jumped out of her dream startled.

Thomas hollered up to Mary from the front of her house that faced the street. There were two other windows to her bedroom that faced east.

She quickly composed herself and went to the window.

"Come on Mary we'll be late for school." He shouted at the

window.

She opened the front window and shouted down to him on the street.

"Almost ready. Be right down." She yelled.

As he looked up at her his heart skipped a few beats. Lord how beautiful she was to him. He had a strange feeling in his belly and his hands got all clammy.

A few moments later she burst through the screen door.

"Hey you." She said playfully.

He looked at her and wanted to say something sweet to her, but his mouth wouldn't work. He tried to say something witty and clever. He decided to comment on her green apple perfume.

He uttered something like "Guderoffapoom."

God I'm such a dork. She going to think I'm a tool. Say something you imbecile. Make a recovery. His inner voice was calling a meeting because they were not happy with the mouth's performance of late.

"Miggosnackeron". He blurted out.

Moron. You retard. What's wrong with you? Now the board of trustees, which ran the matters of his conscience, were hollering and arguing back and forth.

The operator of his speech machine was late for work today. Before he could further berate his inner thoughts, she giggled.

She shook her head approvingly. Her ponytail went swinging to and fro. Then she grabbed him by the hand.

Oh God she's going to feel my sweaty greasy hands, he thought.

If she did, she didn't say so.

Man, was he in love.

The board members cheered at a near miss.

Off to school he went, hand in hand, with his favorite girl.

"OOOOOOOOs" and "AAAAAAAAhs" came from the on lookers and passer-bys. Thomas didn't mind though, not at all.

The new principle though, did.

As he passed by in his new Town Car, he made a facial gesture that only the devil could love.

CHAPTER THREE
The principle

The student's filed into their preordained homeroom classes and received their course descriptions, locations and period determinations. All the rooms were aflutter with chatter and students compared their schedules. After the teachers spoke to their classes about proper etiquette and demeanor required of a good student they began checking over the schedules to make sure there were no errors. After determining that all was in order, each teacher called in to the office over the classroom monitor speaker to announce they were ready to begin school. Then after the 'Pledge of Allegiance' was said, it was a short time before first bell rang. The students hustled out into the halls to find their mates to display a quick fix of comradeship or affection whichever one was appropriate to ones situation.

Mary and Thomas held hands to her first period class, Grammar and Writing, where they unwillingly departed for the long expanse of time which would be fifty-minutes. Doesn't seem like that long, but for young lovers who can't stand to be apart, it is forever. Thomas saw her off and ran to his first class just before last bell.

As first class began and school hard covers were being distributed, a clean- shaven man with his hair slick back strode into the classroom. Thomas' first class was the classroom closest to the general office. His class, by no mistake, would be the first to be greeted by the new principle.

The hair color of this man was hard to distinguish, as with all hair color when it has enough gel in it. It appeared to be black, but very well could have been dirty blonde. He wore tinted glasses, a black suit, red tie and black dress shoes.

Thomas' teacher looked up with her bifocals on the edge of her nose to see the man standing triumphantly in front of the class. The way he stood there you would have thought he single handedly conquered an enemy position.

"Class, this is Mr. Kilcrop. He's our new principle." Said Miss Godwin from behind her desk.

Miss Godwin was the Sophomore History teacher. Miss Godwin was a teacher in her forties and she was a stickler for details. She would often correct lessons with grammar as well as facts pertaining to Geography and History. She was short and chubby with short brown hair. Her hair was fashioned in a bowl cut. She had a cute face and if she could lose about eighty pounds, she would be something to look at. Although no one would probably get near her, for she was acting celibate. She had taken the vow many years ago, when she sought to be a nun at ST. Mary's Convent and Parochial School. But because she could not stem the carnal desires, which haunted her, she decided it would be hypocritical to pursue it.

Thomas liked having History first period. It wasn't too much thinking like Math, or too much analyzing, like Science. There was no diagramming of sentences, like English. It helped him ease into the day before the tedious tasks that filled the High School curriculum.

He liked to daydream about the history of the world and some of its less civilized time periods and barbaric ways.

Sometimes he would dream about pirates in cannon battles on the open sea. Often times he would place himself in these fantasies.

"Batten' down the hatches First Mate." He hollered.

"Aye- Aye Capain." Returned the First Mate.

"We must sack this ship. Take it at all cost." He yelled through the heat of battle.

Musket balls would just miss him whizzing by his head. Plumes of smoke would rise up from the cannon shod. Everywhere would be the screams and pleas for help or mercy. He bent down to aid a fallen pirate who had taken a musket in the belly. "Please Capain' some wadder." Said the fallen hero. Thomas took his canteen and gave the young mate some of the cool drink. Passionately he spoke words of encouragement to his crew. He picked up a musket and fired it into the opposing vessel.

Sometimes he would imagine he was a World War Two pilot, flying over German ports. His racing Hawker Tempest would dive and reek havoc on unsuspecting naval vessels. He would fire his machine guns and rain bullets down on transport boats. The nemesis Messerschmitt Me 163 would be on his six and he would always be trying to shake him loose. Dodging and weaving through the anti aircraft flak. He would always be one step ahead of the Luftwaffe and two ahead of the anti aircraft. The incoming shells from below would be so thick that you could walk upon the artillery flak.

"Hi class I'm Mr. Kilcrop. Burn Kilcrop." Announced the new principle.

What an unusual name thought Thomas. Something was nagging him about the man's suit too, but he couldn't place it. What's with the hair and glasses?

"I want to keep an open door to all you youngsters. So if something is bothering you or you need some helpful advice, don't hesitate to drop by. I'm here for you all." He ended the phrase 'for you all' with emphasis and a slight snicker.

Thomas caught that snicker and moved uneasily in his chair. He looked at the dark glasses and wondered why he wore them.

Something unnerving was gnawing at his thoughts and still it eluded him.

Mr. Kilcrop glanced at Thomas as if to read his thoughts and laughed.

"If you're wondering about the glasses and why I wear them, it's because my eyes are hypersensitive to the light." He informed the students.

How odd Thomas thought. How very odd. Did he know what I was thinking?

Ridiculous.

Right? Thomas was feeling anxious though.

"I know I'm no Dom Gladberry, but I'll do my best and I think we'll get along just fine. Thank you Miss Godwin. Have a great day." He said with a broad smile.

As he began walking out of the classroom, Thomas noticed even though he took normal strides, he appeared to move faster than logic would suggest.

I'm just imagining things Thomas thought.

But he wasn't so sure.

Dom Gladberry was the former principle and a sore subject to bring up, to say the least. He had been the principle for over forty years and people were talking about dedicating a town square in his honor. That however was before the homicide-suicide incident.

Everyone new this tale, but rarely spoke of it.

Dom was found in his home with his pants down around his ankles. He had put a bullet hole through his left temple and exploded the right side all over Penny Downtrodder. Penny was thirteen. Dom's wife was slumped over in the corner with two bullets in the chest at close range. If the local detectives weren't so inept they might have began an investigation into why Dom, a right handed individual, decided to end his life with the use of his left. Some things though in small towns purposely go uncovered.

The incident had placed Penny in the fourth floor of the psyche unit of the local hospital and finally, off to the Worcester County Ward for the Mentally Unfit.

Twenty-four hours a day she stayed in a padded room with no windows, very little interaction and even less information from the outside world. Even if she were to be told about societies charades and happenings she wouldn't respond to any updates or news. Although Penny didn't mind, in fact, Penny's mind was nothing at all. Totally spent. That which happened to her, and she alone knew, had caused her to shut down, completely.

They fed her through tubes and she never slept. Even upon being given massive doses of sedatives or tranquillizers she wouldn't sleep. She never changed her features. She just stared out into oblivion. She had been there three months and no one recalls her ever having a sleeping moment. She just stared into the nothingness.

Poor Penny.

But there was another who did know what happened that day at the Gladberry home.

Class to class the principle went greeting all the students and teachers. He was colloquial and outspoken to all he met. He received a warm welcome from the faculty staff and student body alike. He departed the last classroom and went down to the basement past the gymnasium and up to a big blue metal door. He had finally made it. He was loath to continue that façade to which he just been subject to. He would rather pluck out his own eyeballs before ever doing that again. He hated being polite. It made him nauseous.

"Hi class I'm Mr. Kilcrop and I love you all." He squawked sarcastically.

He punched the cinderblock wall and pulled his hand out from the busted cement. Broken mortar and stone dust fell to the basement floor.

"Ugh. I hate this part." He proclaimed to the empty hall.

At last he was at the janitor's room. He pulled the heavy steel door open and walked into the room.

It was a small room with a locker, a small table and large stool. On the table were some loose papers, school keys, pens and pencils. Some cleaning supplies lined the metal shelves on the left wall as you walked in. Against the back wall was a washbasin and mop bucket and to the right were class hard covers and notebooks stacked on empty milk crates against the wall. They were lined in alphabetical order and placed in groups according to class year and description.

The principle went up behind the giant man standing in the center of the room putting a mop together. Mr. Kilcrop just stood behind the man for a long spell.

The big man felt something amiss in his environment but couldn't place it. I suppose it was like when an animal knows someone is stalking it but its form and whereabouts still elude them.

"Come on Sol. We have work to do." The principle said with authority.

The big man flinched when the principle began talking. He knew it was something in the room. Every time Sol was around the 'man' the air in the room seemed to get sucked out, or in more like it. He hated the 'man' but he had no choice but to obey. Sol Bender was the janitors name and he too was new to this school.

John Bryer, the previous janitor, had retired last year. He went to Florida with his second wife Emily. A much better retirement than

Dom's I might add, and a lot less permanent.

Sol was a large man of at least four hundred pounds with a shaved head. He would have been over seven feet tall, except he was hunched over with humps on both shoulders. When he walked, his arms would sag straight down and his gigantic hands would almost drag on the floor.

His hands were huge, like the size of watermelons. Each finger was half as big as a normal teenager's wrist. They looked like big kielbasa links. The fingernails were like quarters. And his head well, his head was the size of a man's mid section. Upon it was a great big forehead, like that of a Cro-Magnon. It was too large a forehead, even for his head. His ears were huge like small dinner plates and his nose was wide at the bridge of the nose and wider still towards the bottom. His nose was as big as a twelve-ounce beer can. His nostrils were large round holes the size of bottle caps. It looked like his nose was smashed flat upon his face, for although it was wide and flared it was flat and pug. He wore size twenty-eight shoes, and where he got them made one wonder. When he walked, you could hear the footfalls from two hallways away.

But for all his oversized and intimidating features, he was not malicious or cruel. He was much like a giant teddy bear. He was purely, a simpleton. He was always passive and never confronted anyone. He was content with being left alone.

But he was afraid of Mr. Kilcrop. He wasn't worried about himself for he could handle himself very well. In fact he often thought about snapping the 'man's neck like a pencil, and he could too. What had him troubled was that the 'man' was devious and cunning. Sol was afraid of what he might do to his mother. Sol's mother was totally reliant upon him. He knew that if the 'man' wanted to, he could disappear for a spell and call upon his mother, and not in the fashion of courting her. He realized early on what Mr. Kilcrop was and it only bothered him because the principle was fearless of consequence and pain. He would no doubt not hesitate to hurt others to justify his means to whatever endgame he was trying to achieve.

Sol's mother, Dorothy, was dependent upon him evermore. If he were at work or at the grocery store, he would coordinate for a visiting nurse to be in. Often times he would arrive at home to see a different nurse than the week before because his mother was a pest, and a professional nag. She would aggravate and annoy the nurse to the breaking point. Then that nurse would uncompromisingly solicit to be assigned elsewhere or quit altogether.

The reason for her malcontent in some ways could be understood. I reckon if half of us knew her pain we might be less judgmental. She had a medical dictionary full of ailments. Her illnesses included Diabetes, Rheumatoid arthritis, and PAD.

Her body's poor circulation made her legs swell up to twice their normal size. This reduced her to a wheel chair. She hated this most of all. The whole of her life she had been quite able and she was the one who took care of the house. So it was now that she began to detest herself, not others, because of the burden she had inadvertently placed on her son. This made her spiteful. And whom do you hurt when times are tough? The ones you love of course.

She was also showing the beginning signs of the dark, dreary road to senility. She often forgot who Sol was and when she did remember she would berate him for her problems. Many times she pleaded with him to take her life and sometimes he considered it. Euthanasia is not murder but Sol couldn't get past that ethical boundary. He wanted to for his Ma, but he couldn't bring himself to do it. It was quite sad to see this giant man sob for his lack of strength in seeing this small task through, but his compassion always won out over his loyalty to his mother's wishes. You can see a person's predicament in the matters of family devotion. I have to laugh at these pro lifers who think they know what's right for a person to which they need not spend anytime watching them suffer through unimaginable pain. They say it's inhumane to help a person into death's door but I feel it's worse, even uncivilized, to let a person suffer to death. If their dog was struggling with life and couldn't move to piss they would put them down out of care for the dog. Why wouldn't you for someone whom you love? Nothing is less civil than allowing a person to suffer to death. This is not a moral question but it becomes one of economics. The pharmaceutical and insurance companies want these half empty shells to carry on as long as they can. Material vampires have infected the ethics of medicine. Their platform on this is that the 'Hippocratic Oath' constrains doctors to care for a person through any situation or obstacle. I call it splitting hairs.

Anyway, everyday Dorothy would fight with Sol during meals or getting into the bath. And changing her diaper, that was real fun. If she didn't paint herself with the feces, she would throw it against the wall or worse, at him. And she would not go without a struggle to bed. She liked to stay up late watching infomercials. Sol didn't care much. If she was happy, and quiet, he was happy.

That's why he drew back when Mr. Kilcrop approached him in the basement janitor's room. That's why he cringed at what he might have to do.

Thomas went through the day absorbed in his new studies and didn't realize the day had passed him by. It's nice when work passes quickly as if you've just arrived.

Last bell rang at 2:15 and Thomas collected his books for homework and studying, at his locker.

Mary ran up behind him and put her hands over his eyes.

"Guess who." She said playfully.

"Ah, the T.V. repair man." He guessed.

"Nope. Guess again." She giggled.

"The pizza delivery guy." He guessed again.

"Wrong again." She was really laughing now.

"Give me a hint." Thomas said playing along.

Anything so she would keep her hands on him.

"I'm really fat. I have pimples on my face, back and chest. I'm losing my hair. I always have gas and I'm three feet tall." She said trying to keep from burst out laughing.

"So you're standing on a stool?" He questioned.

"Nope, I have wings." She responded.

"You're Marlon Brando." He said assuredly.

"No silly it's me." She laughed and kissed him on the cheek. She had to stand on her tiptoes to reach. Mary loved his quick wit and sarcasm. They had a similar taste of humor. This time was no exception. Thomas had a knack for coming up with one-liners and on the spot clever comebacks. He would send her into hysterical fits and it would make her swoon for him. She keeled over many times in hilarity at his jokes. Some people think that poetry is the easiest way into a woman's heart, and although effective with the right material it is not the truth. The surest way into the center of her affection is through laughter. Women have much strength, and it is proven that they can withstand more pain than the strongest man, however they have one weakness. Laughter. This is their Kryptonite.

Thomas flushed when her moist lips touched his cheek and that warm almost sick feeling gave way to joy. He got a whiff of green apple. He started to feel light headed and got a strange feeling in his belly.

Mary knew her perfume had got him again and she smiled.

She took him by the hand and they left the school for the short journey home. Their eyes never strayed from one another. They were sparkling and gleaming for each other.

Thomas and Mary passed her house because they decided to go

to his house.

Thomas and Mary collected Jasper from his chain before the rain began and went to the front of the house and ascended the stairs.

Laura greeted them at the door anxious for word about their first day. She talked aloud while she prepared plates full of warm chocolate-chip cookies. She had made them for their first day of school. She poured them each a glass of milk.

Laura gave Jasper a small bowl of vanilla ice cream which he licked away one lap at a time. Laura was about to sit down and chat about Thomas and Mary's first day of the new school year but she saw the glint in their eyes for each other and a short smile creased her face. She decided to leave them to whisper words of affection to one another.

Jasper too noticed the lover's intent and he lay underneath the table listening for any sign of threat that might interrupt his master's pleasure.

That night both of them had indecent fantasies of the other.

CHAPTER FOUR

Clowns and Midgets

"Come now Thomas. You've been putting this off long enough. You've been avoiding this for almost a year now." His mother, Laura nagged.

He turned up a grimace.

"It's time for you to earn the keep of Jasper like you agreed." She further argued.

He knew it too. He had been putting it off far too long. He didn't want to get a job but he knew his mother had been patient long past her usual.

She had mentioned it at the start of summer but she had seen him outside chasing Mary and she was happy for him. She knew it to be all too important, that when one finds love, they must adhere to it tenaciously. For it is often found and even harder these days to keep. Many people profess to have love but the statistics show that they are mistaken. The divorce rate is almost eighty percent.

Despicable.

I wonder how many of those couples still together, stay conjoined for the sake of others, like their children. At one time I thought it was more beneficial for parents to stick together for the sake of their children, but now I'm not so sure. It's quite a paradox really. Is it better to stay as one without love to be seen by those children? Or is it better to make a clean break and let the child's lack of seeing the ones they unconditionally love, torment and bawl each other, and begin to mend the wounded loss? I really don't know. No doubt it's better to grow up and put all differences aside. Get back to the always and forever attitude that you began the relationship with. Sometimes however this cannot be. True love eludes even the greatest of people. Someone very close and dear to me asked me whether or not I believed in true love. That person is the reason for my existence and to whom I dedicate this book. I couldn't answer her very well on the spot but now that I've thought some about it, I feel compelled to answer this very necessary all too important question. First we must decide what true love is in order to discover its existence.

True love. Hmmmm. Let us examine this phenomenon. Like the saying goes, it can make a young man weep and a grown man cry. It can turn the most courageous man into a mouse. It can make and break the most fervent woman. But it can also make us Lords and Lady's of the highest realm. It is a recipe for which the ingredients are a mystery but when put together properly, make the best eats ever.

Let me try to explain the riddle. True love is: You've worked a double shift and arrived home bush tired wanting only your pillow, to find your girl in bed shivering and sweating out a fever. She has been defecating and puking all over, sick as hell with the neuro-virus. Instead of getting mad or excited about this situation you pick her up, vomit and shit covered and all. You carry her to the shower to wash her of the filth that plagues her. Instead of sleeping the rest of the night away like you intended, you bring her to the couch and watch the whole night over her because you know she'd eat glass to make you better.

True love is: your wife has worked the day away and then had to host an after hours board meeting which she would rather give blood through her eyeballs than do. At the meeting, fettuccine and marinara was served and she has the worst case of heartburn, only to get home to find you, her loving husband, has let simmer a spaghetti sausage and meatball dinner. Instead of denying you the pleasure of her fine culinary critique, she eats every bite knowing she will soon regret the esophageal revolt, which will soon make its appearance.

True love is: that ability to say sorry. This is much harder for men than woman, but if you truly care you'll eat baby puke before you let your loved one get away. Apologizing is not a sign of weakness. It is the greatest attribute to a nobleman. The highest character trait of a King is mercy and his ability to ask forgiveness of his people.

True love is: making love through a sultry day and then both of you get into the bath together and wash each other. You talk about what makes you crazy about the others parent's and you both laugh. While laughing one of you chases a fart bubble to the surface and you look at one another. Suddenly you both crack up and hold each other from breaking out of the tub to see who can get back to bed the fastest. Only to be thrown about the bed by the other thrashing lover. You stay there making love until the morning. Then in the morning you argue over who still holds the love making title, sure that the other one gave in first due to being worn out. One more time then, eh? I'll bet my last dollar she wins every time. A noble defeat though and a man can live with that.

True love is many more things that only lovers know. Like when you whisper words into her ear that make her nipples swell and a giant smile break across her face. These same words said to a stranger will get your face smacked to the back of your head. There are so many things that true love can be and if you find it hold onto it tooth and nail.

Getting back to Laura, she liked Mary a lot. Mary would often help with chores or cleaning dishes after dinner. She would set and clean the table. Sometimes she would help Laura hang the clothes out on the clothes- line. She was very helpful around the house. There wasn't anything Laura had to ask her to do, before she was already into the deed. This pleased Laura very much. Mary would make a good wife someday. And more than once she hoped it would be Thomas who landed her.

So because she was content to see Thomas and Mary going steady, Laura had taken up a part time job, cleaning houses for the wealthy. She hated it whole- heartedly. But she would do it for her Thomas. She adored him. So she did.

The Morgan's lived in the 'impoverished' part of town, to be politically correct. Some people called it the 'Poor Farm' others the 'Housing Authority' and some still the "Projects'. The Morgan's didn't actually live in the Federally Housed units but just adjacent to it. It might as well been in Harlem, for the social injustices done to those 'without' in a small town is damn near criminal. The small town politicking in the classroom, on the ball field and on the town stage is treasonous. But so goes the world of green and gold. This part of 'Shit Town' bordered the factory district on one side and the State Projects on the other.

Mary only lived four blocks away, but it was like a different country, altogether.

The Morgan's never really had much, and Thomas asked for less. He never complained about not having more, like single children often do.

He never disobeyed or talked back to his parents or other adults. He always showed them courtesy and respect. He never stole or started trouble. He was a good All-American boy.

So Laura felt compelled to do this indemnifying task for her son. She would continue to scrub the floors, toilets and baths for those brats who grew up with someone else wiping their ass.

She often thought about the difference between the rich and poor, or the have and have not, for those easily offended. Like when someone would whisper a snide remark about her attire, or they would gossip about something she may or may not have done.

"Oh she's one of those people." They would jeer just audible enough for her to hear.

It bothered her some, but not a lot.

She determined that the poor, the weary and the meek were the strongest souls on earth. Those who struggled and trudged on day after day to make ends meet, they were the heroes. They kept on through thick or thin, rain or shine. The ones who suffer most have the most strength, both spiritual and physical.

Let's perform an experiment. I et's place two groups of test rats into a survival situation, the 'have' and 'have not.' I bet you can guess who would come out of that ahead. The poor may be faux pas but they know what it takes to get the job done. It's not only that, they always have a hands on approach and things are not done for them. This makes them battle tested and experienced.

That's why they make the best soldiers. Because the bond-ship they carry with them through the trenches makes them taut as a family. What stronger family is there than that of a military unit? That's all you have when you're poor, your family and your friends. You grow up tight with these people. You grow up in the trenches with these people. You may not have a nice car or new clothes. You may not have that four bathroom, seventeen room beach house in the Hamptons. But when you need somewhere to rest your weary legs, you'll never be turned away.

So on through the summer she cleaned houses on the west side.

She did, until she learned she was pregnant. She had missed a few cycles before but never four in a row. She was very irregular anyway, so she thought it must be coming, but it never did.

Finally she went out and got a home test.

Positive.

Crap.

Thomas didn't know, and neither did Henry. She would keep it that way as long as she could. She worried about the strain an extra mouth would place on the family. The strain it caused on her was heavy indeed.

Later that year, she would think back to an incident with Thomas not being forthwith about a mishap between Jasper and Mrs. Copperback. She couldn't help but feel remorseful for the way she had scolded him, now that she understood his predicament.

She thought about their future struggle with a newborn in the house to feed and clothe. She finally said to herself. "It is what it is."

And so it was.

So when she suggested that he find a job, she did it with a heavy heart.

"Thomas the circus is town for the next two weeks. Why not go down and see if they need help." Laura encouraged.

After he ate a sandwich and some more procrastinating, he did just that.

He went off to call on Mary, and they headed to central park to find some work for him in the up coming circus.

He collected her and headed for the center of town. They went across the train tracks by the school and fire station. They crossed over High Street, and went up the northern end of Union St. to the park.

After some asking around, they found the small trailer they were directed to and Thomas knocked upon the water stained door. He could hear some arguing and bustling going on in the trailer. After Thomas tapped on the door a second time everything fell silent in the trailer. Suddenly the door blasted open almost catching Thomas in the chin. Thomas jumped back and stood wide-eyed at the man in the door.

A tall Irish man with a green plaid Fedora and puffy side burns spoke from the doorway. He muttered some sort of unidentifiable language.

From behind him came a much smaller man who pushed the larger man aside and descended the steps. The smaller man was well dressed in a white suit and sea blue tie. His shoes were also a light blue. He winked at Mary who blushed and spoke to Thomas.

"The foreman said we're in need of a clown to hand out balloons." The smaller man said.

Word had reached the two associates by phone by one of the roadies when Thomas and Mary were asking around about employment.

Thomas was hesitant, kind of embarrassed.

Mary saw this and urged him on.

"Come on Tom, it'll be fun. I'll be your helper." She said.

"I'm owy payin fo da clawn." Said the foreman reeking of booze. The Irish man stumbled down the steps and pushed the smaller man off.

The smaller man tentatively walked off with a wave goodbye.

Thomas looked at Mary and relented.

"Okay sir, I'll take the job." Thomas responded in a less than enthusiastic manner.

"Faw ta seven on week-hiccup-dayaze. Eweven ta fide on week ens." He ended the sentence with a whistle as if it was all he could do to spit out the mouthful.

"Seeze ya tamarra." He finished.

"See that wasn't so hard and your Ma will be thrilled." Mary puffed.

"Yeah I guess so." Thomas replied.

Off they went toward town, they stopped at the frozen yogurt shop and each got a frozen treat. From there they trekked off homeward.

The man with the shotgun under his jacket just stood and watched.

So everyday after school Thomas would come home, let Jasper loose and play for an hour. Then he and Mary would head off to work the circus. Mary would blow up the balloons and he would tell jokes all dressed up in his clown guise while he handed them out. It was pretty uneventful until the weekend.

It was an ordinary day when the first day of weeks end started but it ended in a fashion in anything but. On Saturday while he was handing out balloons he saw some boys had cornered one of the midgets for the side- show for the extraordinary.

They started roughing him up a bit and began calling him names. Kids can be the cruelest.

"Where's the rest of ya', shorty." Joked one boy.

"Hey stumpy need a chair." Taunted another.

"How big is your momma? Is she a midget too?" Asked a third.

"How big do ya' think he was when he was born fellas?" Laughed another.

"How big do you think his wanker is?" Questioned the first with a crude gesture to his crotch.

This got a laugh from the entire group.

"We prefer to be called dwarves or little people." Said the little man. "As for my mother, well she's not half the size of your mothers hole. I can imagine your melon head squeezing and busting through it. It's so big it echoes when she farts." The dwarf teased.

Now they were all laughing at the boy who commented on the

dwarf's mother. They started poking and jeering him to egg him on.

"Oh what he said about your momma." They were shouting and instigating.

The boy was all red faced with shame and frustration. He knocked the dwarf in the dirt. He had both fists turned over in a boxing posture.

Thomas saw this and left his station on a dead run.

Mary was off getting sodas or she would have been the voice of reason.

He ran into the unsuspecting boy and they wrestled on the ground. Thomas had him pinned, or thought he did, until one the boys from this wayward crowd pulled him off. The boy Thomas had tackled got up and punched Thomas in the mouth, but Thomas stood his ground. It hurt like hell but he wouldn't waiver. He stood there with his fists clenched and his jaw tight.

"Is that all you got punk?' Thomas asked.

"Who you calling punk?" Returned the boy.

They were about to engage again, until the foreman came and broke it up.

"You boys ain't allowed back, ya hear." Hollered the foreman in a much more lucid voice than yesterday.

He kicked one of the boys in the pants as they scurried out of the park.

"You okay kid?" The foreman questioned.

"Yeah I guess so." Thomas replied sadly.

Thomas could feel tears welling up inside and he was shaking. He had never been in a fistacuff before. He didn't like the feeling. He couldn't understand why people intentionally hurt others. Why do they make fun of or intimidate the less fortunate?

"Why don't you take five and recuperate. Okay son." Offered the foreman.

Thomas tried to speak through a heart- wrenching sob. He couldn't so he ran behind one of the trailers and cried aloud.

While Thomas was relieving his frustration he heard a soft voice. He felt a small hand on his shoulder, and another was patting him on the back.

"Thanks mister you really saved my butt. Those boys were out to make my day miserable but you showed them. Don't think I would've stood a chance but you risked it all for little ole me. Kind off exciting really." The tiny voice said.

"Doesn't feel real exciting to me. In fact it feels like dirt." Thomas spat.

"It's okay young sir. I know how you feel. Fighting ain't no fun. Nope, not one bit. But sometimes it's necessary I think." He proclaimed.

Thomas still hadn't said anything but now he was looking at this unique little fellow.

"Don't you?" He inquired.

"I guess so." Thomas responded a little less dejected than before.

"You knew the others were there and the odds were against you, but you still stood up for me. Not many youngsters would have put themselves in danger for the sake of another. In fact not many adults would have done so either. You are a dying breed, young sir." He said in gratitude.

"I don't like bullies." Thomas said finally after the sniffles stopped. He wiped his nose on his sleeve.

"My name's Jerry. Jerry Littlefeet. Pleased to make your acquaintance." The dwarf said nobly.

"I'm Thomas. It's nice to meet you as well." Thomas replied.

"Are you always that brave." Responded the little man.

"I'm not brave. I just saw that you were out numbered and that they were about to gang up on you and… I don't know, some voice spoke up inside me and told me that it was wrong, to do something about it. That's all." Thomas said.

"Brave and modest. Well that not something you cross paths with everyday. You're quite a character Thomas." Boasted Jerry.

" I feel better now, thank you. I must be going back to my post." Thomas said.

"You got the lion in your belly. When he gets hungry he comes out to feed. I've seen it before. Good men often keep the lion at bay until provoked. Still rivers run deep, eh?" Jerry went on.

Thomas peered at the dwarf befuddled.

Jerry started up the stairs to the trailer that Thomas went behind to hide his tears and told Thomas to follow. Thomas slowly and reluctantly entered the trailer.

"Come, I want to give you something." Jerry said.

"That's not necessary." Thomas answered.

"I insist." Responded Jerry.

Jerry brought him in the trailer and showed him around.

It was nothing short of utter disorder. Quite the chaotic mess it surely was. There was junk everywhere. Well it was junk to you and me, but necessities to the likes of Jerry. There were items blocking the kitchen area, covering the floor, atop the cabinets and all over the stove and table. It covered the furniture in the room he was standing in, if there ever was any. It covered most of the bed except for a small spot for Jerry to curl up in.

Jerry tossed stuff over his shoulder, in front of him and under his legs. He was always trying without success to get the endless stuff out of his way. It always landed on a pile and rolled back down to what little floor was left in the trailer.

"Where did I put ya'? I know you're here somewhere." He spoke aloud.

"This it?" He asked himself.

"Nope." He answered.

"How about in this trunk?" He inquired of himself again.

By this time Thomas was sure he must get back to the balloon station if not for fear of reprisal from the foreman than definitely from Mary.

Jerry stood there thinking. When he did, he lifted up his right leg and crossed it against the back of his left leg. His right leg was bent at the knee and the bottom half went behind his left and rested against the back of it. From a distance he would have looked like a small number four. He turned his tongue over in his mouth and just the curled tip was visible. He put his left hand on his small head and began to scratch it. With his other he pulled at the whiskers that extended sporadically from his chin. Then his eyes opened wide as if he had discovered the answer to the oldest problem in the earth's short history.

"It's not there either so it must be... I know." He said finally.

He walked to his confined bed and he reached under his pillow. He pulled out a long bow. Because of the size of the pillow most of the bow must have been sticking out the other side amidst the junk. Then he jumped up and stood on the bed. He was quite deft and moved with an unusual dexterity for one with such short legs. He reached up to the third shelf over his bed and took down a quiver. He laid the quiver on the bed and took a deep breath. Then he jumped up in the air and did a double flip onto the trailer floor just in front of Thomas. When he landed he did it in a fashion that the bow was in both hands in offering to Thomas. He was on one knee facing Thomas and now his head was lower than the bow as if beckoning him to take the gift. It was as if Thomas was the Emperor of some fabled land and a mere subject was offering his most prized possession to him.

Thomas gently took the long bow from Jerry in anticipation of a great joke in which the punch line was about to be delivered.

"Ah ha. There you are my pretty. This belonged to the chief of an Ancient Indian tribe in South America. Or so they tell me." Jerry explained handing the relic to Thomas. Then he returned to the bed and collected the quiver.

Thomas took the quiver and the bow but was puzzled.

"What about…" he trailed off.

"Arrows?" Jerry asked.

Thomas nodded yes.

"Sorry didn't come with arrows, but I do have a hawks feather to attach to an arrow. You can notch it in the end." Went the dwarf.

This guy is nuts. Thomas thought. A bow and quiver with no arrows.

"Take it. When you need it, you'll know what to do." Jerry prophesized.

Thomas was hesitant to take it, but Jerry insisted.

"Nice meeting you lad." Jerry said offering his hand.

Thomas shook it and reciprocated his thanks for the gifts and for showing him kindness after encountering him. He was very confused and his lip hurt like a bastard.

Thomas felt it was time to leave before things got anymore strange. He said goodbye and exited the treasure trove. When he returned to the balloon station, he found Mary anxiously waiting for him.

"Where were you?" "What happened to you?" She asked concernedly.

Thomas shrugged and said he wasn't really sure.

She just looked at him and shook her head. She looked at his broken lip and about his person to see if he were injured anywhere else. Satisfied that he was not badly hurt she began in on him.

"I don't know about you Thomas Morgan." She complained.

He knew she knew he wasn't that hurt and she wouldn't give him any understanding and tenderness until he told her what had happened. She would be relentless with questions until he told her.

She got the response she wanted out of him. He grimaced when she called him by his surname.

On the way home that evening after work he told her what happened. She listened intently but didn't understand anymore than he did.

When they arrived at his house she took him to the bathroom and cleaned his lip. Big baby she called him. He turned up his puffy lip and put on his sad eyes. Now she was powerless not to feel sensitive to his pain. She bent down slowly and kissed him on his thumping lip. It hurt like hell but he didn't feel a thing.

Two men embraced on the stoop of the treasure trove, which was Jerry's trailer, like old friends do when they haven't seen one another in a long while. Then they shook hands. When they did, they used both hands, one mans hand holding the others elbow deep. They said what few words two humble men might speak to one another and then they parted ways. Then the man with the shotgun strapped to his back walked off into the forming mist.

That night as Thomas wrestled in a fitful sleep the moonlight danced upon his windowsill and climbed up the window pane until it broke free and carried itself to the bow leaning against the clothes hamper. There was a slight mist sputtering in the cool autumn night. When the moonlight fell upon the wet window at the right angle tiny prisms were evident.

The moon was full and it had a blue radiant light surrounding it. Encircled within the blue light was silver and bronze. It was like that of another world or one of a fairy tale. Not often does the moon date blue, silver and bronze. And to be seen out with all three at the same time, people would surely be talking.

The bow which before was ordinary wood, started to reveal intricate markings and drawings. These ancient carvings or runes were aligned as if to tell a story. There were very few alive who knew what these pictures were, and even less could translate them. The history of this tale is long forgotten. The tragedy of man is that they often forget the perils of yesteryear or the reasons for the heroic deeds on the battlefield. They forget what's really important in this short expanse of time we refer to as life. It is all too brief to squander and we should keep the right character within us to remain righteous. These traits are, but not limited to: Honor, Unity, Humility, Bravery and Courage. Now these are the character traits that you want to instill in your sons and daughters. These they are to keep stowed in their hearts. If you do this, I promise it will make you proud.

The moon receded from its place inside the room, some minutes or hours later. How ever long it takes for the moonlight to return from an engagement. It moved out of Thomas' room and fell upon the windowsill once more and then moved to the side of the house. It moved off the house and spread across the backyard. Then it ran off to wherever else the moonlight goes when you are no longer conscious of it.

When it left the room the markings faded away. The bow returned to its ordinary drab wooden self. The ancient story that was so evident and visible was now camouflaged and hidden to the naked eye. However, just because you can't see or feel it, doesn't mean it's not there. This is the true meaning of faith. Putting your belief in something that is not entirely tangible.

When the markings wore away Jasper let out a long shallow

sigh. He had a feeling that his master had missed something of the utmost importance. He put his head on his paws and thought about what he could do.

He knew there was only one thing that he could do.

Wait.

Prepare.

Protect.

From that night forward he slept lightly and with one eye open.

Thomas awoke Sunday with an awful headache. He got in the shower and stayed in there a long time. He let the hot water sink and work its way into his muscles, joints and bones. He tried to let the water wash away the weariness that was creeping up on him.

Jasper sensed this too. When Thomas returned to his room and he was drying off, Jasper nestled up next to him. He rubbed Jasper and patted him hard on the chest. Jasper was staring at his master and knew some dilemma was besieging him. He would not let his King be overtaken.

"At least I have you and Mary to keep me strong." Thomas declared.

Jasper barked as if he approved.

Thomas got dressed in his weekend clothing, which consisted of gray sweat pants and hooded sweatshirt. He combed his hair while he gazed into the mirror and then he and Jasper headed downstairs.

Thomas had an English muffin for breakfast and Jasper ate his large bowl of Purina Dog Chow. He lapped at his water bowl when he was satisfied with his intake of dry dog food. He went to the door and waited for Thomas to return from brushing his teeth. Thomas came down the stairs in a rushed stomp and blasted through the screen door. They were off to Mary's house. Thomas chased Jasper all the way to Mary's. Jasper let Thomas think that he might catch him and then picked up speed and once again Thomas was just out of reach.

Thomas called on Mary and they all made their way to the park where the circus was set. Mary chased after Jasper and he always let her catch him. He either did this to boost her self-esteem, or because he too liked Mary's hands on him. Either way, Thomas laughed all the while. He knew there was no way Mary could catch Jasper unless he wanted it so. It appeared that he did too.

Thomas decided to bring Jasper along with him today. If those boys showed up again they would be sure to stay clear of him now. Thomas felt a little guilty for bringing Jasper along for somewhat protection but he justified it with the thought that Jasper might want to get out and stretch his legs. Plus it would be new scenery for Jasper. It would be good for him. He hoped.

Jasper just lay down with his head on his paws and watched the occasional passerby. When children would come up for a balloon he would lick their hands and they would chuckle. If he could talk, he would tell Thomas not to worry about the guilt for bringing him along for protection. He'd do it anytime and without a moment's thought.

"Can't get any worse than yesterday, eh Mary." Thomas stated.

Thomas was about to experience Murphy's Law. Just when you think things can't get worse, it can. When something can go wrong, it probably will.

Thomas and Mary were filling balloons on this sunny cool day in October. He noticed across from his station that a crowd had formed. Cheering and shouting was coming from the crowd of spectator's en-masse, about a circus game.

It seemed that Mr. Kilcrop was entertaining the assembly by showing his accuracy of sport in one of these games.

He was dressed in your typical recreational Sunday garb. He wore green khaki's, a beige collared shirt and brown boat shoes.

And of course he was wearing dark sunglasses.

"Yeah, good one Mr. Kilcrop." Shouted a member amongst the group of onlookers.

"Ooooo." swooned the crowd.

"That a way sir." Came another voice.

Mr. Kilcrop was throwing small hand sewn beanbags at three bowling pins stacked on a stool. The stool was roughly a dozen feet from the counter that contestants were to stand behind. The counter was waist high so as not to hinder a persons throwing arm.

The man running this rigged game was duped. How in the world is he doing it? He thought. The reason for this wonder was that the house had an unknown advantage. Two of the pins were normal wooden ones, and very light. The other though was heavy and it had a Velcro strip glued to the bottom of it for extra hold. Once knocking them over was uncommon and twice was pure luck. Six times though was surely a marvel. The man had to stop this strange luck before he lost his shirt or worse, before the foreman came and saw what was happening to his fixed game.

"Good show sir, but let's have someone else give a try. You can chose a prize for your efforts." The man finally said.

"Ah." moaned the mob.

The gamekeeper went back to the prize rack and showed Mr. Kilcrop which ones he could pick from.

He picked a large pink elephant and handed it to Mrs. Copperback.

"Good choice sir I'm sure." The gamekeeper announced.

Mrs. Copperback was beside herself in delight. Her head was buzzing with excitement. She was a lady of seventy- two summers who had lost her one true love, two fall seasons prior. So when she had been given this gift her eyes glazed over in adulation.

The horde of onlookers roared their approval. They applauded and slapped Mr. Kilcrop on the back.

He basked in this present glory.

Mr. Kilcrop then turned his attention elsewhere. He spotted Thomas at the balloon station and proceeded to his location.

Mrs. Copperback followed in tow, like a groupie to a traveling rock band. Her loyalty to her new champion was written on her face. Her appreciation for her new idol Mr. Kilcrop was genuine. His kind act of showmanship however, was false.

Like all men who desire power there was a hidden purpose.

"Good afternoon Thomas." Mr. Kilcrop boasted. "Why Mary, you're looking splendid today." He further exclaimed.

Jasper who had been quiet and calm through out the morning was ruffled.

He stood up on all fours and hunched up his front shoulders. He began to let out a lengthy hoarse growl.

"Easy boy." Warned Thomas. "Easy." He repeated.

Then Jasper sprang up at his nemesis. Mr. Kilcrop stepped aside like a ballroom dancer does on the dance floor, even faster. Jasper missed his mark and slammed into Mrs. Copperback, who stood adoring her gracious victor. She landed hard on the ground with a loud thud. Her prized pink elephant fell in the dirt.

For a moment all was quiet, like the calm right before the storm. Then the silence ended and the storm broke loose.

"OOOOOOOHHHHHH!" Mrs. Copperback whined out in pain.

A man and woman passing by came to her assistance.

"Are you okay mam'? Are you hurt?" Asked the woman.

"Someone call an ambulance." The man called out.

"Oooh! My back. My back." Cried Mrs. Copperback in agony.

"What an unruly animal." Shouted another voice from the gathering crowd.

"What's it doing out without a leash? Who's the owner anyway."

A man questioned.

Jasper looked at Thomas and knew there was about to be trouble. He sniffed the ground and made certain that the 'man' was nowhere about. Then he lay down at Thomas' feet and awaited judgment.

The word of this accident traveled like a brush fire. The news on the grapevine had reached the foreman who was serenading a woman on the Ferris Wheel. He damned himself several times before he reached the bottom of the Wheels rotation where he could exit the amusement ride. He demanded the 'carnie' responsible for surveillance and safety of the Ferris Wheel to stop the ride. He pushed open the small door to the ride swing and sprinted to the scene. He came storming into the gathered mass pushing and ushering folks aside.

"Thomas, what has happened here?" He puffed winded from his hurried jaunt.

Before he could answer, someone did it for him.

"This wild beast of a dog attacked this poor old lady." The voice announced. A person who didn't even see how the incident occurred.

"Thomas?" The foreman asked.

Thomas was without words.

"Thomas get that dog out of here." The foreman said sternly. "I'm going to have to let you go son." He went on.

The foreman didn't want to fire Thomas, but he had to save face in light of the gathered crowd. He watched the young man walk away with his head down and couldn't help but feel a bit of remorse. He watched someone he admired walking away distraught. He went back to his trailer forgetting the woman he had been previously trying to impress and settled into a liter of scotch.

As Thomas left the circus and walked through the park gates, he tried to locate the whereabouts of Mr. Kilcrop.

Thomas saw him driving away in his new Town Car with a great big smile.

Thomas thought he had somehow been waylaid but for what reason he knew not. Why would Mr. Kilcrop purposely rile Jasper? He hadn't seen Mr. Kilcrop do anything unordinary or threatening. Jasper though saw something and heard something that no one else did.

Mindspeech.

Jasper could not convey this strange occurrence to Thomas but somehow Thomas knew Jasper did right. Even if Jasper could convey this fact to his master, would he even believe him?

Mindspeech.

Ridiculous.

Right?

An ambulance was backing up through the gates of the park as Thomas, Mary and Jasper crossed onto High Street. It backed up to the fallen woman and began to aid her.

Thomas left this embarrassing moment and awful scene behind him. He kept thinking about the Town Car, because something deep down was bothering him, and he couldn't put his finger on it.

"What do you think got into him?" Mary asked, pointing at Jasper who had taken point. "I've never seen him do anything like that. He's usually a good judge of character." She added.

"He's always a good judge of character." Thomas retorted.

Having said all they were going to say about this occurrence, they walked home the long way. They walked up Franklin St., crossed Main St. and went down onto the trestle running over Small Pond. Then they climbed the hill to Saint Angelo's property. They crossed the field at the basketball courts and traveled through Goreman's field, over the stream, through the playground, across Rigby Rd, onto Woodland St. and into the pricker patch.

Thomas didn't want to let on to his folks that he had lost his position at the parkway. So they stayed there in the pricker patch chatting until dinnertime, when they both went home.

Thomas asked Jasper what he thought of Mr. Kilcrop on the way home and Jasper turned up a nasty look. He didn't growl. He didn't have to. Thomas got the point.

An hour or so later, while the Morgan's were having dessert and clearing the table, the town sheriff pulled up in his police cruiser.

Thomas could see Sheriff Conway from his vantage point at the table before his parents did. A freezing touch of fear set upon him.

The sheriff was a short fat man of sixty years and he often smelled like a boys locker room. He always had body odor and he often wore the same socks for many days in a row. He had a large beer gut and a big red nose. His bushy eyebrows often came down into his eyesight until his wife would nag him to trim them. One of his eyes would wander off every so often until the brain told it to come back to the line for group inspection. This happened more frequently when he would get piss drunk at the local Railway Pub. He was a grotesque excuse for a man.

The Sheriff got out of the cruiser and proceeded to the front porch.

"Evenin' folks." Sheriff Conway said through the screen door.

"Come in Sheriff. We were just sitting down for dessert." Thomas' father declared.

The sheriff opened the door and stepped into the kitchen. The sheriff didn't say so but Thomas could tell he didn't like visiting this part of town. Sheriff Conway's wife came from old money so he had become increasingly self-righteous over time. His sense of entitlement to some was bothersome considering that he grew up in a hovel in 'German Town.' His holier than thou attitude made the townsfolk chuckle because they knew that for a man with only a eighth grade education to consider himself 'all that' was laughable.

"What brings you out this way?" Thomas' father Henry asked concernedly.

"Can I get you some dessert or fix you a plate of Swedish meatballs?" Thomas' mother Laura asked.

Jasper got up from his spot on the rug in the living room and came to the kitchen. He stood right next to the sheriff sniffing at his feet. Jasper did not like the color aura smell he was picking up from this man. Jasper didn't like men in uniforms either and he liked this man even less.

"I just put it away. It's still hot." She added.

Like I'd eat anything made in this dump Conway thought.

"No, but thank you anyway. I just came by to talk to Thomas about the mishap at the circus today. I know it was an accident Thomas…" He said but was interrupted by Laura.

"What accident Thomas? What mishap is he referring to?" She fumed.

Thomas hadn't told them yet. He was trying to think of the right way and the right time in which to drop the news. There was no good time or way now that he had been ambushed. His deceit, or lack of coming forth with information detrimental to his comforts and well- being, was undone.

If the humiliation at the parkway was bad, this was worse.

Jasper was starting to feel the pressure that was being inflicted upon Thomas and he started letting out a growl.

The hair on Sheriff Conway's nape became erect. His tiny penis though did just the opposite. It began its ascent up inside his loins.

"Take it easy boy." Thomas said trying to calm the incensed dog.

Jaspers teeth started to show and the sheriff began to back up until his back was up against the fridge.

Henry stood up and grabbed the dog just before he lunged at Sheriff Conway. The sheriff cringed at the near miss. Goosebumps were present on his arms.

"Come on Jasper. I don't know what has gotten into you but you're going outside." Thomas father announced.

Thomas returned to his frightful situation and thought about what had happened and what he would have to do to make it right. The people who trusted him most were now disappointed in him and he would have to work to gain their trust once more.

"What incident Thomas Joseph?" She asked waiting for a response.

Crap. It was that bad. Thomas Joseph. Thomas was shifting around in the chair like he had sat on a tack or had been stung by a bee and was trying to get comfortable on his wound in the stiff chair.

"Well Jasper kinda'… he trailed off.

"It seems Jasper knocked Mrs. Copperback down hard and then landed square on top of her." Sheriff Conway proclaimed.

Henry had returned to hear this part of the conversation.

Now Henry knew Mrs. Copperback and she was not his favorite person.

Many years ago, in his less accountable days, he and a few friends placed super glue in Mr. Copperback's work boots, which he often left outside. Mr. Copperback worked landscape- construction and he seldom came home with clean boots. So many times he would leave them on the open porch. Mrs. Copperback was always after Henry about something, maybe it was the fact that he broke her daughter's heart. It wasn't really his fault though. Let me explain. Her daughter Janey was ever scornful and was always badgering

Henry about his so called 'recklessness.' Thinking back if she wasn't so damn handsome he never would have dated her. Looking back with 20/20 vision he never would've dated her anyway because now he knew she was f..king crazy. That was to put it plainly. She was a mad control freak, not unlike her mother. She had shown up at the town cinema where Henry and his friends had smuggled beers into the movies. Henry had told her he was visiting family and would be out of town for the weekend. Henry at this point was getting tired of checking in with her every time he did something and this broke the camels back. In the middle of the cinema she made a scene and demanded that he take her home that instant. Maybe it was the beers talking or maybe it was the bravado he felt in front of his pals. Nah, it was the principle of it all. He was fifteen and he didn't need to be controlled every minute of the day. He stood up on one of the theater chairs and pulled down his drawers.

"Janey." He said. "You can kiss my ass."

Needless to say she walked home.

So Mrs. Copperback, and rightfully so, suspected that Henry had something to do with the super glue caper. BUT, she couldn't prove it.

The mention of Mrs. Copperback being knocked in the dirt brought a suppressed chuckle from Henry and with this, ginger ale that he had been drinking came through his nose.

Thomas started laughing. They were both trying to control themselves. The giggles turned into a sidesplitting laugh.

Laura stopped them both cold. Her stare shot into Henry that froze him and he composed himself, mostly.

"As I was saying she landed pretty hard but she's not hurt, that bad. Just sore is all. She doesn't want to press charges or anything but I'm going to have to insist that the dog be tied up. If you take him out for a walk, obey the leash law. Okay Thomas?" He commanded. Not really asking. Sheriff Conway did not like that dog and he knew from Jasper's reaction to his visit that he was not fond of him either.

"Okay?" Laura asked of Thomas.

"Okay." Thomas replied.

"Good. Now I can get off to the Misses. She is making my favorite. Lobster casserole." Conway said.

The Sheriff opened the screen door and descended the steps and carried himself on to his car. He fiddled with his Sheriff's hat. He worked a loose thread where the visor met the hat. He nervously pinched and pulled at the string. He got in the cruiser and thought a moment or two about something and then he drove away.

More collected now from his brief nasal backfire, Henry said solemnly "Son, please do what the Sheriff asks. I don't want to be bothered by Mrs. Copperback." He finished.

Thomas made a half nod through a slight smirk.

"Okay son?" Henry asked with a smile trying to impress Laura although he really wanted to take Thomas in the den and slap him on the back in praise.

"Okay." Thomas whined.

Laura glared at him.

"Okay." Thomas said more assuredly.

"Good boy son." Henry added.

His father always called him son. Never Thomas or Thomas Joseph like his mother and many times he wondered why. Thomas didn't know about Henry's abusive childhood. And Henry would keep that awful time from him unless absolutely necessary.

Laura was about to ask about the circus job but she saw the preoccupation forming on Thomas face. He knew she was on to him. He would have to find another job. Laura didn't bring up this fact because she didn't want to burden Henry with financials.

Men out number woman 50 to 1 in knowing how to play poker and placing in the money. Often I wonder about this because more often than not they're five moves ahead of men in the playing field.

The Morgan's finished their dessert quietly that evening.

CHAPTER FIVE

The Marker

It was a week before Halloween and there was a dance scheduled for the Saturday night before the holiday. The dance was to be held at the Town Hall. Refreshments and finger foods would be served. The dance was formal and it began sharply at eight. The student's wanted it to be a Halloween costume party but the teachers voted it down. They had gone that route before and the Town Hall ended up a mess in toilet paper and egg. Who was to blame? Who could tell? The students were in costume garb so nothing could be proved and no one could be held accountable.

Halloween, which fell on Sunday this year, was forecasted to be clear and cool. Not as if the weathermen ever get it right. It has to be the only job where you can earn six figures and be wrong ninety-percent of the time. And why do the meteorologists give you the seven-day forecast. It's not like the weather in New England doesn't change from moment to moment. If you don't like the weather here just wait ten minutes, it'll change.

Monday morning everyone was talking about the Halloween dance. They gossiped about who would take this person and who would take that person. Rumors spread about this and that, dates were broken and then reformed. Some were mended and some remained in disrepair. No doubt someone stayed home alone in tears and regret. So is the complex world of the modern teenager.

Mary came up behind Thomas at his locker. She had her hands behind her back. Each was folded in the other and resting on her back.

Thomas turned to her and smiled.

"Well?" She questioned with eyes of diamonds.

You see ladies, men and boys alike, can't read the signs. As obvious as the situation might be to you, we are always dumbfounded.

It's like the postman went to drop off the mail, and because of an improper address, the information is returned to sender. Or we just forgot to study for the test. And it is a test. One I might add you do not want to fail. This secret weapon, the simple expectations of the female gender, is something they riddle you with sometimes weeks or months later. They've been using this wild card since the beginning of our short existence. And we love it. Deep down we like chasing them, after we have unintentionally slighted them. It's like going back to the start. And making up, for lack of a better term (and to keep it clean), making up is heavenly.

"Um." Thomas said unsure of what was required of him.

"Da. The dance." She said. "Aren't you going to ask me to the dance?" She asked lovingly.

"Well, will you?" He asked.

"Not like that." Mary insisted. "Say it romantic like. I want you to say it like you mean it." She added sternly with a touch of innocence.

Thomas began to say something but was cut off.

"I want you to think about it during the day and when I call you at your locker after last bell, I want to be surprised." She demanded.

With that, she bounced off to first class.

Thomas grabbed his History book in the mess of his locker and hurried off to class as first bell began to ring.

Man.

What am I to say to Mary? How are guys supposed to ask these things? He was worried and with good cause. He kept going over lines and scenarios in his head. Each time it sounded corny or feeble.

Crap.

Having a girl is harder work than I thought.

Then the board of trustees inside his mind spoke up again.

Are you kidding? Think about what you gain.

He didn't have to ponder on this very long. All he had to do was think about Mary. He placed her face in his mind and he saw her smile and he was happy. Then his eyes kept focusing on her breasts. That was it. He would walk across the dessert if he had to in finding the right words for her. He would make her happy. How hard could it be anyway?

The students were chatting and filing into their respective seats. Miss Godwin assigned seats according to alphabetical order. This placed Thomas in the last row third seat nearest the windows.

"Class, open your hardcover and turn to page one hundred and seven." Miss Godwin said.

They had left off the previous day entangled in the Mexican-American War.

It was 1847 and The United States was expanding its territories. An army outfit invaded and sacked what is now New Mexico. This was one of many bloody conquests of aggression and forced will upon the indigenous people in our nations history.

"Jennifer, could you start reading aloud?" Miss Godwin asked. Then added "We'll follow along silently."

They all followed along with Jennifer and Miss Godwin lipped the words as if she knew them by heart. As she was reciting this knowledge to herself she paced up and down the aisles to be sure that everyone was paying attention.

In unison, the class turned to page one hundred and eight.

Miss Godwin had started down Thomas' aisle when he noticed that his book was defaced. In big black bold letters it read 'Miss Godwin licks donkey crotch.'

The moment he finished reading it, he felt Miss Godwin grab him by the ear. She would escort him, with her hand tightly fixed on the lobe, to the hall and on to the principle's office. Before he could express his surprise, Miss Godwin was pulling him toward the door.

"Come now Thomas. Let's go see what Principal Kilcrop thinks of your filthy humor. Really Thomas I never expected anything of this sort from you." She fumed angrily.

"But I didn't..." Thomas refuted trying to pronounce his innocence.

"I personally went through all those books before the new school year and none of them contained anything of that nature. We'll see what the Principle has to say about this." She barked.

She pulled him through the Secretary's office and then passed the Guidance Counselor's office and onto Mr. Kilcrop's office.

Dom Gladberry's name had been removed and the new principle's name had been added.

This was one of Sol Bender's many tasks since he had arrived.

"But you have to believe..." He stammered.

They entered the Principle's office without knocking and charged right up to the front of his desk. Principle Kilcrop was looking out the window at the gym class playing a game of baseball in the field behind the school. He had the phone against his shoulder and ear like he had been on the phone for a long period and was tired of holding it.

"I'll have to call you back." Principle Kilcrop said into the phone receiver, although no one was on the line.

Thomas could hear the dead line through the receiver and was puzzled, although he had no time to contemplate this fact. Miss Godwin was so consumed with rage she neglected to hear the dead tone in the phone. Even if she had she would make herself reason it out. For who would sit facing out the window talking to no one?

Silly.

Yet?

Couldn't be.

Miss Godwin alleged that Thomas had defaced his hard cover History book. She told him about the contents of the comments there in.

Thomas professed his innocence.

"Well let's go have a look." Principle Kilcrop declared.

So off they went, returning back to the History class. All the students were gossiping about what Thomas had done.

The principle pulled out the tote desk below the table that ran along wooden runners. In the tote was a single item.

A black bold magic marker.

"Really Thomas you had me fooled for being a nice young gentleman. I guess I was wrong." Stated Miss Godwin.

"Thomas I didn't take you for this caliber of person either. I guess you deceived us both." Declared Principle Kilcrop.

"It wasn't me I swear." Said Thomas earnestly.

"I'll see you after school Mr. Morgan." Publicized Mr. Kilcrop.

Oh God a detention. Mom will kill me. First I lost my job and now I'm after school.

Thomas just seated himself, defeated.

He could hear the students whispering around him.

Miss Godwin kept glaring at Thomas through out what seemed like eternity, which was the rest of the class.

The rest of the day wore on like all days you want to end. Seconds become minutes, and minutes become hours. Finally it did come to an end and he shuffled to his locker with a heavy burden.

He was digging through his locker for his Science book to bring home to study for an upcoming test. As he looked up he spotted Mary marching proudly his way. When she had reached him she stood and waited for her surprise.

Oh God.

I forgot about Mary's small request thought Thomas.

Then he said words that he never intended for Mary. Words he thought he would never say to her.

"Now is not a very good time Mary." He said.

As he said the words he saw the way they took hold of her. Her heart was breaking right in front of him. He would never forget this look till the end of his days.

Her bottom lip started to quiver. Small crows feet gathered around her eyes and pointed down toward the top of her ears. The look of sadness gave way to utter dejection. Her eyes glossed over and tears shed from them like a leaky faucet. Down they came running into her mouth, off her chin and onto her red sweater. She was sniffling and her nose was running.

She bolted off crying hysterically.

He went after her.

"Wait." He cried.

But she was determined to get away.

Sometimes it's best to let people air their feelings before you confront them. It gives them a chance to breath and reflect on their present crisis. Often times it's better to let a woman, who is hot with you, have space. You might find that their mercy and understanding is stronger than your resolve.

Thomas wiped a tear from the corner of his eye, lest anyone should see him and deem him soft.

He lumbered on to the Principles office. He sat down in a seat in front of his desk waiting for Mr. Kilcrop, who was speaking with the janitor in the next room. Then, after much waiting, the Principle entered the room closing the door behind him.

This caused an uneasy feeling in Thomas.

This is a fear tactic often used by police or military to let the subject know that they are on their own, with no one to help them.

Completely alone.

Solidarity is not a tool used in getting information or making someone concede. They strip you down to nothing until you give up and tell them whatever it is they want to hear. They will use force if necessary although most times fear is enough to sway a person's silence and trust.

It's deplorable that seventy years after thwarting a nation of evil we have employed similar techniques in the name of national security. However necessary you think war crimes are remember they are after all illegal and immoral. We are supposed to be the driving force behind the United Nations, which was intended to be an oversight committee for just such situations and yet we are the first to jump on the torture wagon. What we should be doing instead of saying these people are fanatics and beyond reason is asking ourselves why the hell would someone blow themselves up. Is there something in the water? I think not. Or is there some hidden agenda in the air. Who knows?

So Mr. Kilcrop sensing Thomas' uneasiness and fear feathered his hands together and cracked all his knuckles at once. They made a giant snapping sound. It sounded like there were too many knuckles cracking.

"Now Mr. Morgan. I've thought about your situation and feel that you don't need a detention this time. But I do want you to think about what you've done." Spoke Mr. Kilcrop.

"But I didn't do anything.' Thomas replied.

"Really Mr. Morgan, I think were past that." Mr. Kilcrop shot back.

"I didn't." repeated Thomas.

But Mr. Kilcrop was past that already.

Like a parent dismissing their child's story as nonsense or rubbish. This is not healthy for a child. They have to know that their parents believe in them. A parent should listen and understand their child's point of view. This is necessary for them to build trust in others. This is necessary in building a foundation for their identity, which is always taking shape.

"I want you to go home and do some thinking. I want you to apologize to Miss Godwin tomorrow. Consider this a warning, next time you won't be let off so easily." Mr. Kilcrop said finally.

Mr. Kilcrop waited for a response but none came. In some ways he liked Thomas. Thomas wouldn't yield to wrongness. Even though he had been undermined he would not admit wrongdoing. Strong conviction makes for a formidable adversary. Mr. Kilcrop liked playing against a difficult opponent, it made for a much more interesting game. He liked playing games for that was his favorite thing of all. Especially when he controlled the rules. The principle watched the young man exit the room without another consideration about his alleged crime. Mr. Kilcrop thought that this would be a chess match for the ages.

Thomas was upset that he had to apologize for something he didn't do, but that took second place to making up with Mary. He knew someone had duped him but Mary was more important. He set off to apologize to his best girl.

He burst through the Secretary's office nearly knocking over the girl's gym teacher, Miss Liklot. He apologized in passing and ran through the double doors in the front entrance of the school. He sprinted down the paved runway leading up from the front stairs and onto the sidewalk. He flew by the courtyard and someone waved to him but he ignored it. He was not interested in anything but making it right with Mary. He hurried down School Street and across Elm and on to Woodland St. He ran like the wind to Mary's house and flew up the front stairs. He knocked on the door as he huffed for breath. He was trying to get the air into lungs when Mary's mother, Brenda, came to the door.

She opened the storm door and spoke through the screen one.

"Mary doesn't want to see you anymore, Thomas. And I don't want to see you hanging around waiting for her. Now go on home." She stated.

The words fell down on him like a hammer to a nail. He couldn't move. His legs wouldn't work.

"What's the matter with you? Didn't you hear what I said?" Brenda asked becoming angry.

Thomas was vanquished.

Brenda relished in his anguish and savored this scene. She liked inflicting pain and humility on men. This displaced aggression came from her messy divorce with Mary's father.

He dragged his heavy legs down the stairs and began the lonely trek home.

The weight of the world was resting on Thomas' shoulders and he felt wearier than ever.

Up in the window facing the street, Mary looked out. Her right hand rested on the window glass as if she was saying goodbye. She was watching her best friend walk out of her life and she began to cry all over again.

That night Thomas lay on his bed, staring up at the ceiling with his hands behind his head, underneath the pillow. He had cried for sometime and now he was beyond tears.

His mother heard him crying and knew it must be something bad. Thomas closed his door too. She went to his door and tapped softly on the door. He didn't answer. He didn't want to. He knew confiding in his Mom about this tragedy would make him all the more sad.

"Thomas?" She asked. "Thomas, can I come in?"

"Yeah." He said half-heartedly.

She opened the door and came into the room. She petted Jasper on the head and sat on Thomas' bed.

Jasper was worried too. He had never seen Thomas like this and it made him sad and perturbed at the same time. Who had made his master like this? He had better not find them, for they would be sorry evermore.

Thomas continued to stare at the ceiling so as not to make eye contact with his mother.

"Is everything all right Thomas?" She asked.

"I guess so." He replied.

"Has something happened between you and Mary?" She further inquired. She knew the answer of course because she was skilled in these ways. Like all women they know when someone's been dumped or dismissed as it were.

He began to come apart. He bit his lip but tears squeezed their way out of their ducts anyway.

Jasper let out a whine.

Laura saw his tears and held his hand in hers.

"Thomas I don't know what has happened between you two but I can't believe that you have done everything to make it right. I know how much Mary cares about you. I'm certain that if you go to her with all your commitment and loyalty, that she will forgo whatever happened between you." She finished.

"You really think so." He said.

"I know so." She declared. "Have I ever been wrong in the affairs of the heart?" She asked.

He liked when his mother talked poetic and romantic like, it made him feel good inside. No other can match a mother's love for her child. And besides she had never been wrong about these matters. Who knows more about a woman's feelings than another woman?

"Thanks Mum." He responded.

She patted him on the head and kissed him on the cheek.

"You'll find the answer in your heart. That's where all truth and faith comes from." She proclaimed.

"No matter how corny it is?" He asked.

"In the matter of making up, the cornier the better." She responded.

He laughed at this.

She smiled at Jasper and left the room.

Jasper was more cheerful now that Thomas had returned from the land of despair. He went to Thomas and put his paws up on his belly. Thomas rubbed Jasper behind the ears and started thinking.

He was focused now.

He must make it right. He was determined that nothing would keep him away from Mary. He would chew his arm off before being stuck in this trap that someone had laid for him. He knew what he must do. He would make it right with his best friend, and he knew just how.

The next morning Thomas woke up at first light. I say he woke up but he didn't sleep a wink. He threw on some old clothes, tied up his New Balance cross trainers from last year and headed off to do his duty.

He and Jasper headed to Goreman's field.

He didn't place Jasper on a leash because he couldn't bring himself to do so.

There was the stream that ran directly through the property. This stream divided the property in half. The property on the far side bordered the playground. Where the stream ran underneath Rigby road, there were wild rose bushes of many colors. He crossed the stream and walked down to the roses. As usual, Jasper played in the stream. He liked drinking the cold fresh water, which ran down from Mudjets Hill, via the orchards. There was an underground stream that ran through the orchard. This made the ground fertile and well irrigated. It showed in the huge apples it produced every autumn.

Thomas approached the array of rose bushes near the road and saw they were in full bloom. He pulled his Swiss army knife out. He opened it up to the scissors. He snapped off four roses. He picked a pink one, a white one and then he chose two red ones. When he was finished, he closed up his knife and headed home. Jasper led the way.

He got home and quickly changed into school appropriate clothes. He brushed his teeth, grabbed his school- books and started out the door.

"Aren't you going to have some breakfast Thomas?" Laura asked.

"No Ma I'm on a mission. Oh I almost forgot." He said walking out the door.

He turned around and gave his mother a red rose.

"Here Ma for you." He proclaimed as he kissed her on the cheek.

"You're going to make your father think it's a special occasion." She responded.

He just smiled and blasted through the door. The screen door crashed back on its hinges.

His mother smiled too, for she was anxious to see what she might get out of her husband when he saw she had a freshly picked red rose. He'll think Thomas remembered and he didn't.

Laura watched Thomas run up the street holding the roses like a kingly gift.

"Young love is something to be desired." She whispered.

She had the strange feeling that all was going to be right between her son and his best girl.

As Thomas neared Mary's house he could see that she was already up ahead of him and almost on Elm Street.

He ran up behind her.

"Mary." Said Thomas tenderly absent of breath from his run to her.

She just stopped with her back to him. She held her books tight.

"I have three roses for you. The pink one is for friendship, that you've always shown me. The white one is for faithfulness, which I pledge to always be to you. And the red is for love, which is beating in my heart to which you are the blood." He said awaiting her response in quiet desperation.

She dropped her books to the ground and turned around and ran into his arms. They held each other tight. Tears filled her eyes. She felt guilty for being angry with Thomas and even more culpable for having told her mother she didn't want to see him. How could she think that she would never want to see Thomas again?

Silly.

"I'm sorry. I was having an awful day yesterday and took it out on you. Said Thomas. "Can you forgive me?" He asked with his big brown sad eyes.

"I'm sorry too." Mary sobbed.

She pulled his head down to hers and gave him a big kiss.

Thomas could taste the salt of her tears that had run into her mouth.

"Does this mean you'll take me to the dance?" Mary asked playfully after their lip lock.

"Well Jessica Alba said no, so I guess…" He jeered.

She smacked him on the arm in fun and they walked off to school.

She was guarding her roses and he was carrying their books, all six of them. But no matter, He and Mary were going to be fine. And he was happy. He carried the books and a great big smile.

An atomic bomb could fall on his head and it wouldn't bother him in the least.

CHAPTER SIX

Jonas

Now we haven't talked much about Jonas Lightbringer up to this point.

You know, the one who carries the eight gauge shot- gun attached to his back. It's not for lack though of knowing what he is about. He's just been busy making preparations, like his enemy.

Jonas was old.

Well he appeared old to you and I, but really he was only middle-aged for his race. He was one hundred and eighty three years young. I know what you're thinking, crazy right? But there are things on this planet amongst our existence that are beyond our understanding. Many of these creatures we have not even found yet and maybe we never will.

There are things that we are starting to discover in the ocean, that don't follow any living processes previously known to man. There is the money pit in an island in Nova Scotia, that some believe, holds the remains to the Ark of the Covenant. The contents found in the hole are like nothing scientists have ever encountered. They are from the future and the past. What? There are countless numbers of documented cases of extra-terrestrial abductions. I'm not even going to say how many people have seen a UFO. I know it sounds like an X-Files episode right, but hear me out. There are things out there that, by a mere defense mechanism, do not want to be found. This self- preservation technique is mother- natures way of insuring life goes on. Much like an animal that is sensing it is about to become extinct because of encroaching settlers or changing climates. If there are only males left to that species, mother- nature might play a funny trick on them. She may make the species asexual and cause the males to give birth. Stranger things have happened. It's like the onion. When you cut apiece off and place it under a microscope, it begins growing again by regenerating its cells. If you leave an onion in the cupboard long enough it will begin sprouting into a new plant, until there is no longer any part of the once living organism to feed the new.

My philosophy is that, if you can imagine it, it can be.

But before I reveal all of nature's hidden ploys, let me get back to Jonas.

Jonas like I said is middle-aged, for he is a descendent of the Silverfish Blue Clan. This ancient race is one whose people are now all but extinct. There are only three that remain. Jonas, a small girl and her guardian are the last of their kind. But I'll save them for another story telling.

He was born in a small fishing village in the territory we now refer to as Alaska. There were only a few means of employment in this remote area of the world. If you lived in these parts when the territory belonged to the Russians you would find yourself with but three choices for work. They were fishing, working lumber and trapping.

His mothers husband Jack, had taken to the lumber industry. He worked long hours, high in the trees strapped to the trunk of a tree whose age only the soil knew. He would come home with pine pitch and grease all about him.

Many hours his mother, Sarah, would try to scrub out the grime and grease stains from his clothing in the running stream in back of their cabin. It didn't bother her none, for she was quite content with her simple life.

She would spend much of her time in the small garden she had planted on the south hill overlooking the little settlement below. She planted cabbages, onions, potatoes, carrots, garlic, tomatoes and several spices, like fennel, basil and parsley. The window for cultivating these crops in Alaska was something to get used to, but she managed just fine.

One day though, her world changed.

Her husband befell a terrible accident. He was relieving himself near the tree he had just felled and a rookie atop another nearby tree marked for death called out those terrible words that no one near wants to hear. If you hear them all too clear that means you all too close.

"Timberrrrrrrrrrrrrrrrrrrrrrrrrrrrrrr." The young lumberjack called out.

It was a bit too late.

Jack was too close.

The tree came down and barely missed him. It would have been better if it had landed right on top of him killing him instantly. But it didn't. It bounced up knocking him backwards into the fallen tree behind him. He was pinned against the fallen one, with the larger one landing on him, smashing his lower body. He was so damaged that he felt no pain, and he knew he would die. In his dying remaining moments, he begged God to take care of his Sarah whom he loved with all his heart. The Lord heard his prayers and gave his grace.

The rookie lumberjack came down out of the tree in two leaps like a damn panther. He ran to Jack and fell to his knees and grabbed him by the back of the head.

"No. Oh No. Oh Nooooo." He cried.

Jack looked up at the young whipper -snapper and just smiled.

The medical team arrived on the scene and there was nothing they could do.

He was gone.

His body was beyond repair, and so, he died.

It was several hours before they could pull the large tree off of the dead man. No one felt compelled to do it except an old timer. He was appalled that they would be reluctant to remove the felled lumber and give this hard working family man a proper burial. The old timer worked late into the night with the depressed and sullen rookie right there with him. Finally they got him free and placed his broken body on a horse pulled wagon. They brought his body down to Sarah and they buried him that night. The rookie cried all through the dig and service. Sarah delivered his vigil and gave his eulogy. The old timer never left her side. The rookie could not look at her. At the end of the service the young lumberjack felt a hand upon his shoulder. He slowly glanced up into Sarah's eyes and she forgave him.

"I'm not angry with you." She said softly.

"I'm sorry mam.' I'm so sorry." He said.

"I know." She replied.

His tears and sorrow were sincere and she knew it was not his intent to cause the death of her husband.

"Who will look after you?" He asked crying. "This country is very unforgiving Mrs. Lightbringer." He added through a tear soaked face.

"I will survive, I'm sure." She responded.

The rookie never felt the same after that, taking to alcoholism and gambling. He would never marry. The girl for whom he was intended he could not face. Although she had understood his foreboding, he could not forgive himself and sunk deeper and deeper into substance-abused depression. He would carry this guilt for the rest of his days. To ease this guilt, he would sneak up to Sarah's cabin and place money in the coffee can left outside.

Jake used to throw his hand rolled tobacco stubs in there.

So with the help of the blood money and the sale of her vegetables, Sarah managed. People would often call her green thumb because the fruit and vegetables she cultivated were two or three times the average size.

The old timer, who everyone called Colonel, often paid a visit and always bought far too many vegetables. He would always leave too much money too. The next time he would come by, Sarah would insist he take it back. He would until he was about to leave and then he would hide it somewhere it could easily be found. Each time she would find it she would curse the old man, then she would feel grateful for men like him.

One night, some time later, a stranger came calling.

She opened the door expecting to find the old man standing in the door with a fresh cut of cattle or a catch of fish and instead she saw this weary traveler.

"Could I bother you for some water My Lady?" He asked rather parched.

"Of course, I'm sorry. Please come in." She said hyper apologetically.

He said he was a trapper and was just passing through. She obliged him with two large glasses of clean mountain water. She fixed him a bowl of hot fish chowder. She broke off a piece of bread and spread some recently churned butter over it.

I don't know if you've had freshly made butter, and not that naturally made store bought stuff either. I mean right from the source. It's delicious, like a totally different product.

I have to laugh at the people who go to the market and want a cut of beef, cut fresh. They don't realize that the beef is all sectioned and boxed, shipped out from thousands of miles away. The cattle they're eating from, is probably three weeks deceased. That's why the freshest beef comes from the slaughter yard, although those are far and few between nowadays. The difference though in the product will astonish you.

The man was pleased, for not many welcomed unknown travelers into their homes. She had nourished and comforted him with open arms.

When the man finished his fine meal he said to her "Young lady you have shown me a courtesy not common to this world and I grant you a wish."

She was puzzled by his statement, and dismissed it as a kind gesture or service. She just cleared his place at the table and began to clean the dishes.

He just stood there waiting for an answer.

She felt him staring at her from behind.

Finally she turned and said. "If you will grant me one wish, I wish you would stay and keep me company."

"That's all?" He asked as if stunned.

"That's all." She responded.

He smiled.

He was pleased.

And it was so.

They talked and laughed. He spoke in great detail of the outside world. He educated her on the ports of the orient. He told her about the unique spices and exotic plants relative only to that region of the world. Then he went on about the silk trade and the lucrative market it brought to the rest of the world. This was her favorite story.

He went on about the tribes and cultures of the Indians on all continents. He described the differences and similarities between the groups residing in their respective places and climates.

He talked of the diamond excavating slavery camps in Africa, which in many ways still exists today. He told her of the ways that indigenous people were coerced and manipulated into working cheap for the traders.

On and on he spoke of the world south of heaven.

She wondered if he had really been to all these foreign places in the world, or if he was in fact just well educated.

As night approached, the man began to get his belongings together and threw the nap sack that he was carrying when he arrived, over his shoulder. It made a clinking sound like metal objects clanging together.

"I must be off. The road is long and time is short." He said as he walked toward the door.

"But where will you stay?" She asked. "And you promised to keep me company." She replied.

"And I have kept you company." He reiterated.

"I didn't say for how long." She said.

"Well that's true enough." He replied with a smile like he had no choice but to concede.

"Won't you stay the night?" She begged.

"Well it does appear we have a storm approaching. Yes I think I will stay, since you've offered." He went on.

This man had a charm and aura about him that Sarah had never witnessed in a man before. She was drawn to his shyness and overly polite manner. She was overcome with desire by his large stature and broad shoulders. He was a handsome looking man, very pleasing to the eye. She was also terribly lonely.

Late that night, the man would challenge her loneliness and she would willingly succumb to his advances.

The love they made throughout that night, and next day, she would remember for the rest of her life.

That stormy night when the rain fell hard pelting the roof and buckets outside, feeding the garden its necessary drink. They were engaged, rolling back and forth in her bed amidst the throes of passion. He caressed her body. She kissed, bit and scratched his. It was a time not to be forgotten.

Around mid afternoon the next day when they had finished, the traveler sat up in bed and spoke to her.

"You won't be lonely anymore." He stated.

She just smiled at him as though there was no one else in the world.

She thought that he may stay on and began preparations for a bath. They went out with buckets to the clear clean mountain stream several times to get water to heat for the tub. She poured the water into the large pot the man had gracefully picked up from the corner of the room and placed on the rack over the fire. After some time the water came to a simmer and it was well hot enough for a bath. She transferred the water into smaller buckets and took them to the large wooden bathtub.

She finished pouring the last of the hot water in and began stripping down.

He came up behind her and gave her a kiss on the ear. He was already naked and they got in the tub together.

The hot water brought goose pimples to Sarah's flesh. Sarah poured some scented oil in the water. She had purchased it some years ago from a Chinese merchant going door to door. He had come in on a merchant ship and stayed only a short time for the lack of need of his merchandise. But Sarah bought a small bottle of his slippery lilac potion.

They slipped and rubbed and fondled.

She straddled on top of him and rode until she came again. But he wasn't finished. He bent her over the side of the tub and sodomized her. The rumble that came from her legs shook her right to the core.

She stayed in the bath a bit longer than him because her legs were useless.

When she was finally able to work her legs, she wobbled out of the long wooden tub and got up and dressed herself.

When she entered the main room she found that the stranger had gone. She was a little dismayed but understood the man's clean break. She was not one for long goodbyes and she reckoned neither was he. She went to the dinner table and looked upon the items that lay there.

First to be noticed on the table was an old Bible. When Laura opened the sacred book she saw that the pages were blank, void of any literature or history. Strange she thought. To carry a Bible which had no scripture.

There, also lying upon the table, were two long bracelets made of pure gold. Inscribed in the bracelets were two Angels. Their wings were unfolded to full wingspan and their hands were clasped together as if in prayer. 'These are for Jonas' it said on a note. 'The Book and Bracelets are to be given to him when he becomes of age' it informed her. She was bewildered. The man was quite an enigma that she couldn't riddle out.

Later in life these tools would make themselves useful to Jonas.

The bracelets were six inches long and were to be pulled over a man's wrists.

They had a small extension at the end where the wrist meets the backhand. It almost reached the knuckles to give the wearer extra protection.

Later in Jonas' life he would discover that this one of a kind artifact was a protection against physical harm and magic. These were Bracers of Defense, defense against Dark Magic. No physical craft could bend or maim the bracers. No dark energy or force could expel or threaten the wearer.

Sarah put these items away, into an old trunk that she and her husband brought with them on the journey to this frontier. Sarah buried them, so Jonas would not ask about them and where they came from. She let Jonas believe that Jack, her husband had impregnated her before he died tragically. She had Jonas believe that Jack was his father.

Many years later and also three days before she passed on, she told Jonas the truth about that night, and day, nearly fifty years before. He wasn't angry or sad that she had kept this from him. In his heart he knew that she probably did this to protect him, like she always did.

The book appeared empty to all but Jonas, for he alone could read from it.

Later on when he opened it to read the pages, they would light up with golden hieroglyphic letters. It contained material information about things he must do and targets he must protect. These tasks that he would perform, would take him far and wide. He would meet many people along his journey and he would change their lives forever, mostly for the good.

Oftentimes Sarah would think about pawning them in at the small town store, or the hovel that was posing for a store, when Jonas was just young. There, they exchanged gold for coin, in the merchants favor of course. But she kept these unique items to remind her of the time she came through the night, and day, with the mysterious wish granter.

I'm getting ahead of myself though. Let me tell you how Jonas came to be. Then I'll fill in the mystery of the relics and unearthly possessions.

So having put these odd objects in the trunk, she went back to her daily routine. That is until her belly started to round up. She tried to keep this hidden from the people in the settlement. She didn't want to arouse suspicion or have the women think that maybe one of their husbands, being 'charitable or concerned', went to visit her.

One day this became unavoidable.

She was tottering around the house, eight months into term and she heard a rapid knock upon the door. Then a fierce and frenzied banging started falling on it.

She heard a women speaking frantically in a language she did not understand. Sarah opened the door to see a half-clothed Spanish women crying and screaming. She kept looking over her shoulder as if someone was pursuing her.   Sarah let the woman in and gave her some clean clothes. She then gave her a cup of hot soup. The woman was going on and on about who knows what, when a less fastidious knock fell upon the now closed door. It wasn't hurried like that of the Latino woman. They were slow intermittent knocks followed by heavy thunderous blows with the side of a man's fists. It seemed like the person didn't know how to approach his current state of affairs. Should he bang on the door and demand that the Spanish girl face him or should he beg for her mercy?

A slurred voice began yelling unintelligible talk at the door.

"I Donna figa matha graz." Is what it sounded like.

Sarah crept over to the window and saw a man with his head against the door, barely conscious with drool hanging from his mouth. Then he vomited right on the stoop. After that, he began whining about how he wanted the woman back.

Just then a posse came up the trail to her cabin and detained him.

Later Sarah found out that this man had lost her new house-guest to another man in a poker game. When alcohol, desperation and gambling come together to stay the night at your house, you can bet it will lead to trouble, if not disaster. The previous 'owner' of this woman was not thrilled about having lost her. He drank and stewed on it, until he finally shot the other fellow in the back. Subsequently he was hanged two weeks after being arrested. He was tried, arraigned and put to death all in a fortnight.

"Too bad so sad and who will cry for me." He said upon his hanging.

Never mix booze, woman and gambling for it will only bring you misery and nothing but the worst of troubles.

Some good did come out of this situation though. The Spanish woman, later to be known as Juanita, would stay on and help Sarah with anything that needed doing. Juanita was so grateful, for Sarah having opened the door to her, she insisted she do everything. Every time Sarah would go to do a simple chore, Juanita would take it from her. She would rub Sarah's belly and speak her sweet romantic language to the child inside. Then she would press Sarah to sit down. Sarah was content, and thankful that Juanita had come along.

The Lord works in mysterious ways.

As my Grandmother used to say 'there is a silver lining to every dark cloud.' This is often true unless that cloud is a hurricane.

So nine months and six days after that sweet romance with the stranger, Jonas was born. He was late on his arrival. He stayed in longer than most because, well, he needed more cooking than most.

Sarah was very fortunate to have Juanita there to help deliver the baby.

Juanita had helped deliver two nephews for her brother in Spain six years prior. So she was very capable and Jonas came out just fine.

Sarah was grateful for Juanita and although the Spanish woman knew not the words spoken in praise to her, she grasped their true identity and she was happy to have been granted this fortunate fate.

Jonas was around six pounds at birth and was a very good baby. He never fussed except for a short while when he developed colic. But Juanita the Spanish vixen was more than just a pretty face. She was skilled in the ways of herbal medicine and she went into the forest and got the necessary ingredients to formulate a remedy for Jonas' gastro-intestinal problem. Soon Jonas was back to his normal quiet but attentive self.

Jonas grew up fast and strong. His mother was very fond of him. She taught him to read and write. She taught him the difference between right and wrong. She taught him discipline and she gave him much love. She nurtured Jonas with all her attention and affection. He became a strong soul because of it. He would keep the lessons she taught him close to his heart.

She began to teach him the word of God at an early age. He liked the ancient stories of tribes in conflict. He liked when his mother would read to him before bed. He always asked for one more page, and she always obliged. He would do this until he descended into a deep sleep.

Juanita would listen from the main room with wondrous intrigue, about the language she was foreign to.

At first it was hard for them to communicate with Juanita, but as with all things, the more practice, the more able. They picked up one another's language and before long they were finding it easier to converse. It became less and less problematic to communicate.

This experience was good for Jonas growing up, learning two languages from birth. He would become fluent in many languages in the future because of his basic understanding of a primary romantic language. Of all the romance languages he would come to love the French one most. Only the listener of the words understands the true reasons for a person's preference or appreciation of one language over another.

There is culture and depth to different languages and this helped to make Jonas well rounded. He would come to understand the different and sometimes dual meanings of words, which are prevalent in all languages. These teachings would add depth to his perception of people's races and genders. Several languages have words that cannot be translated. His broad knowledge of literature and linguistics helped him bridge this gap when communication came to a halt in matters of great concern.

Very often he would just sit and listen to Juanita speaking and imagine the words and their hidden meanings. His ability to listen and hear the words helped him much in his learning of the world.

All was good with the world on their small acreage. They planted more and more as the years went on. They would experiment and if something didn't take they would try something new the following year.

Jonas became an excellent fishermen and one of the best and most accurate hunters ever to grace that part of the world. He never killed for the sake of sport or just to do so because he had the means. He only hunted when they were in need of food. Before the winter, Jonas would often go off for days on end, hunting to meet the necessary need for meat supplies through the cold hard winter known to that part on the frozen tundra. His going away for several days and sometimes weeks would genuinely distress his mother. He would return unscathed though and with many hides for skinning and smoking.

All was well for several years and the three were joyful. Around the end of each year, they would celebrate the new coming year with drink and dancing.

Juanita lay with Jonas one night and took his virginity. Sarah knew this but pretended not to. Sarah thought it was a good thing for him to know the ways of a woman so she intentionally turned the other way. On his fifteenth birthday Juanita gave him the best gift a man, young or old, can receive. And let me tell you something, I'm still not sure which women move the best in the art of love. Is it the Asians or the Spanish? The Black girls or the Europeans? What a dilemma to have to reconcile, no?

It's hard for me to say which is best, for I don't have enough information to form a hypothesis. But I will continue in my research so I can formulate an answer someday. Do an experiment yourself, to find out which type of women can shake your lemon tree the hardest. Whichever race you pick, you're sure not to be dissatisfied.

Jonas was thrilled to unwrap his present and he would try to score gifts often. Juanita in the prime of her life was all too ready to give. She was very charitable in this sense, and Jonas loved her benevolence.

All remained well until Jonas was seventeen, when Juanita got sick with Typhus and soon after she died.

He was grieved. For many weeks he was sloth. He couldn't perform his normal chores or duties and Sarah was moved by his heartache. She took him aside and talked many hours with him and slowly but surely he came out of the gloom. He would never forget Juanita, his first love. He could not, for most women were pale in comparison to her. Some could move as well as she and some were tender enough to compare to her and others were as romantic and caring as she had been. But she was all of these things combined and a whole lot more. He would find only one that would ever come close. She lived seventeen thousand miles from his home in a small village just outside Bangkok. He would be seventy years older than her, but that was fine. She was a real woman of real respect and dignity. These traits are very hard to find in today's times. If you find them in a woman make sure she also holds faithfulness dear to her heart.

This young woman would make him feel like he was the only man alive and she believed it too. Her hands were small and soft but were mighty strong. She could wash your clothes all morning, beat out the rugs during the day and do the other chores as well. Then she would cook dinner and after the meal she would rub you until you were Jello. Then she would climb on top of you until you were worn out. When you woke she would have your coffee and breakfast ready. If you were able, she would rock you again in the sack and then go about her daily tasks. She was like an ever -ready self-reenergizing battery. I have to save the erotic details for another time or I'll never get off this subject. Man, what a woman.

As I said, Juanita died from Typhus. Jonas' mother though, lived thirty-four more years, to the age of eight-nine. She was able until the day she died. She passed in her sleep without pain or turmoil.

Jonas was much distraught by her passing. He mourned for many days. But she had told him that death is not the end of this. Death is but a change she would tell him. A change we all must make. It is a metamorphosis of mind, energy and spirit. Although he heard these words, it still stung his heart that she was gone.

Later in life he would learn to keep his distance from people and ones who grew fond of him or at the very least try to. He knew that watching them die would always break his heart.

Since that time he has chosen to give much of his time and energy to helping mankind, and completing his tasks, in any way he can. Oftentimes, picking up the broken pieces these experiences left behind.

He had many experiences, both good and bad. At times he would get the itch for a woman but he would never again become embroidered in someone's heart. He tried to lessen the experiences of heartache and adulation from people around him but sometimes it was unavoidable. Because however hard you might try, sometimes love happens and when it does, you are helpless to resist. This drama and conflict are necessary elements of human interaction and existence.

Adversity and conflict is what makes us who we are. If we took back all the mistakes we thought we've made over the years, it would make us someone else. These changes would change the course of history not only for us but also the rest of the living world.

Let's do another experiment. Let's say we change something, as small as say, the death of a dinosaur. One that escaped the lethal jaws of T-rex, instead of being killed. Now the dominoes start to fall. The young archeologist that was supposed to find the remains of this not yet discovered species does not. Someone else does, some five years later. The notoriety that he was supposed to gain, that would have led him to funding by an esteemed university, goes to another. This gives way to money problems. This turns his once supportive wife to anxiety and grief. Finally his wife concedes to the bickering and undermining of her parents and friends. Also because she's so tired of living on the cuff. She divorces him and takes custody of his only child. He turns to opium and excess. One night driving high in the distant dreams and visions that only opiates can take you, he strikes and kills a young Asian boy. This boy was supposed to grow up to be the next Dalai Lama.

Now this is quite ridiculous and very far- fetched but the point is, that one small change can alter the events and course of history.

So when Jonas visited places like Beirut, Vietnam, Cambodia, Somalia, Germanys siege at Stalingrad, or the Missouri/Kansas border wars during the Civil wars, he treaded lightly.

He witnessed people trying to maintain their way of life by fighting under the black flag. There was nothing civil about war.

These units would raise the black flag and offer no quarter to opposing forces. This may sound cruel but like I said war is not civil and often times the rules of chivalrous engagement often go to the wayside.

Both sides in any war are guilty of being less than gracious to the overtaken force.

History is not written by the vanquished but is written by the champion of the battlefield. These are sometimes less than factual events scribed for students and scholars because who would slander themselves. This is however how the truth gets skewed. The spoils of war go to the victor and often times when brigands clothe themselves in wool they will pull out the card calling for the necessity of revenge. This necessity is constructed to rid the winner of any further opposition of events not privy to their tastes. They pull that sheep's wool over the eyes of the public and scream reprisal for the conquered. They would do it to us they'd say. Watch with vigilance for these wolves for they are the nastiest vermin of all. Those who profess to do things in the better good and trade off small injustices for betterment of all are the real criminals. They work tirelessly creating a vacuum of fear to justify encroachment of civil liberties with domestic criminal and treasonous activity. It always starts with small bites but soon the fascist monkey becomes a hungry gorilla and needs to feast more and more until the only thing left is the dirty war machine and its corporate masters. Two wrongs don't make right.

Jonas saw men getting shelled by some fascist bastards trying to protect their own state. Free men washing up ashore, sea sick carrying boys blown apart by the perils of war. They would forever wonder about the merit and necessity of war. This is for the seasick veterans who washed up onshore while getting shelled by some fascist fucks trying to protect their own state. This is called D-Day. 'Washing up ashore a seasick man, trudging his ass across the land, washing up ashore a friend of his, all he can smell shit, blood, piss. Ah! Over the wall the rifles busted, hand over heart in god we trusted, over the hill and in the bunker, rounds fired off from a fascist fucker. Come on!' Sometimes like I say it was hard for Jonas to stand idle but he had his assignments. He did what he could not to get too involved in these frays.

Jonas observed men crawling underground, to thwart enemy invaders trying to interfere with their daily lives. He watched many times, foreign legions, trying to convince these indigenous people that they were killing their sons and daughters for their better good. Sometimes he would intervene if some great injustice was happening but for the most part he did not participate. He did this with the exception in the cases where a target needed protection and/or training or a child was at risk of a wrongdoing.

There were many wars where men decided it was beneficial to their efforts to fight underground. In Stalingrad, snipers on both sides were so prevalent that both forces decided to fight in the tunnels and sewers underground. This fray was known as Rattenkrieg. In Vietnam the Vietnamese Peoples Army had dug tunnels underneath Cu Chi, and it consisted of a large network to hide guerrillas during the Vietnam War. This extensive tunnel system covered much of the country and all citizens loyal to the party were obligated to do weekly excavation in the effort to stave of colonialists. These tunnels helped hold caches and were a living quarters to many military troops. The living conditions these men and women were forced to endure was nothing short of degradation. Malaria was rampant and at any given time one hundred percent of people had intestinal parasites of some kind or were struck with dysentery. Operations held by U.S. military officials were not blind to the importance of this tunnel system and so launched two campaigns against this guerrilla tactic. Operation Cedar Falls and Operation Crimp were implanted to drive out the 'rats'. Another form of Rattenkrieg, which when translated from German means "Rat War.' Although 'Tunnel Rats' or 'Ferrets' from the 1st and 5th infantry division seized some primary intelligence in a major raid on a tunnel system in Cu Chi, the major objective of destroying these very important and effective means of guerrilla fighting was unsuccessful. The enemy had lived long enough to fight another day. By the time U.S. bombing had done any significant damage to these areas, public opinion about this conspired war had diminished. The Paris Treaties recognized the end of fighting in 1973, although engagements were still in effect until 1975 and the fall of Saigon. There are classified reports of soldiers having to jump in already over manned helicopters and being forced to sit upon corpses just to evade being overrun. What a tragedy war is.

So like I say, before you send your children to war, make damn sure it's unavoidable and your reasoning is righteous.

So with all these factors and his confined rules of engagement, Jonas tried not to get directly involved into the fray of conflict.

Sometimes though, it was unavoidable, especially in the cases where children were being affected or hurt. This was a point that stuck in Jonas' craw. As long as he was present during these circumstances he would not stand idle. These decisions would have dire consequences, as you will see later in this tale.

He had seen and taken part in many battles. He had seen the immorality and horrors of warfare. He had seen the best and the worst that men could do to one another.

The other thing is this; when you attack a country to rid it of insurgents or rebels be sure it is in the best interest of the indigenous population. If you do not win the hearts and minds of the people you are professing to be there to assist then the war is futile. It becomes a war of aggression and the only people to suffer are the assailing troops and the civilians of that state.

Many times, God has unleashed the Dogs of War. He does this to keep men humble and thankful for what they have. He does this to challenge good men to stand in the face of tyranny and oppression.

Edmund Burke once said. "The only thing necessary for evil to triumph is for good men to do nothing." This is the truth.

Now Jonas found himself in a sleepy little town in Massachusetts. He wondered what troubles would befall him here. For he had seen the 'man' and knew that something awful was about to happen. It always did when 'he' was around. The 'Bible' had directed him to come to this rural place and wait, watch and learn. When the time presented itself he was to do what he always did. Help the target overcome his quandary and lead him to make his stand.

When he arrived here a short while ago he needed to search out an abode which would give him privacy, help him store his cache and be a base in case the fighting came to him. He found such a command post.

He had taken up residence in the basement floor of an abandoned telephone factory warehouse. It was in squalor and disrepair. Jonas didn't mind though, he was accustomed to living in the less fortunate of places. This place was kingly for some of the places he'd seen people forced to live in. This would be a perfect center of operations for him. It was wide open and centralized in this small town, so if needed, he could return to it promptly.

The warehouse also had running water, so that was a plus. It didn't have electricity but he was used to that. In today's day and age, you could run most minor electronics on batteries or a small generator so this did not pose a problem. It also had plenty of room for his 'stuff.' And he had plenty of 'stuff.'

A small mattress lay about the floor. It was ripped on the side with the springs showing through. He had taken this from the curb in the state projects.

Lying next to the mattress were two Army duffle bags, two water canteens, a lantern, which ran on propane, several candles and a tinder kit.

He had removed his overcoat, which contained several small

and somewhat significant items. In the right front upper pocket was the 'Bible.' The inside of the hooded coat contained many hidden pockets. The pocket closest to his left breast was where he stored his chewing tobacco pouch, from which he had just retrieved a bit. Jonas spit heavy black goop from his mouth on the dusty floor for he didn't suppose anyone would mind. In the hidden pocket on his right hip is where he kept his traveling essentials. An old passport last stamped 1976 J.F.K. airport. There was also a domestic identification card from New York State, which no doubt was from the same era as the passport. Whether or not these old ID's were valid or not only Jonas knew. He had bundles of U.S. Currency in both hip pockets for easy and unhindered purchases, because cash is still king. Even though this 'Fiat Money' is becoming more and more useless like the paper it's printed on. However, I won't get into the state of financial stability of our 'affluent' nation. He possessed matches, a flint and steel tinder kit, fishing line and miniature pole handle, a Swiss Army Knife, pen and paper, some loose change and pepper spray.

There was a stool for him to sit on while he worked at the work-bench left behind when someone decided that the business was no longer profitable. Jonas worked away at the project in front of him occasionally spitting a black stream of chaw juice from his mouth.

Upon the table was an array of objects.

1) A battery operated am/fm radio, which he was now listening to.

2) A hack saw for sawing off the end of his eight- gauge shotgun, and anything else that needed shortening.

3) Two Ak-74 Russian assault rifles were fully loaded and lying in front of several loaded clips.

4) Two Desert Eagle semi-automatic handguns were at the ready, also with several clips.

5) Many grenades with electrical tape around the triggering

clips were in a small wooden box atop the bench. Jonas is working carefully on this right now while surveying his arsenal. Then came his favorite, the object with the biggest bite.

6) The Panzerschreck. A rocket propelled grenade launcher from WWII. Against the wall in front of him was a large green box with ropes for handles. Inside rested six rockets. These rockets were made custom since production for a Panzerschreck is well out of operation. He cleaned the rocket launcher often so that if he needed it, it would be ready for use.

Strapped to his back was the eight-gauge. Around his belt were shells embedded in it for easy access. On his right hip he had a holster for one of the Desert Eagles. His leather pants had several pockets sewn into them for his loaded magazines. Strapped to his shoulder was a holster which was sewn into his dark green vest that earlier was hidden under his dirty overcoat. In this holster was an ivory handled revolver. He kept the butt of the revolver faced inward because it was known by experienced gunmen that this was the fastest way to draw.

This was the first weapon he ever owned. He purchased it from a storekeeper in Deadwood Dakota. This merchant claimed it belonged to a prominent lawman, turned outlaw, turned poker player. It was often disputed but, this sometimes vigilante and other times law enforcer was rumored to have been the fasted most accurate draw in the country for his time.

The Dakotas were very kind to Jonas over the years and he often returned there to the hospitably poor people. These poor folk always insisted on housing him even though they had very little. Ask your self this; is it more of a gift to receive the last ten dollars someone possesses or a million dollars from a billionaire? I'll let you decide on this. Anyway, Jonas always left more money for them than they had ever made in their lifetimes. Funny thing is that when he did leave it, the citizens of this depressed area never left the region and would not use the money for individual gain.

Whomever the money was left with that person or persons would spread out the money evenly with as many neighbors as they could. This continued the somber prosperity and sovereignty of that area. It ensured that no one had to ask outsiders for assistance.

Jonas learned from this weasel of a man/storekeeper that this Marshall/Gambler/Gunfighter was playing poker at Saloon Number 10. He had been deceived and shot in the back of the head during a poker game. In his hand were Two aces, Two eights all black and another card rumored to be the Jack of Diamonds. It is accounted that, at least on two occasions, the man who was shot asked to switch seats with another player because he never sat with his back to the door. The other man refused to change and relinquish his chair and the rest they say is history.

Like I said, Jonas positioned the gun in the holster so it was almost horizontal with the handle butt tilted slightly upward and in towards his heart. This enabled him the quickest draw and several times for this reason he was spared being shot.

He had killed a man with this method in Wyoming before the turn of the twentieth century. The man had Indian women and children locked upon in a cage upon his large wagon. The twisted man was using them to sell and trade in the upper Mexico Regions for money, favors or property.

Sick.

True.

History.

This brute had taken one of the young girls and was having his way with her. Jonas had come upon this group by accident and heard the girl screaming for help. Jonas came upon this grizzly scene and challenged him in a duel. The man feigned disinterest and prepared to make off with his human loot. Then as he crossed his leg over his horse saddle he drew the rifle from his saddle holster. In luck, it misfired and Jonas drew and shot him right through the right eye socket. The young girl to whom Jonas was credited to have saved gave her honor to him. Jonas tried to insist it was not necessary but the young girl was tenacious and resolved in this matter. Even if he didn't want her for his wife she was resolute to follow him everywhere he went.

Jonas freed the remaining enslaved and accompanied them back to their tribe in the Dakotas. This is where he came about his rather unusual clothing. It was tough and sturdy wear. Although he would have to mend them several times over the years, they lasted.

This is where he shared a piece pipe with a famous Indian Chief. The name given to him by the elders and tribesmen was 'One who challenges the bear.' Jonas liked the Native Indians because their cultures had depth and meaning. Just in the names there was great significance in distinction, which is something lacking in the modern world.

The Native Tribe married Jonas and the girl, Titaqua, and all was well. Jonas lived and traveled with this young able-bodied woman for twenty-two years. Titaqua died of pneumonia on the trail to the Colorado Basin on the first day of the Twentieth Century. Even though Jonas had come to love her, he would not express this to anyone but the Lord on the day of her burial, at the base of the Rocky Mountains. Those were simpler times and with a lot less surveillance. Now he had to contend with the Electric Eye and the age of 'necessary' privacy invasion from the video surveillance cameras.

The project Ricochet was introduced by the ever -inept Ronald Reagan in the 1980's. This project was basically in all accounts a satellite sent into space for the purpose of spying on the people. Now many would argue that if you've nothing to hide then why does it matter. A person's right to privacy is an essential element in their emotional state of love and trust. Also it is a Constitution right afforded to all men in their pursuit of happiness and their right to confidentiality. You wouldn't want voyeurs spying on your daughter showering would you. I know what your thinking. That wouldn't happen because our government is good and just. This is true in many extents. But what happens when the watchers of the watchers become corrupt? What happens when oversight boards and committees all fall under a similar veil of deceit and fraud? Think it couldn't happen, just peek into the history books and you won't have to go back that far to find similar tactics of foreign and domestics states and administrations. If you want the account of truth and facts open your encyclopedias and history reference books. However after having read this excerpts follow up with an investigation of who wrote, published and produced these articles of past endeavors and you might realize of why I am sometimes, and often to a fault, ultimately cynical.

Now as Jonas brought his attention back to the task before him he gazed down upon the arsenal before him and thought that he was about ready for the fight.

Just one more item was needed. It is something very crucial to effective warfare. Something needed in defensive and attack offensives alike. If you can't have radar you need some other means of knowledge of the ensuing raid. Advanced warning or stolen battle plans are the best defense but this is almost always impossible. So another alternative was usually necessary.

Reliable information and communications is a must.

So he set out to town to get it.

The school week passed by uneventfully for the most part and Thomas was content that the week was coming to an end. On Monday morning he apologized to Miss Godwin through clenched teeth but overall the week went well. He and Mary were an item again and nothing made Thomas more secure in his identity.

On this Friday before Halloween while Thomas was reveling in his recovery of his best girl, Sol Bender was up to something too. The janitor was fiddling with one of the lockers. He was going about some sort of mischief and he wasn't sure he cared for it. No as a matter of fact he didn't like it one bit, but it was part of his concession with the 'man.' So he went on about it in silent grief.

Mr. Abrams, the Civics teacher, had noticed this waywardness. He would certainly investigate this matter. Mr. Abrams was coming out of the teachers lounge, when he thought he saw, no he definitely saw, Sol hurriedly put something in the waste basket he had on his push- cart. Sol crumbled up some waste paper and threw it on top of what he placed in the trash. Mr. Abrams noticed he had plastic surgical gloves on too. Sol was aware that Mr. Abrams was on to his malevolence and he aimed to get away.

Mr. Abrams' mother, Ellen, God rest her soul, had always said he had eyes of the eagle. Even at this stage of his life, who some would say was past his years of teaching, he had perfect vision. And he saw Sol doing something like a kid trying to get into the cookie jar and someone noticed. Now the big man was trying to evade detection and being found out.

The push -cart that Sol was pushing around contained cleaning supplies and items to restock the bathrooms, teacher conference rooms and lounges. It also had soap for the locker rooms that Sol would restock after school, when the rooms would be devoid of students.

Sol had just come from the teachers lounge where Mr. Abrams was reading the newspaper enthralled in the world news. Sol restocked the paper towels and emptied the wastebasket. Mr. Abrams noticed Sol and greeted him, although the janitor went on like he hadn't heard the salutation. He knew Sol was a private man and he didn't bother him for a response. So it was because of this that Mr. Abrams was overly curious about the wrongdoing that the giant man was now engaged in.

Mr. Abrams spent last period everyday in the teacher's lounge reading the newspaper, for he didn't have a class last period. He felt that it was a nice way to unwind from a day of rowdy teenagers. He exited the lounge and having seen Sol's reaction to being spotted approached the janitor to question him.

"Whattcha ya doin' there Sol?" Asked Mr. Abrams.

"Nottin' sir." Replied the big man.

"Thought ya were up to somethin' there big fella'." The Civics teacher proclaimed.

"Nope, just wiping down the lockers to make 'em clean-like." Responded Sol.

With that, and being only partially satisfied, Mr. Abrams started off, but not before he glanced up to see which locker Sol was messing about.

Number 317.

He was anxious to see whose locker it might be.

Mr. Abrams was leery of all men, lest they be wicked.

Really the only people he trusted were those he grew up with or those who fought and died next to him in the jungle. He distrusted men in power. He distrusted cheats and sneaks for they were usually sent as messengers by the real troublemakers, the hidden thieves in the night.

That's why he had become a Civics teacher. It was his way of joining the Civil Rights movement. He would educate and empower young people about the necessity of having their voice heard. They were to question authority if they thought that the authority or administration, was abusing its powers. If they sensed something was wrong to stand and speak up, not sit on their hands and do nothing. Remember Thomas Jefferson's motto 'A little civil disobedience is required in a republic.' If the Republic should become a Socially Democratic Oligarchy, run by corporate dictators and capitalist regimes, then they were to join together to bring it down. Either peacefully or by force they were to do this, but only if absolutely necessary.

He was angry at the industrial complex. The industry Eisenhower warned us all about after WWII. He was angry with the defense contractors and natural resource companies. He was angry with the oversight committees set up to overlook these crooks, who turned a blind eye to their treachery and treason. He was angry most at the politicians who professed to do things in the name of the better good.

Their own better good that is.

He was mad because he knew the lobbyists sent to Washington, by foreign and domestic organizations alike, were doing the bidding of corporate dictators who lined Congress' coffers to achieve their goals.

These were the people who caused war. They were the ones who created a volatile environment for chaos and revolt to exist. Then they fed those areas with weapons, armor and promises, taking the side most sympathetic to capitalism. If it were found that this approach was not in the best financial outcome or the monetary forecast was bleak, they would reroll the dice. Sometimes this meant staying idle and other times it meant switching sides. It was all relative to fiscal victory and gain. It all comes down to the demographics.

The people who fight these wars seldom even know what they're really about. The men caught amidst the disorder are the ones who fight the war. The men who profit from them wage war.

Mr. Abrams, consumed by a conspiracy theory, went down to the secretary's office and to the bookcase that held the information he sought. He would find the root of this plot and make sure he was apart of its demise.

The double door glass bookcase, which held class attendance, schedules, locker distribution and combinations, was locked.

"Dana, where's the key to the cabinet?" Asked Mr. Abrams of the secretary who was going diligently about her work.

The young beauty looked up in reply to the Civics teacher and responded in her passive young tone. "It's in the bottom drawer of the front desk." Informed the secretary.

Then, as if she remembered something she forgot to do, she said. "Mr. Kilcrop doesn't want anybody in there."

"Really." Mr. Abrams replied.

Mr. Abrams was not confined to the conformities and regulations installed by others. He had learned the hard way that sometimes these rules and policies must be bypassed in order to find the truth. If you couldn't rattle the snakes by beating at the bush then you must go stealth and find their whereabouts. Often times it was the holder or purveyor of the stick trying to locate the snakes that was the real culprit.

She said stop but she didn't physically try to stop him.

She wouldn't because she was a timid young woman fresh out of the University of Umass Lowell, and all she knew was to be passive. She was naive to the outside world. She existed only in the parameters of her everyday tasks. She didn't know about wickedness or grief, nor did she want to. She stood idle while Mr. Abrams obtained the keys and delved into the student information book. She surmised that this would cause her future trouble but she was unable to summon the courage to stop the trespass.

She was shy and not very gregarious and for this reason she was also still a virgin. She remained in waiting for her dark, tall and handsome to come along. She had never been with a man. There was a boy in her sophomore year of high school that came close once but that was about it. It wasn't for lack of being handsome enough. More than once she had been told she was very beautiful and so she was.

Dana, the secretary, was five foot five lean and very toned. She worked out at home forty-five minutes a day and twice a week she participated in a Tae Bo class. This kept her in very decent form not so much as to be overly muscular but enough to define her striking curvature.

She was one hundred and eight pounds and had loose curly blond hair. Her hair was just below her shoulders and she often wore it in a ponytail. Today it was tied up with a baby blue ribbon to match her outfit. Her hazel eyes were hypnotizing to look at and many times during the day the male students would make excuses just to be able to gaze upon her. She knew this and it made her long for some contact with a gentleman. She longed for a partner to share intimacies with although she often distracted herself from these yearnings. Occasionally though, it was not to be staved off and she succumbed to these temptations.

She had never felt the brush of a mans ruff hands against her breasts or the sensation of him running his fingertips over her body until she got goose bumps. She didn't know of the power that a man could hold over her when he tongued the canals, impressions and valleys of her body. She wasn't familiar with the desire and need that would infect her mind after a man had done this. Nor had she experienced the euphoria when a man grabs a handful of hair from behind his partner and whispers words only the lovers know. She dreamed of these experiences often.

Mr. Abrams took the keys from the bottom drawer and proceeded to open the locked bookcase. He grabbed the book containing the references to all students and their designated school property and looked up the locker number he was searching for.

"306…310…315, ah here we go 317." He said aloud.

"Thomas Morgan." Mr. Abrams stated.

He closed the book and thought about this revelation.

Very peculiar, Very peculiar indeed he thought.

Mr. Abrams liked Thomas. He liked him quite a bit, because,

although he was innocent and not very experienced, he possessed strong beliefs and conviction. He knew he was the kind of lad not to be swayed into wrongness for any reason and he wouldn't compromise his ethics. He was fond of this kind of youngster most of all.

Word had reached him about the incident with the magic marker and he didn't believe for a minute that Thomas was responsible. He didn't take Thomas for a vandal or rabble-rouser. He was quiet and content to spend his time in recreation and adventure. Abrams also knew Mary. He was sure that she was equally of sound character and doubted that she would be with a person of a less than honest disposition. He also didn't deem it likely that his dog would have a temperament far from Thomas' own.

He kept his ear to the ground so that he would know when something was up.

He had heard about Jasper supposedly attacking Mrs. Copperback and dismissed as rubbish. He had heard that Mr. Kilcrop had been present at this fiasco and wondered about his involvement. Jasper according to Mary was a great judge of character. Mr. Abrams was no slouch in this field either. He suspected that the principle was hiding behind some mask but his true nature was still concealed.

Mr. Abrams felt there was something else going on here, some hidden agenda, but the whole picture eluded him. He would however keep his eyes peeled.

That evening just before five o'clock, Mr. Kilcrop came into the secretary's office to sign off on the day's necessary reports before locking up for the night. After they had finished all the tedious filing work, Dana began to log off her computer and Mr. Kilcrop went to lock the front doors to the school.

The teachers parked on the side of the school and Mr. Kilcrop would lock that door behind them when they both left.

Dana and Principle Kilcrop just had to finish signing the necessary student progress forms for the next day. These reports were left on the front desk and delivered to the appropriate classes for review and adjustments. After this tiresome and mundane task, Principle Kilcrop addressed Dana.

"You all set Dana?" He asked.

"Just about, one more thing." She answered.

Just then, Principle Kilcrop looked down at the bottom drawer of the front desk and saw that it was slightly ajar.

"Dana, were you in there?" He asked pointing to the bottom drawer.

"No Mr. Kilcrop sir. Um…" She hesitated.

"Dana I entrusted you to keep every one out of the front desk." He fumed.

He told her to enforce the policy of the 'need to know' basis. He wanted this area off limits to curious people. He wanted to know who was peering into his plans.

"Who was in the desk drawer Dana?" He asked demandingly.

"Mr. Abrams sir. I told him not to, but he went ahead anyway." She said.

Principle Kilcrops eyes flashed with anger and a frown started to break across his face. He kicked the desk drawer shut and clenched his fists in rage.

Dana could hear him grinding his teeth in frustration.

"Why didn't you stop him?" He questioned her, although he already knew the answer. He knew she wasn't strong willed enough to handle the task when he gave it to her. He knew she wasn't capable, but he liked toying with a prey that doesn't realize it's been spotted for the kill.

"I'm sorry Mr. Kilcrop, sir. I promise it won't happen again."

She replied.

"OH I KNOW IT WON'T!" He exclaimed this prophecy, arrogantly.

Just when Dana thought he might explode and do something rash the look of mad frustration left his face and he was calm. He composed himself and gingerly strode to the front of the room. He went and turned out the lights.

Dana was anxious now. Her heart started beating and Mr. Kilcrop could sense this. He started sniffing the air. He could smell the fear in the air like an animal that suspects its prey is consumed with terror. This is when the predator attacks.

And so it was.

He came to her and he took off his glasses. His eyes burned with yellowish green hellfire. He always kept his glasses close to his eyes so that the true color and constitution was hidden. This helped add to the dread when they were discovered.

Dana was now locked up in a state of shock. She tried to run but she was powerless to move. She was so terrified with fear that, she could not escape.

He kept his eyes glued to hers as he approached her.

She realized that his hands had transformed into claws and his breath smelled like stale, wet dog.

"Soon Dana you won't feel a thing. But not soon enough." He said and the room reverberated with a demonic echo.

He tore open her pink blouse, which buttoned down the front. A scratch at the top of her breast from his claws drew a tiny hint of blood.

He sucked at it.

A feeling of embarrassment flashed through Dana, but still she was paralyzed.

He flicked the strap on her pink bra that hooked in front between the breasts. Her perfect subtle breasts fell out. Mr. Kilcrop put one in his mouth and squeezed the other almost too hard.

This can't be, Dana thought. I'm appalled and no... I can't be... turned on.

Someone help.

She was starting to breath heavy so her chest was heaving in and out. Moisture was forming between her legs that she only felt when she was fantasizing. A fire started to grow in her loins.

With his mouth still on her breast he tore her baby blue skirt off. The skirt buttoned up on the side and all the buttons came popping off. He flicked the strap on her pink polka-dotted undies and they fell to the floor. He picked her up and pulled her legs over his shoulders. She hung on by wrapping her legs and arms around his head to keep from falling down. He licked at her glistening patch and she began to quiver.

Oh God this can't be happening thought Dana.

"So it appears you like this treatment." He said.

She was desperately trying to speak.

She must get away.

No.

Help.

"D-D-Don't... Please... Don't... Stop." She stammered.

"Don't stop. But I never thought of it honey." The principle laughed.

He grabbed her by the buttocks, lifted her from his shoulders and unzipped his pants. Out sprung his huge wanting member. The veins running up and down it were throbbing and pulsating.

Then he slammed her down on it.

She let out a terrible scream.

"AAAAAAAAAAAAHHHHHHHHHHHH!" She wailed.

If anyone had been in the school, they would have heard it all the way down at gymnasium on the other side of the school.

He broke through her hymen like a water balloon smashing on the ground and he drove himself his full length up inside her.

All she could do was grunt as he banged away on her.

"UH! UH! UH! UH! UH." She went.

He grabbed the handful of her blond hair tied up in her ponytail and pulled it hard, resting his elbow on her shoulder to give him leverage to drive it home harder. Her arms hung limp by her sides and she was whimpering through the grunts.

She was both ashamed and excited.

Oh please let me run away.

I'm so ashamed.

Then guilt made its appearance.

Needless to say, she came several times.

So did he.

As much as a horse stallion put out to stud. It poured out of her and made a splat sound on the floor. He let out a massive groan in doing so.

He smiled.

Finally, it ended.

Thank God.

The real horror though was about to begin.

He dropped her, like a full grocery bag, on the secretary's desk. She fell to the floor kneeling in his semen and her blood, holding her lower belly in pain. He reached down and lifted up her chin with his index claw.

His eyes turned from green hellfire to lava red. It burned inside his head and looked like iron ore at its melting point. The red sockets stared into the eyes of the abused secretary.

"You will get cleaned up. You will go home. You will forget this dance of ours ever happened. Right Dana." He commanded.

"Yes." She uttered in a trance-like state and then the pain was gone.

"You will always do what I command." He stated.

"Yes." She said as if stoned on PCP.

To me, being hypnotized or blind to the truth is worse than rape and murder. Sometimes this is the kindling used by usurpers and brigands to start their corrupt campaigns.

Later that night two men pulled into the scrap metal yard on the northeast side of town. The car was standing idle for a time before any movement was made in the car. The 'man' took his time for this made the victim sweat and it was easier to convince a trapped person than that of someone with nothing to lose.

The engine to the red Toyota Camry stopped and the driver turned off its lights.

The man in the passenger's seat had a video camera and switched it on.

The screen- play that came through the camera was nothing short of disgusting, pure debauchery. It was so immoral and despicable that I won't even describe the details. The man in the driver's seat started to shift about uneasily when he saw this footage. He pulled at his collar as if he was desperate to breath. He began to sweat profusely. His penis shrank up to the size of a cashew. His balls climbed up inside his loins.

The 'man' knew he had his mark but he liked to hear them submit.

"So we have an understanding then?" The 'man' asked. It was

not so much in the manner of a question but rather a statement of fact.

The driver who was now in a cold sweat, with clammy fists, gulped. It was as if he was trying to swallow something too large for his throat to handle. A giant apple was caught in his throat and he had trouble making audible sounds. What came out first was a squeak like that of a wounded mouse.

The 'man' reveled in his dominance.

He chose to get stern with his quarry and see how much torture he could inflict on this pathetic creature before it gave in.

"I've had about enough." He said. "Would you like me to go to the tabloids with this?" He asked.

The driver's eyes widened to their limit and he forced words to his tongue. Before he could speak the passenger went on berating him.

"You know, it would make for an interesting and revealing story. Wouldn't you say?" He finished with a smirk.

Finally he said. "Yes sir, we do.

"Yes we do what. Want to go to the newspaper and media. Is that what you mean?" He asked. He was really toying with the other now.

"No that won't be necessary, I assure you. I get the picture perfectly." He stated.

"Good." Said the 'man.'

The 'man' in the passenger seat grinned and exited the vehicle and walked out of sight with the video camera. He was pleased his plan was coming together.

The other man took a shot of liquor from an old flask.

Then he began to fidget with his hat.

CHAPTER SEVEN
The nursing home and the dance

At the Morgan house, Thomas and his parents were sitting down for dinner.

They ate and talked about the day's events. Thomas thought he might escape another meal without being pressured for employment. Then Laura said the inevitable. He knew it was coming and now he had to face the music. Laura had explained to Henry that Thomas was forced into retirement from the circus for circumstances beyond his control. Henry either understood this to be reality or the leg lock that Laura had on him when she told him wasn't letting enough blood circulate to his brain. In either case he was willful to comply and understand. If these were the benefits of forfeit or compromise, Henry would gladly look the other way.

"Thomas I see they have sent you home with some job listings from school." She stated. "Have you looked them over?" She asked.

Thomas knew this time would come. It was just a matter of time.

"Look they have two part-time positions at the nursing home." She informed him.

Great. Just what he needed, A bunch of old people with nothing better to do but complain and make messes for attention. Incessant nags and full-time whine bags beckoning his every movement.

"I want you to call Fallon's after we eat supper." She went on.

He started to protest but he knew it would be in vain.

She looked at him with that look like a shark prepared to strike. And once it smelled blood it would start a thrashing frenzy, in which his father would most likely join in.

"Okay I'll call." Thomas replied.

Thomas didn't know that he had the abridged version of the listings. The significance for this will be discovered later. There actually were many more part time jobs available, but someone made it appear that he had only the nursing home to chose from. The other ones, on the list available to him, were full-time employment and jobs out of town for older kids with transportation. Positions he certainly was unable to fill. His only option was the nursing home.

His mother Laura changed the subject after she thought Thomas was onboard. Laura asked Henry about his workload and then they went on to talk about relatives and other boring talk.

Thomas feigned interest.

Boring.

He was thinking of a way to approach the job opening at the nursing home.

He detested the interview and meeting process. It made his stomach uneasy and he didn't care for letting strangers in on his personal life. But that's life.

They finished dinner and were clearing the table when his father brought something to his attention.

"What's on your hand Son?" Asked Henry.

He hadn't noticed because he was so excited about tomorrows dance with Mary. He turned his hand up to see what his father had caught before he did. On his right index finger, thumb and palm was red paint. Where had he picked this up from he wondered.

"I don't rightly know Dad." He responded puzzled.

Thomas brushed his teeth after dinner and when he thought he was prepared, he picked up the phone. He dialed the number on the job sheet sent home with him that was offered as the listing to the nursing home. Thomas called it and a woman answered. The woman talked as though she had a head cold and her nose was stuffed up.

"Fallon nursing home." Came the subdued voice.

"Hi I'm calling in reference to the job opening." Thomas replied.

"Yes, one position has been filled, the janitor's position, but you can come up tomorrow and apply for the nurse aid opening in the morning. Say around 10a.m." She finished blowing her nose loudly and Thomas held the phone away from his ear.

"Okay I'll be there in the morning." He stated. "Whom should I ask for?" He then asked.

"Ask for the facilitator who will be here half a day, 'til about 11am." She responded with a restrained voice.

"Okay I'll do just that. Thank you Miss." Thomas responded.

He hung up the phone satisfied he had done all he could and went off to take a shower and prepare for bed.

That night Thomas was in the shower, trying to get the red dye off his hands but it wouldn't come off. He went to bed that night mortified that he might have go to the dance with this on his hand. He didn't want anything to ruin the night. He went to sleep with a worried mind.

In the morning Thomas put on a pair of tan slacks and a red sweater with a white turtleneck underneath. He combed his hair and brushed his teeth and glanced at himself in the mirror. Then he went downstairs, with Jasper following and made his way to the fridge to grab a glass of orange juice.

"Good luck." His mother wished as he headed out the door.

"Don't you want some breakfast?" "Thomas?" She asked.

He hadn't heard her call after him because he was caught up in his upcoming appointment at the nursing home, and he knew how important it was.

Jasper followed him to his chain on the side of the house and Thomas set him on it. He rubbed Jasper's chin and asked him for luck. He said goodbye to his dog and made off to his interview. He crossed his back yard jumped the fence at Cooper's Barnyard and cut through the old mans property. He went under the bridge at the bottom of Greeley Hill Rd. and walked along the Supernaut Building. He continued his way toward the western part of town where his engagement was. He walked up through the old school yard, which was really an old D.P.W. operation center. He hiked up into the cereal factory warehouse parking lot and up the small hill to the nursing home. On the large wooden sign in the front walk were the words 'Fallon Nursing Home'. All the way there he'd worked over what he would say to the facilitator in his mind. If all went well he would no longer have to hear his Mom's excessive nagging. He entered through the automatic doors and approached the information desk.

"Hi I have an engagement with the facilitator. Could you tell him I've arrived." Thomas said to the middle-aged woman behind the desk.

The woman seemed perturbed to be interrupted from her article in Readers Digest. She peered up from her magazine and looked at him up and down as if to measure his status quo. She spoke with a sense of privilege that made Thomas' blood boil. The woman was a brutish type and she had long gray hairs sticking from her nose. Short thin one's inhabited her upper lip. Her short gray hair was pushed to one side and she wore thick brown glasses. A real ball breaker Thomas thought.

"I will tell HER you're here." Remarked the woman behind the desk. She said this with a real attitude.

She picked up the phone and rang the facilitator.

"Yes Sonya your 10 a.m. has arrived." Okay I will." The snooty woman finished.

The woman hung up the phone and went back to her reading material.

Thomas just stood there awaiting some indication of what might be expected of him or what he should do.

The woman looked up at him and gave him a nasty reprisal.

"Well sit down already junior." She barked.

"Excuse me?" Thomas asked.

"Are you deaf? Sit. Sonya will be here momentarily." She said in utter wickedness.

"I'd appreciate it if you wouldn't talk to me like that." Thomas informed her.

"Are you dumb as well as deaf?" She accused.

"No it's only my clothes that make me look like dumb, sir." Thomas joked.

Her eyes opened wide and she was so stunned she couldn't formulate a comeback.

"Sir? Sir?" Was all she could spit out.

Thomas was satisfied with his quick wit and his ability to tongue-tie this nasty bull dyke and so he sat down to wait for his interview.

Just then a woman with long red hair tied up in a bun came through a frosted glass office door to the right of the information desk. This smartly dressed handsome looking woman came over to greet him.

She wore a smile and had straight white teeth.

Good sign thought Thomas. At least he didn't have to conduct an interview with the crass woman behind the desk. The woman, to whom he had shunned, glowered at him all the way to Sonya's office.

Sonya was a woman in her mid forties and she looked stunning for her age. In fact she could put ladies half her age to shame. She often did too.

Thomas found himself feeling a little awkward, as she got closer. The woman was the type that got more beautiful the nearer she got. That's not always the case with some women. Usually it's the other way around. The closer you get and the more the image comes into focus, you realize the person you were gawking at isn't exactly what you initially thought. All the imperfections and miles make some woman appear hard ridden and wet when put away. Others though and very infrequently, get better and more beautiful with age.

The lines around her blue eyes were distinct, as if she was one who liked to laugh. Her mouth was perfect. There were little indents on both sides like a parenthesis. The left side was a little bigger than the one on the right and extended to roughly an inch below her left nostril. When she smiled it got bigger and almost touched her nose. She had a thin straight nose that slightly flared at the nostrils.

Thomas was awestruck, for she was beautiful. Sonya had red hair, blue eyes, perfect mouth with large pouting lips and a slender body. The kind of woman that would make a man or a particular woman I guess, cross the dessert without water or food because it was the quickest way back to her. Her body was tight and fit in every area and Thomas noticed too. She wore a red stretch dress, which hugged her body just right. Thomas wondered what color her under garments were and what she thought about in the morning before she put them on. He was starting to become excited. I better control myself he thought.

For all this though Thomas noticed she didn't wear any make up. Men call this quietly beautiful, for she didn't need all of the frills and get up to look smashing. She was all that without the accessories. She was like the librarian with glasses who is very studious and shy. But don't be fooled. When the lights go out and she lets down her hair, the inner animal comes out to feed. The animal is always hungry because it has an insatiable appetite. The kind of woman you can wake up next to, with her hair a wreck, her mouth all funky, smelling slightly of yesterdays sex and sweat and still you find her as wonderful as the night before.

Let me try to explain it in terms to which we can all understand.

A young woman who is pleasing to the eye of her man is like a good whiskey. Hot going down but quickly returns to normal. She is cute, sweet and built for speed.

An older woman however, in the same situation is like a well -aged expensive brandy, becoming finally a delicious cognac. A little warm going down but keeps you warm all night. Hot, saucy and built for distance.

The fine looking woman snapped Thomas out of his mind-altering daydream.

"Hi my name is Sonya." She said.

Thomas was silent for his tongue was stuck. He was getting nervous and he started to sweat. He pulled at his turtleneck collar and hoped she hadn't noticed him staring at her.

"Hi I'm Thomas." He blurted out too fast.

She sensed his awkwardness and his attraction to her and thought, if he were ten years older she'd show him how she could hurt him using only her inner leg muscles.

"You've come to fill the position." She stated with a smile.

"Yes if it's not taken." He remarked slightly regaining his poise.

"Come let's go fill out an application and get your identification." She said.

They went through a side door in her office into a smaller office with the words Administration Room labeled on the door. He gathered this was the room that Human Resources kept for employee records and identification information.

He entered the room behind her trying to keep his eyes off her buttocks and surveyed the room. It had a file cabinet, a copier a desk and chair. There were certificates and plaques upon the wall. She had a picture of her and her family next to the computer in the middle of her desk. It appeared that she did the Human Resources bit as well as managing the home.

Upon the desk was a computer monitor that she went to work on, pulling up the proper documents for employment. She ran them off through the printer scanner and placed them in front of Thomas. He filled in the necessary information, signing them all. He showed her his Student Identification card and she made a photo copy of it.

At the conclusion of this monotonous task, she stapled them together and placed them in the employee section of the file cabinet. Then she came back and looked him over. Yes she thought he would make a sturdy lover some day.

"Well. That's it." She explained.

"That's it." He remarked surprised.

"Can you start tomorrow?" She inquired.

"Yes, Yes I can." He said quickly.

"Good." She said. "Why don't we call it 10 a.m. again? How's that?" She asked.

"Sounds good Miss." He replied happily.

"Please. Call me Sonya." She responded extending her hand.

"Thank you Sonya." He returned and shook her hand.

She noticed his clammy hands.

She grinned and saw him to the front entrance. As he walked away she wondered how many hearts he'd break before he met the 'one.' If only I knew then what I know now she thought strolling back to her office.

Off he went. He went home to tell his mother the news.

She was pleased.

That night so was Henry.

Henry quietly thanked his son for the spoils he was about to receive now that Laura was no longer worried about his job quest.

Henry slept later than normal the next morning.

Saturday night was here and Thomas was getting ready for the Halloween Dance. He had showered and brushed his teeth. He then sprayed on the Polo Cologne he had been given last Christmas. He put mousse in his newly cut hair. Laura had done some trimming and styling when she was younger and she forbade him to go to the dance without a clean cut. He resisted to no avail. She was not budging on this matter so he gave in as usual.

He put on the suit that his mother had purchased at the mall the weekend before. It was a gray suit with a white shirt and gray and black striped tie. His mother made sure he had new black dress shoes. Henry insisted he wear his old ones but Laura was adamant about Thomas looking good for the dance. She was proud of him working and she would do whatever it took to help him impress Mary. Henry argued just enough to let Laura know that it would take some convincing to make him understand. He was getting spoiled. Laura had given him a bone to chew every night this week and he was chewing at the bit for more. She didn't mind though, for she liked it as much as he did.

Laura knew they couldn't really afford the new apparel and shoes, but she realized how important it was for Thomas. She took money from the grocery fund and gave it to the dance fund. They would go a little short, but she knew Henry would approve. That night after very little convincing he was onboard.

She was proud when she saw him smiling and admiring himself in the mirror. She was glad she had a son who cared so much about his girl. She was pleased when she thought of Mary and Thomas together. True happiness can only be found in love. She was happy for him. His father was too.

"Knock 'em dead kid." His father shouted slapping him on the back as he walked out the door.

Jasper was happy and wagging his tail as though he knew about Thomas' big night. Jasper barked approvingly.

Thomas smiled at Jasper and waved back at his father as he and his mother got into the little Honda Civic and left to pick up Mary. Laura backed up out of the driveway and pulled onto Fitch Road. Then she turned right onto Woodland St. Mary's place was two houses up from Pine St.

They pulled up to Mary's house at quarter until eight. Thomas strode up to Mary's and rang the door- bell. Mary's mother answered the door and invited the sharp dressed young man into the foyer. Mary's mother called up to Mary who was putting the finishing touches on.

"You're looking very handsome tonight, Thomas." She said.

Thomas was taken back for Brenda never complimented him.

"Why thank you." He replied.

Just before he felt respite she took him by the arm.

"No funny business Mr. Morgan. I know you young boys, with your quick hands, charming wit and dirty minds. Mary is not for handling. Understand?" She finished.

Thomas was sore that he felt that he and Brenda were finally connecting. He just nodded for he didn't want the wrong message to be delivered to her on this special occasion.

Mary came down the stairs slowly savoring the gaze Thomas was burning into her. She wore an eggshell white ruffled dress. Her strawberry blond hair was long and straightened, held back by two pink pins. Her shoes were red with a low heel and a strap across the foot.

She did this to imitate the roses Thomas gave to her. Thomas noticed this too and his heart swelled with joy.

He remembered what Brenda had said to him but he was certain at some time during the night the board of trustees inside his mind would meet and dismiss this warning as disinformation. It was not to be trusted and that he should make a full assault.

As they entered the car Thomas said "You look…" He didn't have the words to finish.

"Charming." Laura finished.

"Thank you Mrs. Morgan." Mary said mockingly, sticking her tongue out at Thomas.

She was thrilled and smiled with glee. One reason was because of Laura's comment. Mostly though, it was because she had stunned Thomas into a tongue-tie. The thought of Thomas' eyes upon her made her chest swell. Thomas wasn't the only one who was thinking about going over the wall to escape the prison of sexual confinement. Mary's motor was running hot too.

They pulled up to the dance hall in the town square across from central park. They said their goodbyes to his mother and ran into the hall. She had his hand and was pulling him because he was bashful and more than a little apprehensive to dance.

Thomas was so nervous about dancing that he tried to put it off, but Mary pulled him out to the dance floor before he could argue.

No one else was dancing, and seeing them out there loosened up the other dates. After a short time the floor was full of bodies shaking their moneymakers.

Thomas and Mary had a great time. Thomas forgot his fear of dancing. All he could see was Mary. He swung her around and around. They twirled and spun holding each other tight, to Thomas' delight. He was so happy. He was exhausted but kept on going. Mary could've gone all night with her athletic tight body. However, she noticed Thomas' fatigue and they broke from the dance floor for some refreshments.

But Thomas wasn't the only one to have eyes for Mary that night. Mr. Kilcrop saw her and he felt a sensation too. It was a lot less innocent than Thomas.'

When Principle Kilcrop first glanced at her that night, he was filled with a lust that just about overcame his control. It was all he could do to manage his burning desire and corruptness. His only thought was to have her. He wanted to utterly subdue and violate her. He would have her and he would defile her, his thought in his demented mind was bent on it.

Thomas and Mary sat down for a breather and Thomas got up and poured two glasses of punch for them. He asked her if she wanted any of the finger food arrayed for the students and faculty alike. She declined and they sat talking quietly about the little things that partners do when they're in love. Thomas put his arm around her and she smiled.

The principle saw this act of devotion and the feeling of lust Principle Kilcrop recently experienced turned to pure rage. He was losing control of reason and his mind was frantic. He left the dance room and went off to the men's room. He went down the old corridor leading to the janitors closest and broke right, down past the Town Offices by the water bubbler and into the men's room.

He slammed the door against the inner wall and began punching the stalls. The wooden stalls splintered and cracked. There were fists holes and knuckle prints in the wood. He put his foot through a closed stall door and the door smashed off the hinges. He tore the mirror off the wall and busted it into pieces. He ripped down the overhead lights by punching his way through the Plexiglas. He destroyed the effervescent lights inside. He busted one with his hands and the other he broke into pieces with his teeth, crunching on the busted shards. He welcomed this pain. He fed his lust for Mary with the blood in his mouth.

The dance was breaking up and Thomas took Mary by the hand as they left the dance hall. They exited the Town Hall and said their goodbyes to friends and teachers. Then together they sat upon the granite stairs and waited for her mother to pick them up. Thomas put his brand new suit coat under Mary to keep her off the cold stone steps. She was moved by his chivalry as usual.

"Mary." He said shyly. Like a puppy, who has done something wrong and is now trying to get back in the owner's favor.

"Yes." She replied lovingly.

"Can I kiss…?" He was interrupted because she threw herself into him and pressed her lips against his.

He felt her tongue trying to find its way into his mouth. He was all too ready to oblige. Their tongues wrestled and they were engrossed in one another. He put his right hand under her chin and the other on her waist. The hand on her waist set off an electrical charge in Mary's young body.

A heat was growing in Mary's loins. There was a brush fire spreading into her honey jar. Her cheeks flushed and her nipples swelled. Thomas could feel them against his chest. She was slightly moaning and Thomas too was getting excited.

A fire inside Mary was not the only thing that was growing. Suddenly Thomas' pants were too small in the area where boys need extra room.

Just then they heard a horn beeping.

CRAP.

NOT NOW.

BEEEEEEEP.

The board of trustees was trying to convene but the stock market had closed and business was done for the day.

Both of the young lover's minds were buzzing and keyed up. Mary wished her mother would go away. Thomas tried to imagine what would've happened if Brenda hadn't arrived at that moment. Oh well another time he thought, but when? When men and boys alike are turned to the off position nothing happens, like there is a faulty switch or bad wiring. You see it's impossible to stop. The only time we understand, once the motor starts running, is now. Blue balls is not a myth, just ask any man who has experienced this torture, it's hell.

When they were engaged they hadn't realized Mary's mother, Brenda, had pulled up. They unwillingly broke embrace and headed to the Mercedes-Benz. Thomas walked slightly behind Mary with her backside being blind to Brenda in the car. Thomas gently placed his hand on Mary's butt to gauge her reaction.

Mary just grinned.

Thomas opened the door and Brenda gave them both a spiteful look. She shot Thomas a second look of disdain in the rear view mirror after he had climbed into the back and adjusted his seatbelt.

Thomas' fire was extinguished by the guilt he felt for violating Brenda's trust. How would he ever get her to like him if she couldn't trust his word?

You see Mary's mother and father grew apart when she was just young.

Her father's family was very rich. He had left Brenda for a younger woman and left her sour. He did not however, leave unscathed. She kept the house, the car, the child and eighteen million dollars.

Hell hath no fury like a woman scorned.

But he also left her with the load of raising a child alone. Money is great and money is grand but a broken home is more than I can stand. Raising a child alone is no small feat and those who do, get my praise. So Thomas understood in some degree why Brenda was very protective of Mary and the reasons for her trying to shield her from harm.

As they were about to pull away from the curb a knock came on the driver's side window that scared the wits out of them all. Brenda stopped the car and rolled down the window to see a much more composed Principle Kilcrop.

"Hi, I'm Mr. Kilcrop." Said the principle. "But you can call me Burn, my friends do." He continued.

"Hi I'm Brenda Smothers, Mary's mother." Replied Brenda.

Brenda had taken to her maiden name after the bitter divorce, but her driver's license and all her bills were still in the name Talisman. This is the name that Mary kept, maybe because it was the only thing left of her fathers.

"Oh my, I had you mistaken for an older sister." He joked.

"You're too kind, but flattery will get you nowhere." She played along.

"I was being all too sincere." He replied.

"Well then thank you, kind sir." She laughed.

"Nice to meet you Brenda." He said.

He turned his attention to the back seat where the two young lovers were holding hands. He spoke to both of them but stared directly at Thomas.

"You kid's have a good time tonight." He went on.

Normally Thomas probably would have been uneasy but Mary had his hand and he could think of nothing but her.

The two young lovers just nodded. They were still relishing in that warm moment just minutes ago.

"Good. I'm glad." He said, not meaning a word of it. In the back of his mind he was starting to think that maybe he had lost a step or that he had underestimated the resolve and courage of this green kid.

Nonsense.

"It was nice to meet you but we should be going." Brenda stated.

"Brenda would you like to go out and get a cup of coffee or catch a movie sometime?" He asked.

She hadn't been asked out in a long time. Her sense of longing for a partner to share intimacy with was all but snuffed out. A flicker of flame kicked in and a small combustion started growing.

"Ah sure…" She stammered.

"So I can call on you sometime?" He questioned.

"You can." She responded.

She was about to pull away and motioned to Mr. Kilcrop that he had something on the corner of his mouth.

He brought his bent right index finger up to his mouth and noticed blood on it from the lower lip.

"Oh thank you Brenda. I had a bloody lip earlier from a game of handball. The wound must have reopened. I better go get it cleaned up. Goodbye." He said waving.

She gave a speedy awkward wave back and drove off rolling the window up as they pulled away.

As the car pulled away, Kilcrop was deep in thought. Then he grinned. He would break that sturdy resolve of Thomas' and he had a plan on how.

CHAPTER EIGHT

Halloween

The next morning Thomas awoke in high spirits. He had a smile painted on his face that he didn't plan to let wear off all day.

"Last night was a success, Jasper my boy." He announced while throwing on his slippers and sweatshirt. He went about the room gracefully like a figure skater whose crowd is hoping that he is not quite finished with his routine.

He told Jasper about the evening with Mary at the dance and how they kissed. Jasper seemed to listen and understand perfectly what his master said, or maybe it was just the feeling radiating from Thomas that made him pleased. Jasper put his paws up on the bed, while Thomas was reliving his victory, and wagged his tail. His huge pink tongue fell to one side out of his open jaws. It fell out before his four-inch bottom canine teeth. He went on huffing while Thomas spoke and petted him.

After a while of revisiting his dream night, he went to the hall and hurried excitedly downstairs to get some breakfast, then, he would shower and get ready to go off to work. He whistled and hummed some ancient anthem known only to his imagination and finished his descent with a hop from the third step landing soundly on the small foot carpet at the bottom of the stairs.

When he got downstairs and entered the kitchen he could hear his mother talking with some neighbors.

Mrs. Hadcat and Donna Winer had come to visit. Thomas stopped his melodic hymn and let his auditory system spy out the meaning for the morning's rude intrusion. What was the meaning of this visit?

Thomas could soon tell it wasn't meant to be a cheerful one. He couldn't quite hear what they were saying but he guessed he was involved. He heard his name and Jaspers' too, so he peered around the corner to get more details. Laura had caught him out of the corner of her eye, for she was sitting facing the kitchen and Thomas knew by the glare in her eye, he was in trouble. She had the look of utter contempt. The demeanor of his neighbors was worse. The smile of happiness he was wearing, turned to a frown of discontent. What was the reason for their malicious destruction of his fine morning? He was not about to stick around to find out.

He decided to skip breakfast and go get changed before the flak started flying. He went upstairs and got dressed in blue jeans, a red sweatshirt with blue and white bold letters across the front spelling out the word Boston. Then he went to the closet to retrieve his gray boat shoes. He slid them on, threw his dark blue windbreaker and headed for the light of day.

The facilitator said it was okay to dress down on Sundays, so he wasn't really concerned by his appearance for his first day of work. When he got there he would see what attire was standard for the weekdays.

He went into the bathroom, brushed his teeth and combed his hair quickly.

He and Jasper then scurried down the stairs through the screen door and out of the house. When he rounded the house to put Jasper on his chain and bolt off to work, he froze. He was in sheer disbelief of the awful scene in front of him.

Hanging from the clothesline poles were three mutilated cats. All that was left of them was a head and a shoulder for one, a head and half a torso with its bowels hanging down for another, and just a head and two inches of vertebrae for the third. Thomas saw that his father, Henry, had taken one down already. He placed it into a large plastic garbage bag. He was wearing plastic household gloves like the ones used when cleaning greasy pots and pans.

His father realized that Thomas and Jasper were now present and he turned to chastise them. Thomas was not the only one to wake up in a great mood only to find misery waiting to besiege.

"Son, is this some kind of sick joke? What's the matter with you?" He asked angrily.

Thomas was speechless.

"Son, you have some explaining to do." He added.

"You don't… Jasper and I…" Thomas broke off befuddled.

What is this? Thomas thought in horror. Who is doing this madness?

"If not you." He said perturbed. "Then who and what did?" He inquired.

These questions and accusations put Thomas into a tailspin, and he couldn't focus. His mind was bouncing to and fro. This can't be happening. I woke up to a perfect day and now this. Why?

Finally Thomas spoke irately.

"You know Jasper ain't like that, Dad." Thomas shouted. "And neither am I." He shouted.

"I didn't think he'd knock down an old lady either." Henry fired back.

Thomas was about to blow. His temper was reaching the top of the dikes. When the levee breaks will he have no place to stay? The walls came down and all the pressure that was being held back came spilling forth.

"That was an accident!" He hollered at the top of his lungs. "Someone's out to get me!" Thomas exclaimed.

Thomas' eyes were glazing over with wrath. He heard his father talking in some sort of muffle. They were just distant nonsensical sounds. His fists were clenched on his sides and he couldn't make sense of any of it.

"Son I'm not talking to my…" Henry would have kept going but Thomas rushed off.

NO. Thomas said in his mind.

NO.

HELL NO.

Thomas ran down toward the twin Dogwood tree's at the edge of Cross' Cove and on towards Mary's. Jasper who normally took the lead stayed close behind following his master to whatever peril might befall him. He was sure that something was terribly wrong and if the fight came to his master the assailant better bring the thunder because he was tired of Thomas being distraught. When he confronted the culprit to whom his master was suffering at the hands of, he would even the odds. When Thomas cleared the pricker patch, he and Jasper proceeded to the front of Mary's House.

She hoped he would come to her because word had reached her through her mother of this ordeal. Her mother was already biased toward Thomas and all she needed was another feather to place on the camels back. She had piled so much upon it already that now it was sure to break. If he thought she was less than affable before he would surely be in for it now.

Her mother was without an intimate partner, but she was not dead to the 'ways of the hen.' She was part of the branch on the gossip tree. There were many branches on this tree and they all were apart of the same trunk and network.

Mrs. Slanders told her that it was very 'possible,' that the cat massacre 'was' a product of Thomas' subterfuge. He was letting on as a nice young man, but in fact he was really devious and malignant at the core. This was his stratagem.

Like all hens clucking in the hen house, they spread the information on to their family. In turn their members of that family spread it to their friends and their families and so on. Until finally what you have is an entire community filled with half- truths and mere speculation. It's laughable when you think that people would rather have circumstantial evidence than fact. This way they can create conjecture and assume the worst. This is a favorite pastime for the grapevine tenders and their merciless associates.

Brenda ate this up and defecated the untruths onto Mary. But Mary was having none of it land on her. She knew her Tom wouldn't do such a thing. Who ever it was that was doing this to her best friend, was barking up the wrong tree. She would find out who was planting these weeds in her garden and show them what happens to people who mess with her harvest.

Mary was looking out the side window when Thomas and Jasper were approaching the house. She dashed out of her room down the hall, slid down the cherry wood railing, scurried into the living room and into the foyer.

At this same time Brenda was cursing Thomas. She opened the screen door and was holding it open with one arm and castigating him from the porch. Thomas was at the bottom stair, for he was ambushed with his head down when he arrived. He had started up the stairs with his head down and Brenda had fired her rebuke upon him before he was prepared. He was frozen in place, like he had seen the Gorgon Medusa and he was now a lost Legionnaire. It was like he had become another stone victim for her collection.

"Thomas Morgan you and that beast stay away from Mary. You're a bad influence on her and I don't want you spoiling her future." She berated him shaking her index finger on her free hand at him.

Before Thomas could respond to this badgering, Mary blast by her through the open screen door.

"Mary you get back here this minute." She yelled with authority. "That dog is a menace, and Thomas will only cause you trouble." She added.

"I don't believe it for a second." Said Mary assuredly.

She grabbed her harassed lovers hand and made a run for it. Together they all ran off toward the pricker patch. As they were running along Mary assured Thomas she believed in his innocence.

"Thomas I know you and Jasper are not responsible for this." Mary said assuredly.

She did too in her heart. She trusted Thomas since the first day they met in third grade. This is the true account of boy meets girl.

Mary had come from St. Joseph's seminary school in Fitchburg, which she attended for first and second grade. Some boys and girls made fun of her when she transferred and arrived at the public school and this was one of those days.

"Mary, Mary, from the seminary, eats the dirt and rotten dog berries." The kids would shout. This was a schoolyard favorite. I know this ridicule sounds foolish and utterly absurd but to an outcast child the taunting accusations are very hurtful. Children are a product of their parents and some of them are far from innocent and have less than proper role models.

There was one though who was happy about this teasing. Eddie Spagelli. Before Mary had gotten to this Elementary School he was the subject of snide remarks and constant jeering.

"Eddie Spaghetti with the meatball eyes, put him in the oven and make French Fries." The kids would sing in unison every time one caroler would take up the song. I know they are just words but remember these are children and the sneering goes right to the core.

Today a boy, Marty Hitch, was picking on Mary. It wasn't the normal day of name-calling or talking behind her back. Today it was more physical. He liked her of course, but he was a 'meanie' and she didn't reciprocate the fondness. In fact she was afraid of him, and maybe he sensed it too.

Mary was feeling nervous and intimidated by him on this particular spring day. He was chasing her threatening to pull her hair and by accident she bumped into the desk that held the class fish tank. It was a project that the class was doing for the year. It was mostly just for show, but it helped the children think that they were all part of something. The fish tank fell to the floor with a crash. All the room was hushed. You could hear a pin drop.

"Uh OoooooH." The class started. "You're in trouble." They didn't actually know who did it but they were waiting for the suspect to break down.

Mrs. Seems heard the breaking glass from the coat- room. She was assigning a new student a cubbyhole, for their jacket and boots. She came running into the main room to see gold fish, guppies and other small fish flopping on the tile floor. Some were underneath the desks and were wriggling all over. The kids were trying to pick up the slimy creatures and laughing all the while. Bedrock and tank decorations were all about. Fifteen gallons of water soaked the floor and rug.

"Who is responsible for this?" She demanded. "Kids stay away from that, there's glass everywhere. Billy stop it right now." She hollered.

Mary was terrified. What had she done? The class will hate her. It was only her first week and she had ruined everything.

"Who?" She yelled again.

"I did." Reacted Thomas. "I was running and bumped into it." He went on.

Mary's heart stopped.

It swelled like all the blood in her body came immediately into her heart and it was about to burst. She immediately fell in love with Thomas. The look of shear gratitude she displayed for him in taking the blame for her, made Thomas feel righteous. No, it was more than gratitude. It was adoration. Her eyes were starry and she thought only of him. Later when the teacher called on her she just stared off into fantasy. She pictured how he would take the punishment too for her. She was sad. He would probably be cast down into the alligator pit in the principle's office. He would never come back. Maybe they would throw him into the fire under the big stew pot in the cafeteria. Maybe he would be the stew. Oh no! Then out of the ashes, Superman! Thomas would come, pick her up and fly away.

Cute, eh. But it's the truth, I swear.

This is a loose description, but it isn't even close to how she really felt.

For I can describe it in words but it loses a great deal of substance in translation.

Mary, now six years later, would stand by him.

They sat in the pricker patch and talked quietly.

"I knew you would believe me Mary." He said sadly. "I don't know who is doing this to me. I have to go to work but I'm afraid for Jasper. I can't go home because my parent's think we did this. I'm afraid to leave him at home cause I don't want the cops or the animal officer coming for him." He sobbed.

He began to cry.

She took him by the head and placed it on her chest. She let him shed tears until he was dry. She ran her hands through his hair and cooed until he stopped. He peered up at her in worship.

Oh Mary.

"Thanks Mary, I can always count on you." He said truthfully.

"You go to work and I'll take Jasper and talk to your parents." She stated.

"Mary they're pretty upset right now." He replied.

"So am I." She declared.

Thomas smiled and ran off to work because he didn't want to be late his first day. He hoped Mary had the right stuff to convince his irate parents. He was certain she did.

Mary and her protector Jasper went to Thomas' house. She spoke to him softly as they approached the side of the house, the scene of the 'house cat slaughter.' She placed Jasper on his chain and continued on to the front of the house. She was fuming. Laura was at the door.

"Mary have you seen Thomas? Did he go off to work?" Laura asked. "He's in big trouble." She said. Though only partially believing Thomas was responsible.

"That's what I've come to talk to you about." Mary emphasized. "Can I come in Mrs. Morgan?" She asked.

Mary always called her Laura and this proper salutation threw her off.

"Oh God I'm sorry Mary, come in." Laura apologized.

Mary had a way with Thomas' mother. Laura really liked her. Laura knew something was amiss with this whole thing but wasn't sure of its origin.

Mary explained how Thomas was not the kind of person to do that and Jasper was even less likely to have committed this heinous crime. The fact that Mary truly believed in Thomas and his innocence, made Laura feel guilty and ashamed she ever questioned his humanity.

"You know this. Right?" Mary asked.

"Yup." Laura said in tears.

How could I think for a moment that my Thomas was involved in this offense, surely I am not worthy. She was being harsh on herself and berating her inner fiber but Laura was like that. Her loyalty to her family was unwavering.

His father too was proud, and ashamed. He felt guilty for having scolded Thomas when he didn't really think he was at fault either.

Sometimes things are not what they seem. Believe in your children. They believe in you. Loyalty and trust from our parent's is what makes us who we are. Nothing is more important to a child than the acceptance of their accounts.

He was glad that Mary came to Thomas' aid. It reminded him of Laura.

Laura always stuck up for him when he was less than responsible. And boy did he have some reckless days.

Once he had landed in jail on a 'Shitty Time' and he had to call Laura to help him out of his predicament. He forwent the idea of calling his parents in his current condition and phoned his savior. She put all the money together she had saved to buy a new car and put it up for bail.

Now that's true commitment.

What's more is that, at seven-teen years old, she stood up on his behalf in court and told the judge that community service was all that was required. She assured him that he had learned his lesson and if he knew what was good for him he'd smarten up. If he did it again he'd lose more than his freedom. And the judge believed her too. He thought to himself, if he were in those shoes, he'd fly straight as well.

So he got community service.

Not so bad for launching his Chevy Celebrity, in reverse, through the barbershop window on a 'bender.'

Man.

How did I ever survive those wild times?

And booze was not the least of it.

Anyhow, for the rest of the summer, Henry's community service was to help rebuild the shop. The barbershop owner Terry Hack wasn't angry with him, so that helped. He told Henry some things that he did in his day that would make the devil blush. They laughed and drank cold beers while they labored. Good thing Laura didn't know he was drinking on the community service job. Thinking back now, he got shivers thinking what part of his body she would have grabbed and the force to which she would have removed it if she did know.

Laura got back the bail money after he finished repairing the barbershop and Hacks Barbershop was back in business. Terry's business tripled after the backward racing and flying automobile episode. The want of gossip about the incident and the rascal who had done it was the topic of all conversation. Talk was bountiful about Henry's accident and the old timers ate it up.

Laura also did the driving for the next two years. Henry was reduced to the passengers seat. And not just once did he crave to blast the music so the speakers thumped when the car would begin to pick up pace from his heavy metal foot to the delight of the rowdy teenage passengers.

Hustle!

To race to a great tune.

To pick up his feet and enter the drivers seat.

Oh yeah.

So after Mary had easily convinced Thomas' parents that Thomas wasn't to blame, they went about getting out the candy for the neighborhood kids for the holiday. They put up old Halloween props and got out her and Thomas' costumes.

They awaited Thomas' return and ate brownies Laura had made, though not without much on their minds. Laura and Henry both worried, like Mary, that someone was sabotaging Thomas. They hoped that this was the end of the sick farce.

Thomas arrived at the nursing home with two minutes to spare. A male nurse came to greet him at the time clock.

He was a young man, thinly built and he had a goatee. His hair was dyed black and styled in a Devilock. He had a stud through his nose and bottom lip. He had large ring holes in his ear lobes. All the way up the outer ear were more studs. He wore black army boots, green jump pants and a yellow T-shirt. Engraved on it were the letters ST. They were upside down and intertwined. The S wrapped around the T. Thomas deemed that dress down day meant way down, if you could limbo that low.

"Here you go. You need to punch in and out so payroll can determine your pay. That, and they haven't installed security cameras yet. It's a way for them to know whose here and who isn't. You know, to be accountable." The nurse rambled.

Thomas punched his time ticket.

"You must be Thomas, I'm Jez. You'll be working with me." He said.

"Hi, nice to meet you." Responded Thomas who couldn't take his eyes off Jez' get up.

Jez noticed this and was thrilled because he loved getting reactions and attention from others. There is an underlying psychological condition for people like this but I wont bore you with the diagnosis and details.

Okay, I will.

Jez didn't have the kind off parents that were attentive enough even to care and watch out for their selves. Oftentimes they would

155

be out at the local riverbed engaged in hallucinogens and orgies. Jez would sit in front of the television watching cartoons while his grandmother did crosswords, belched and farted cabbage gas. This lack of attention, family unity and concern destroys children from the start. As they grow up and gather a mutated identity, they always yearn for attention and adoration. Where I grew up we have many names for these people. The guys are called 'Sinkers' and the girls are called 'Hussies.' Usually the guys turn into punks and take to drugs and broken relationships. Finally they often end up in and out of jail. The girls often do the same but are more impressionable than men. A 'Hussie,' which is often confused with a whore, is a female who constantly requires the attention and affection of her partner. If that affection becomes less or displaced they look for it elsewhere. They often confuse sex with love. They are trying evermore to fill the whole in their heart, which was stolen from them by their sad excuse for parents. A whore on the other hand just likes being abused and throttled. There is a much deeper condition with these folks.

Jez didn't like to think of these times so he filled up his time at hardcore shows and punk forums. There he would meet people not much unlike himself. These conditions occur regardless of social stature in fiscal deficiency or abundance.

So when Thomas stared at Jez it made him feel noticed.

"Nice to meet you too. We will be working the west wing. That's our zone." While he said this he handed Thomas a yellow name-tag. Jez just kept on talking.

"There are four color coded zones. The red is for east. White is for south. Yellow, our zone is west. Orange is for north. You must stay in your zone, unless, you are accompanied by someone with that color or someone with clearance. The ones who have total clearance are the facilitator, Sonya, and the shift managers. You'll meet them as we go." He finished. When he spoke he didn't pause between phrases.

ANCIENT ARROWHEAD

Later that day Thomas found out that he drank four or five red bulls a shift. This was the basis for his caffeine induced body tweak.

"Any questions?" He asked hurriedly.

"No." Replied Thomas trying to soak it all in.

Things at home were still on his mind.

As he walked with Jez to put on a smock he ran into an unexpected surprise. Coming out from the men's room was a man that was buttoning up his shirt. When the man looked up after he finished tucking it in, Thomas noticed it was his uncle Bobby.

"Hey, they said you were coming in today." His uncle said.

Thomas was surprised to see him. He hadn't seen Bobby in some time. Bobby and Laura led very different lives. Bobby liked burning his paycheck up at the racetrack and drinking away his sorrows and sometimes winnings in the pub. He often hooked up with a bored housewife or a younger girl mad about her boyfriend's unfaithfulness or lack of interest. On at least one occasion, after last call, he took both home.

Great nights.

"How are you Thomas? How's my sister? Is she still in control at home?" He went on to ask.

"I'm doing okay. And Mom is well. And well, you know that she is always in charge." Thomas said rather glum. He was talking to his uncle but that thing in his mind wouldn't quit.

Bobby was Thomas' uncle and godfather. Bobby is Laura's only sibling. Bobby wasn't sure everything was all right with his favorite and only nephew. Bobby was no less steadfast in his loyalty for family than Laura. Even though he didn't come by all that often to the Morgan home he cared a whole lot. If something were wrong, he would call on them pronto.

Bobby was very close to Laura growing up. He was four years older than her and if anybody gave her problems, he dealt with them accordingly. Laura had a deep admiration for her older brother and when he came by she waited on him hand and foot.

"Why are you here today, Bobby?" Thomas asked. I didn't know you worked here. I thought you were still an EMT." He said puzzled.

"I still am. I come here one Sunday a month to give CPR lessons, the Heimlich maneuver and stuff like that." He told Thomas.

Thomas nodded showing his understanding.

"Well, I'll let you get off to work. Say 'Hi' to the folks for me." Bobby said shaking his nephews hand.

"I will Bobby, take care." Thomas said.

Booby went off to the red zone and Thomas and Jez went in to the cafeteria to retrieve meals and drinks for the patients. I should say residents. They gathered the necessary trays and refreshments placing them in turn on a dinner cart and went back to zone yellow to give lunch to the residents.

In the first room they entered, there was a woman sitting right in front of the T.V., and it was so loud it was ear-piercing. Jez pushed the dinner cart over to her bed and began removing her items and placing them on her dinner tray.

"Hi Miss Sourdough." Jez said with a smile turning down the T.V. with the remote.

Her name was Miss Sowado. Jez called her this because it would get her riled up. She probably didn't deserve this treatment but Thomas would find out that she was a cold calculating woman so he could see Jez' reasoning for teasing her. It was the only real way of trying to make her understand that her constant bickering didn't affect him. Thomas found out that the more aggressive you let these people become the more they complained and took advantage of you.

This is a sad reality really.

"It's Sowado you young scoundrel. You better not have forgotten my pudding again." She fumed.

"I didn't forget it today and I didn't forget it yesterday, Miss Sourdough." He gloated.

"Just give me my lunch." She demanded.

As Thomas got her dinnerware prepared she asked. "Who is this? Another juvenile to harass me?"

"This is Thomas and be nice to him, it's his first day." Jez acknowledged.

"Hi nice to meet you." Said Thomas genuinely.

"We'll see how nice it is." She shot back with a frown.

"Let's turn that frown upside down." Said Jez harassingly.

She spat on the ground to show him what she thought of his sunny day advice. She went back to eating her meal with a frown on her face like she was eating nails.

Thomas and Jez finished laying out her lunch and went off to the next room.

Jez told him that the other resident, Mrs. Dower, had died last Thursday as they left the room. That's why there was an open bed in Miss Sowado's room. He told him there was a lot of that and to not get too fond of the residents.

Thomas thought if they were all like Miss Sowado, it wouldn't be a problem.

In the next room they entered, they encountered two men playing cards. Mr. Sham and Mr. Chete. They didn't talk much and didn't really want to be disturbed.

Jez motioned to Thomas to keep quiet by placing his index finger over his lips. They laid out their lunch and utensils on the men's dinner trays and briskly left the room. When they did, the two gentlemen stayed enticed in their cribbage game. It was as if

Thomas and Jez weren't even present. He heard one of them shout out something about how he'd been cheated.

"They play cards from 9 a.m. sharp to 3 p.m. sharp. They always fight and accuse each other of cheating but they continue to play day after day. They've both been here over three years and everyday it's the same thing. Other than that though they are nice guys." Jez finished.

Then they came to the next room. There was a couple in this area of resentment. Thomas could feel the glowering bitterness in the doorway before they entered. Mr. And Mrs. Crassman started in on the young men before they could run for cover.

"What kind of crap they feeding us today?" Mrs. Crassman complained.

"I can go to jail if I want to eat this slop." Mr. Crassman said rather snooty.

"Isn't that where we are?" Mrs. Crassman asked sarcastically.

Mr. Crassman nodded to his wife.

"You've had Sheppard's pie every Sunday for lunch for five month's Mr. and Mrs. Crassman, you know that." Jez replied.

"Hi I'm Thomas." Thomas proclaimed trying to break the tension.

"So. You a movie star or something." Mrs. Crassman said arrogantly.

"Oh honey we have a movie star." Taunted Mr. Crassman.

They both roared at this.

The rest of the day went on like that. Jez said to Thomas that he'd learn to 'tune' them out.

"Don't worry after a while you'll just roll with the punches and it won't even bother you." Jez promised.

Thomas wasn't so sure.

They checked Mr. Chete's blood pressure. It had to be checked daily at Four o'clock. It was always 110 over 58. But he insisted that his wife said…

Miss Sowado complained of a fever, so they checked that. She was fine.

They passed out dinner at 4:45.

"Just be lucky that all of them can eat by themselves. They can all get themselves to the bathroom. They can all shower without help. We've got it lucky. Not all zones run this easy." Jez informed Thomas.

Easy. Thomas thought. My God what are the other aides going through?

They gave out the Salisbury Steaks to everyone but Miss Sowado. She couldn't eat steak. It had to be fish or chicken. Today it was fried chicken. Mr. And Mrs. Crassman could smell it and complained.

"I smell fried chicken. Miss Sowado getting the royal treatment again." Mr. Crassman complained loudly enough so the woman might hear it in the first room.

She did.

She smiled.

She ate her food with a sense of elegance, like she was on a different level of the pecking order than her peers.

"Why must we eat this processed crap and she gets fried chicken?" Mrs. Crassman barked.

"You know she can't eat red meat Mrs. Crassman." Jez responded.

"RED MEAT?" Mr. Crassman asked rather loud and sarcastically. "You call this hockey puck meat." He went on.

"I'm not going to listen to anymore of this." Jez announced and

JASON HANCOCK

they both left the room after having dished out the meals. Jez left the dinner cart in there so that when they collected the half eaten meals, after the residents claimed to be finished, they could work backwards from the Crassman room.

After they collected all the finished meals, twenty minutes later, they took break at 5:05.

At 5:20 they did their last rounds. Jez informed Thomas that when he got more comfortable with the job their breaks would get longer but for now there was much to learn.

Jez told Thomas he could leave after they picked up the dirty dishes and took them back to the cafeteria.

"Why don't you split a little bit early." He said. "It's your first day. Don't want to burn you out. It can be a little overwhelming the first few days but it will get better." He said trying to instill confidence.

Thomas nodded.

"Okay. That sounds good." Thomas replied.

"Plus it's Halloween. Go out and raise some hell." He said.

Crap.

Halloween, he forgot.

Mary is waiting Thomas thought.

"Okay Jez I'll see you tomorrow." Thomas replied exhausted both emotionally and physically. But he had no time to be worn out. He must hurry home and fetch Mary.

Thomas sped off to drop his dirty smock in the used linens chute and went to use the bathroom. He did his business. Then he washed his hands and face. He dried them off with the automatic air dryer and burst through the door. He ran by the nurse's station and out into the evening air.

He was in such a hurry he forgot his windbreaker and something

162

else very important.

When he left, Jez was entering his daily data into the computer. One eye was on the computer and the other eye was on Melissa Willing. She was able to keep his eyes on her by bending down to the bottom drawer in the file cabinet making her plaid skirt show a small portion of her purple undies. The important portion.

They didn't see Thomas run out the door in haste to get home, for Mary was waiting to go out trick or treating.

The man in the mausoleum in the rear of the local cemetery was making some tedious preparations. All about the crypt were items essential to his tasks.

Upon a sheet music stand was an ancient book. The book was thick and brown with a worn binder. The words on the front weren't legible but it appeared to be in Greek. The age of this book was three thousand years old. The Macedonians saved this book from ruin from many invaders both from religious sects and from the pagan barbarians. It might have been better to let it burn. On the floor were designs and symbols drawn in blood. What these depictions are I can't tell you. In the wrong hands they could be very hazardous and detrimental to all. You mustn't open a door, unless you can handle what comes through it.

When one speaks of magic oftentimes they refer to the powers of these arts as Black and White. I though, like to call them Light and Dark. Let me explain.

The reason for this is that, the people or entities that use magic, will often borrow from both fields to achieve a goal. It is the intentions of these goals, which determines their nature. Believe me, if you were to summon an Angel or a Demon, neither would be very thrilled and both would certainly subject you to their will.

Halloween or All Hallows Eve is a time of great significance concerning these powers. The elements are open to manipulation.

The hours between sun down that day, and sunrise the following morning, is the safest time to access and control these factors. Five minutes before the witching hour and five minutes after, is the optimum point for transference. This is the time when, a caster can alter the fabric of time and space to pull something from another plane or dimension to their desired location. It requires much education, skill and confidence. It also requires the preparation of several materials, objects, positioning of the symbols and one's person about those symbols. These are but some of the necessary tools needed to pull off this feat. Timing is everything. Stray just a little and the outcome could be disastrous and/or fatal. The mess you would leave behind could be catastrophic.

All he needed was the proper fuel to feed the imp he was about to transport through the astral gate. It was some time since he had seen her. He was looking forward to their reunion.

The man had done all the other preparing. He would set off to get the food needed for his pet. Then he would wait until the midnight hour, to begin.

When Thomas arrived home he went to Jasper and he brought him into the house. Thomas decided if they were to face persecution, it would be together.

Thomas entered the house to find a much different mood than he was expecting.

Laura went to him with comfort in her eyes and gave him a hug. Laura had something in her right hand when she embraced him.

"Sorry Thomas that we didn't have as much faith in you as Mary." She sobbed still stinging with guilt. She finished hugging Thomas and put her hands behind her back.

"Son I apologize too. To you and Jasper." Henry announced.

Jasper was sniffing out something since he came in. Something sweet was on the edge of his discovery. Laura had her hands behind her back. Jasper was curious. Has she something for me? Jasper approached her and sat up on his back legs.

Jasper would do a funny thing when he was waiting patiently for something. He would stare at the person until they revealed what they were about. His left ear would flop down and the other would stand-straight up. This was unlike when he was on alert, when both ears would stick straight up.

He sat patiently to see what Laura was up too. He had a suspicion that what ever it was, it was good for him. From behind her back she produced a cattle's femur bone. She had picked this up at the local Butcher shop when Thomas was at work. Jasper wagged his tail and with a pat and apology from Laura, he made off for Thomas' room to enjoy his treat. Jasper, like Thomas had a deep love for Thomas' parents. His appreciation for them was never more than it was now. Although the reasons for the affection he felt for Laura was different than that for Henry.

Not more.

Not less.

It's just different. It's different but equal.

Animals, like children, learn the hierarchy of principles and character from their parents, or masters in this case.

A true man of integrity will carry honor and humility in his heart. He will protect his family at all costs, even unto his peril, if that ensures his family's survival. He will stand up for those who cannot stand on their own, because it is right. Might for right, not might is right.

A real woman will carry in herself mercy and unconditional love for her family. Love is the strongest magic that can be performed in this world and it's something beautiful when you learn its origin. It's not something that can be cast though, only absorbed. As hard as magic users have tried they cannot duplicate its power. Many have tried by magical manipulation to make another love them and it always ends in destruction. To be another's beloved both parties must give the greater part of themselves to achieve it. It is seldom captured or understood and even less of it transferred or conveyed. However, if you do find it, you will know. For no power, no matter how fierce, can destroy it.

These are the necessary ingredients for a fruitful family structure.

We love our father's out of respect and our mother's for their mercy.

Both are commendable characteristics, but you can see why our adoration for them is slightly different, but equal.

If you endeavor to pursue this logic, you may find it helpful.

Jasper felt these feelings for his masters today and Laura thought she saw him grow a little.

Crazy. She thought, couldn't be. She shook her head and dismissed it.

Mary and the Morgan family sat down for a quick light dinner. Laura fixed some hot pastrami sandwich's, with Deli mustard and French fries. After dinner they began getting their costumes together.

A man in a black ninja suit peeked through the window.

No one was in the hall.

He pushed up the screen and the slightly opened window and began to crawl through. It was open to let a little breeze in. It was dark already, having set the clocks back the week before, but it was unusually humid. It felt as though the sky would open up and dump the moisture it had sucked up all day down on the earth below.

He climbed through the window and proceeded to the first door on the right.

A woman sat with her back to the door listening to her alarm clock radio. It was on a talk radio station. The world news was spitting out its normal foreboding script.

"Today a man catches fire lighting his own flatulence and suffered second degree burns over most of his body. A man in Oregon won the lottery and while returning from the lottery commission drove his car off a bridge. Police are listing it as an accident. Two other cars were involved in the crash. In other news a small Mexican village claims to have captured the ever elusive mythical creature the Chupacabra…"

The man quietly crept up on her. In his hand was a strip of duct tape. He reached over her head and put the duct tape, that he had torn off the roll stored in his belt sac, over her mouth. Before she could react he punched her in the stomach, disabling her. He wrapped more tape around her hands and feet. Her eyes were wide open and she was trying to scream, making small muffled sounds. He took the blood pressure measuring machine in the far corner of the room and brought it over to her on the bed. He took the Velcro-strap, intended for an arm, tore it open and wrapped it around her neck. He let out the valve and the pressure filled the air pocket.

The woman's eyes bulged.

Suddenly, he heard the toilet flush from the room's interior bathroom. The man thought they were alone. No matter, he would neutralize the threat of being discovered.

"Fran are you…" The man who was speaking to his wife from the bathroom and about to reenter the main room spoke with a gurgled sound in his throat.

Sticking out of his chest was a thin four -inch blade. The man wearing the ninja suit swung the other man around. He pulled the knife from his chest and slit his jugular. Blood jetted out and sprayed the wall. He threw the dying man against the wall and held him up with one hand fastened around his neck. He then cut out the man's heart, kidneys and liver. He did this with the precision of a trained surgeon. The man slumped to the floor. He was still alive and shock was over taking him. The ninja shoved the kidneys in the dead man's mouth. The bloodied victim suffocated on his renal organs. Then the man in black wrote a message on the walls in the man's blood. He took the heart and liver.

He returned to the room to see if he needed to do anything further with the original intended victim. Nope. She was quite dead. Her eyeballs were bulged out and it seems that her blood pressure was 0/0.

Then he pulled two large zip-lock bags from his belt pack. He placed the heart and liver in one. He placed the knife in the other. He then took off his gloves and placed them in the bag with the knife as well.

Abruptly the door swung open.

Jez had forgotten his sunshades and came back to get them. He had the day off tomorrow and had a trip planned with some friends to go to Old Orchard Beach. It was probably too cold for swimming but his friend Tory owned a house on the water.

Well too bad for him he would never make it.

He switched on the light.

Then he met those eyes.

The nurse, who had replaced Jez after his shift, was about to do his rounds. He was late in doing his rounds today. It was Sunday he thought, no managers are on, so what's the rush. And to whom would the residents take their complaints anyway? To their families, I think not. The families that visit once a week, once a month or not at all. Who would listen to them at the nursing home? Everyone who worked here thought all they did was complain anyway. This would surely be another ploy to get attention and sympathy.

It was eight-fifteen and he made sure that Miss Sowado got her medication and helped her to bed. She complained all the way.

"You're an hour and fifteen minutes late, you twit." She argued.

He got her into bed without a word even though he wanted to tell her where to go. He just smiled and this made her even more furious. When someone is berating you, the best thing to do is just smile away, like you couldn't be bothered. Don't give the prick the satisfaction of rising to the occasion.

He went on to Mr. Sham and Mr. Chete's room to find they were in bed watching Jeopardy. He shut the door behind him and went on to the spoiled duo, Mr. and Mrs. Crassman.

When he opened the closed door of Mr. And Mrs. Crassman he shrieked.

"Someone call an ambulance! Call an ambulance!" He screamed.

He reached down to see if Mrs. Crassman was alive and she was dead cold.

He was terrified not only because they were murdered on his watch, but it also appeared that they were dead for quite a spell.

Jez was not present.

"Let me help you do your hair, Mary." Said Laura. "Won't you? She asked.

Mary was so excited that Laura had offered that it made her glow with anticipation. She felt like a younger sister might when her 'big sis' is going to fill her in on a big secret. Mary nodded her approval with a rapid shake of the head and plopped down in front of the large downstairs bathroom mirror.

"You have beautiful hair, Mary." Laura proclaimed.

Mary just beamed.

"I wish mine were as straight and flawless." She said.

"I love your hair Laura it's very… distinguished." Mary replied.

"Mary? Are you patronizing me?" Laura asked with more sarcasm than attitude.

Mary blushed and tried to say something, but decided against it. She wanted to assure Mrs. Morgan that her hair was sharp, but she was afraid that with more struggling, she might sink deeper into the quicksand.

Laura broke the uncomfortable situation when she saw Mary's embarrassment and spoke.

"I wish it were smart rather than distinguished." Laura informed her with a stout laugh.

Laura did Mary's hair in a fashion where there were two tight circular buns on either side of her head with both circles running over half of each ear. Laura sprayed some salon style aerosol hairspray over Mary's improvised hairdo and then Laura pulled out her secret weapon. The weapon when applied in the right measure was the bane of all men.

Hypnotic poison.

Wonderful.

"It smells delicious Laura!" Mary exclaimed.

Mary protested letting Thomas' mother apply this expensive perfume. She could not possibly replace such an offering but Laura would not be turned down.

"It's not your choice when it's a gift." She told Mary.

Mary and Laura kept on sniffing at Mary's wrist. Both of them giggled and whispered like a couple of naughty schoolgirls.

Mary left the bathroom to start putting her costume on.

Laura excused herself for the moment claiming she needed to relieve herself. When Mary had gone to Henry and Laura's room to wait for Laura to help get her costume together, Laura took the one-ounce purple bottle and sprayed a smidgen on her neck. Laura put the perfume away in her secret hideaway under a loose floorboard. This hidden compartment contained some other rather unique items, including money, which Laura had frugally saved over a long time. Then she washed her hands and dried them. Then Laura went to her bedroom to fix Mary's costume. She was anxious to go downstairs and gauge Henry's reaction to the 'Sacred Water.'

So they began doing up Mary's costume. Mary was going to be Princess Lea. Laura had sewn some flannel white sheets together into a thick robe. Laura fished out a black belt from her dresser drawer and Mary put it around her waist. She quickly found the right notch. Then, she pulled out some old black boots. The leather boots went up to the knees. Mary wondered what their previous purpose was.

Laura knew.

Mary didn't mind the used clothing, the old decorations, that they had hand made costumes or any of that. Even though Mary was rich, she was not materialistic at all. She didn't care that she had money and they did not, because they had something she did not.

They had one another.

Love between two parents for their children, trumps any amount of money.

When you grow up in a loving family, you grow up strong. Mary wasn't even that close to the one remaining parent she did have, Brenda. Her mother was so busy playing the jilted wife that she neglected her duties as a mother. That's not to say Brenda didn't buy Mary everything her heart desired but that in the end is not the same thing. Is it?

No doubt everyone has problems and skeletons in their closet. I don't think anyone's personal demons would stand up to another's scrutiny. So in Brenda's eyes, she was doing the best she could.

Mary loved just being here in the Morgan home. The house was filled with a kind of warmth and laughter that cannot be purchased at the local mall. You couldn't send away for it through a corporate magazine. It was something that was built from within.

Sometimes Mary would spy out Henry romancing Laura. The record player spinning and the speakers emitting the sounds of the Carpenters, Elvis or Dean Martin, whatever the mood called for that particular day. They would dance all night looking each other deep within the eyes. They would hold each other like lover's do and when they were finished, Laura would lead her champion by the hand and stroll off to the quiet offerings in the night.

Mary often wondered what happened upstairs after those nights of soft music and tender caress. This is what she wanted for herself and she was sure she had found it. So Mary was happy to be here anytime she could and happier still to be Thomas' girl.

Mary and Laura were satisfied with their job of replicating 'Princess Lea's' outfit and went off to see how Thomas was faring.

She looked at him dressed up in his costume and smiled. Thomas was going to be Han Solo. His father had given him an old black suit and coat that he found in the back closet to the den. He went into the downstairs closet to find his black boots. They put the finishing touches on their outfits and got their gear together.

Thomas sprinted upstairs to the linen closet and produced two old pillow sacks for their candy. He took his old backpack from the bottom of his closet. He had to beat the dust and crimps out of it before he could open it. He placed sodas and a flashlight from Henry's workbench in the cool cellar in the backpack.

The young couple said thank you and see you later to Thomas' parents and dashed off into the night.

Jasper sat on his hind legs with his front paws straight down to the floor like dogs often do. He sat in front of the screen door and watched his master and his girl walk away. Jasper had a feeling of

172

impending doom. He didn't want Thomas to face this foreboding fate alone. He was genuinely worried. He would stay at the door and wait for his master no matter how long it took. Dogs only know two kinds of time. Now and forever, and often times they feel like the same to them.

When law enforcement and EMTS arrived at Fallon's Nursing Home, they discovered the grizzly scene that Tony the nurse had the unfortunate privilege of doing so almost twenty- minutes before.

Deputy Sheriff Jerry Collin's was on duty and parked himself in the doorway. He gazed at the gruesome double murder before him.

Jerry was a young man of thirty-three and was acting Deputy Sheriff. The previous Deputy Tom Crapier was stricken with Crones Disease and had a class action lawsuit pending with a major pharmaceutical company.

Jerry was a very fit young man. He wasn't very tall, only reaching five foot nine inches but he was rather broad at the shoulders. He weighed one hundred and seventy pounds and was known to have done some prize fighting while in the National Guard. They called him 'White Dynamite' when he carried that torch.

He had short blond hair combed forward with the front bangs being spiked up. The young ladies around town thought that he was adorable and no doubt would one day make a special lady very happy. He was well groomed and never showed signs of a beard or mustache. He claimed that the trick to less stubble and smooth skin was shaving with cold water rather than warm or hot. His abdomen was chiseled into a fine six-pack and he had a small tight butt, which was sometimes subject to pinching from his female cohorts at the station.

Jerry was a true gentleman and if there ever was a more tedious or better mannered soul, I didn't know one. He had worked tirelessly to obtain his position. He often worked double shifts covering sick calls or vacations and anytime there was something no one else wanted, he'd take it. It paid huge dividends for him. He became acting Deputy five months ago and he commanded as much or more respect than Sheriff Collins.

And Jerry didn't get his job through small town politics or nepotism. He did it the old fashioned way. 'He earned it.'

Jerry had very little in the way of bad habits. He wasn't one to succumb to the woes of substance abuse or excess. His mother and father instilled in him long ago never to taint his body with the evils of man's creations. And never, his father said, never ever gamble.

One thing he did do though was, he drank a lot of coffee. He liked it black with four sugars and he would wait until it was cold to drink it. If he weren't sipping coffee, he would have the stirring straw between his teeth. He would swirl it to and fro and eventually he would chew on the end until finally the whole straw would find its way into his mouth. There it would become a crumpled waste of plastic useless to all except the garbage man.

Jerry had that straw in his mouth now and took it out with his left hand and spoke to the detective analyzing the murder scene.

"What do you make of this, Gary?" He said to Detective Schleper. The detective was already into investigating the dead couple when Jerry arrived. He arrived five minutes before.

"Not sure Jerry, but it's certainly messy as you can see. Personal too." He stated pointing to the wall.

Upon the wall was a written confession in blood. Although the meaning of it Jerry wasn't sure.

'Mary I'm sorry for what I've done. These pompous shit's had to die.' This is what the ominous statement proclaimed. The motive and culprit were still unknown.

If Sheriff Conway would have been on duty that night he might have guessed, but that would have to wait till morning. Although, maybe he wouldn't have put it all together, Conway wasn't that sharp. In fact the reason for him holding the position he had was because his father-in-law was a district judge.

And even though Conway knew about the 'man' and some of his true intentions, he didn't know of the details.

If Bobby, Thomas' uncle the EMT were on duty, he would have some insight. Although, he surely wouldn't have offered it because Bobby kept family close to his heart and safe from any unwanted discovery.

Mary and Thomas were off on their journey of trick or treating. Thomas had his backpack containing the flashlight, the sodas and two brownies that Thomas had snatched from the table on his way out the door. The two brownies were wrapped in tin foil. His mother had made them for him and Mary. He didn't know Mary already had two while Thomas was on his way home from the nursing home. Mary carried the pillowcases and they headed up Woodland St, to start their candy harvesting. When they approached the first house Mary handed one pillow sac to Thomas.

Thomas was thinking now about his decision to leave Jasper at home. The neighbor's were still sore about the feline massacre and he didn't want any more problems. It seemed best to leave him home. Besides he had a femur bone to keep him busy. Right? The thing he didn't know was that Jasper hid the bone for later enjoyment and waited at the front door worried about Thomas. Thomas hadn't noticed Jasper sitting in the doorway when he left home. They had been ready with their gear and costumes, so off they went. He was consumed in everything that was going on and he had forgotten to check on Jasper. He felt kind of guilty.

They went house- to -house collecting candy. Up Woodland St. and over to Park St. they went knocking on doors and were greeted with the courtesy, charity and compliments that the holiday brings.

They crossed over Main St. to where Beacon St. meets Duck Pond and finished their trick or treating in Farmers cul de sac.

"Mary I think we should be getting back, it's getting late." Thomas said concernedly.

She just shivered and nodded. It was getting cold and a mist was spitting.

Thomas saw this and immediately took off his suit jacket and put it around her.

He was cold too, but he gave up his jacket for her. He would never admit he was cold to her, because he wouldn't want her to feel guilty about taking it. Besides he determined long ago that he would do anything for her, like walk on his face across hot coals if he had to.

He would too.

It's funny when you're a kid the distance you will go to in protecting your loved ones. Only your truest friends keep this fire inside. As you get older they are less than you think. You will find out who they are when you need help the most.

After Thomas gave his jacket to Mary he pulled the flashlight from his backpack and turned it on to ward off cars as they headed home. As they approached Woodland St. and were in sight of Mary's house, they saw Mr. Kilcrop's Town car next to Brenda's Mercedes. They both glanced at each other and shrugged continuing their trot to her abode.

Thomas and Mary entered her house to get some hot chocolate. They dropped their stuffed pillowcases next to the door and took off their shoes. Thomas took off his backpack and plopped it on the floor next to the coat rack and put the flashlight on top of it.

Thomas was skeptical of going in to see Brenda, since she warned him off that morning. He expected to get a lot of hostility from her, but in fact she was rather civil. Obviously she was basking in the idea of having a male guest.

"Did you guys have fun?" She asked.

"Yes Mrs. Talisman." Thomas replied shyly.

Crap.

Was he supposed to say Talisman or Smothers?

She just smiled.

Wew! Close one.

"Well Brenda I must be going. It was nice to have spent some time with you." Said Mr. Kilcrop.

"You sure you won't stay for another cup of coffee?" Brenda asked desperately. "You only just arrived." She said reinforcing her desperation.

"I must be getting home. I have some preparing to do for school tomorrow." He responded. With that, he kissed Brenda on the hand.

"Oh my and I thought chivalry was dead." She blushed.

"Not yet." He said putting emphasis on 'yet'.

Thomas and Mary caught this and looked at each other.

Brenda though, did not.

If she had, she could have saved them much trouble, in the near future.

Her starry eyes just stared into the emptiness of bliss. She longed for him to stay the night but I guess that was not to be tonight she thought.

"I'll show myself out. Please don't get up. Until next we meet." He went on.

Brenda flushed and watched her Charlemagne walk off, out of the kitchen and into the foyer. The kitchen from the angle of the coat rack and front door was out of sight.

Mr. Kilcrop looked back to see if he was beyond view and

saw that he was. He then took his long jacket from the coat rack and reached inside. He pulled out a bag and placed it in Thomas' backpack. The flashlight fell off the backpack and Mr. Kilcrop caught it before it hit the floor. He did this as nimble as a swan on water. After he zipped up the backpack he placed the flashlight back on top of it. Then he put on his jacket and opened the door. He sauntered out on to the porch and took a deep breath of fresh air. He stood at the top of the stairs for a short while thinking about the upcoming chaos that would no doubt unfold and reveled in it. He smiled and looked up into the sputtering precipitation and let it fall upon his face. He skipped down the stairs and hopped a three-step five-step dance to his car. As he opened the door to his Town Car he began to hum. After he sat down and turned on the ignition, he switched on the radio and tuned in to a station to his liking.

"Ah." He said finding a song to his approval.

He backed out of the driveway and put the automobile in drive. Off he went.

He sang along to the music on the radio.

Highway to Hell slammed out of his speakers.

"AC/DC, the regiment of mayhem themselves. Too bad for the original band though for Bon Scott's over indulgence that ultimately led him to his destruction. They rocked every night with him at the helm, until he was 'shot down in flames.' Better to 'Burn' out than fade out, right?" Kilcrop said in a cold laugh to no one.

He continued his croon down the road pounding on the steering wheel and tapping his fingers on the dash.

A man stood watching from the swamp across the street not to far from Mary's. He had a shot -gun attached to his back and he wore a long dirty overcoat.

"So it begins." He said.

Back at the cemetery, the man approached the mausoleum carrying the ninja suit in his hands. He set them down on the damp earth. He went in to the crypt to grab a can of lighter fluid he'd left there the day before and went back out into the dank night air. The heavy pitched door closed behind him. He put some lighter fluid on the ninja clothes. He lit a match that he pulled from his pocket and proceeded to burn the clothes. He stood over the fire and let the hot energy dance before him under the night sky. He liked the nighttime. He had always considered himself to be nocturnal, a creature of the night.

After he had watched the small blaze long enough he opened the door to the mausoleum. Then he proceeded to strip down. He took off his jacket, dress clothes and shoes. He got totally unrobed. He lit up the candles, which were placed in the several evenly spaced holders along the wall. The interval between candles was two feet six inches. There were three on each side of the tomb and it illuminated the room perfectly.

In the room were several marble caskets of a famous family from this town.

This family had ties to the first settlers in Massachusetts. This family was responsible for the first mill in this area. At least two presidents can trace their lineage to this family. They built a settlement here and eventually it became what it is today, because of them. They persevered against terrible winters and ruthless Indians who felt they were being encroached upon.

The Mausoleum was made mostly of granite and fieldstone. However the grave vaults were constructed of marble. This would be a very expensive venture today but in those days of yesteryear they made things proper.

In the center of the large granite and marble structure was the largest sarcophagus. This is for the first of this prominent family. There wasn't any remains in it because his body was buried somewhere else which is long forgotten, but the memory of him rests in this place.

On the top of the doorway inside and out were stone-sculpted gargoyles. The ugly faces were sculpted displaying rude and disgusting gestures intended to ward off unwanted spirits. Unfortunately sometimes they worked in reverse depending on the strength and fortitude of those invading spirits.

After the man burned his ninja clothes and disrobed he moved his naked body above the symbols written in blood on the floor. The blood had since dried and was showing signs of flaking when he passed over them.

He opened the book that was resting on the sheet music stand and began his summoning. Out of his belt sac he pulled a silver cup and small cow- bell. He took the human heart and liver out of the zip-lock bag that he had taken from the unfortunate donor, Mr. Crassman, at the nursing home. He threw the liver on the ground. He picked up the heart and squeezed it until the dark life force liquid fell into the silver chalice resting on the center sarcophagus. The chalice he'd taken from his sac, which was now resting on the granite coffin in the center of the room directly in front of him, was filling up.

He was facing the door of the mausoleum. He filled up the chalice with as much blood as the heart would yield and then threw the spent organ on the floor. He took the chalice and dipped a finger in. He drew a circle on the tomb in front of him. Then, he drank the rest of the blood. He began reading excerpts from the book. As he chanted louder and louder the passages that came in the book he could feel a pulling force yanking on his body. Then he stopped the chanting. He finished reading from the book and he prayed. He prayed to whatever sick Deity that he worshipped. Then he picked up the cowbell and rang it three times. The echo filled the room with a small vibration.

He waited.

Then it appeared.

A blinding red flash emerged atop the granite tomb in front of him and then it was gone. Upon that sarcophagus and through the astral doorway a foul creature from the netherworld materialized.

It was a horrid looking beast. It looked liked some one had placed three creatures in a microwave and they all melted together. The face around the eyes and mouth drooped as if melting from his face, or had some kind of mutant muscle disease. The features that you could make out on the beast, created the appearance of a huge wild boar. These features were only relative of the facial and torso sections of its body though. The back end of the beast was, well, something else.

Its top tusks were five inches long. One of them was broken in half. The bottom set, were slightly bigger. The top tusks were bent back slightly towards the ears. One side only started backward a little ways and was broken off in some long ago tussle perhaps. The jagged tooth stopped next to its chin. Where his ears should have been there were horns like that of a ram. The horns spiraled out from the side of his head and came to points above him. They extended about a foot from his skull. In the center of the spiral were two slits substituting for ears. He had a large snout with hair protruding from his nostrils.

His back end like I said, that was quite different.

His rear legs were like that of a goat and dog but less hairy. His legs were bigger in the back than front, so when he sat down or ran, his back legs were bent, like a dogs. The only other thing different was that he had hooves in the back. Big, black hooves. He had a long tail like a dog and it ended with a sharp tip.

"Hello Helyza." The man said.

The animal responded by snorting. Thick hot air came from her snout.

181

The man petted the beast and showed her the meal he had brought for her homecoming. The beast jumped down from the sarcophagus and tore into the organs with delight.

Thomas picked up his pillowcase and backpack. He grabbed the flashlight, switched it on and proceeded out the door into the misty cool night.

Mary came out onto the porch and grabbed his shoulder. She turned him around and kissed him deep.

He descended the stairs with his belongings and walked home in high spirits.

CHAPTER NINE

Red

Monday morning in the shower, Thomas was still trying to remove the red dye from his hand. It wasn't as pronounced as it was the Friday prior, when he discovered its presence, but it was still there. It was like the shade that cherry cool aid leaves behind after you've had a glass or two. It's not necessarily distracting to the onlooker, but it's definitely noticeable.

After showering, getting dressed and putting his schoolbooks in order, he went down to get some breakfast. He had a couple pieces of toast, grabbed his schoolwork and kissed his mother goodbye.

He and Jasper went out through the screen door. Jasper was unusually anxious that morning. He kept pulling on Thomas' jeans.

"What's the matter boy?" Thomas asked.

Jasper let out a long whine. Jasper was trying to tell him about the warning in his heart.

"It's okay boy. I'll be home soon enough and we'll play awhile." Thomas assured him.

Thomas went off down the road on his way to collect Mary and head off to school.

Jasper watched his master walk away. Then the alpha dog from the Breed Of The Blue Diamond lay down and began to gather all of his strength.

Several detectives and CBI specialists from the FBI were analyzing and investigating the double homicide at the nursing home.

They had the room taped off and were taking statements from employees and residents alike.

Deputy Sheriff, Jerry Collins, welcomed Sheriff Conway on the scene.

"What the hell have we got here, Jerry?" Sheriff Conway asked in concern.

"It's a real mess chief." Jerry responded.

Jerry went through the evidence that they had up to this point with the Sheriff. Conway was wide eyed and in disbelief. His face was changing color because he knew he would have to go in and peek at the gruesome murders.

When Jerry finished he said he still needed a statement from the controller of the nursing home and went off to question Sonya about her employees and anything else that might be pertinent to the investigation.

Sheriff Conway went into the dreadful scene apprehensively.

When he got to the room of Mr. and Mrs. Crassman he saw Mrs. Crassman upon the bed. Her eyeballs were bulged out of their sockets. The skin in her face had turned a deep shade of blue. Her body had succumbed to rigor mortis. The tape was still around her feet and wrists but her elbows had surrendered to the death stiffening. Her wrists were taped so that her arms were tied behind her and the rigor mortis made both of her elbows come in contact with each other so that it pushed her chest way out. The left side of her upper body was pointing up in the air and all her weight was down upon her other elbow. If she were alive she wouldn't have been able to maintain this posture long because her shoulder and arm tucked underneath her body would have long ago fell asleep. It was an unearthly position for someone to be stuck in. It was like she was frozen in this state.

Sheriff Conway had never seen a corpse, especially someone he knew. He didn't like looking at this twisted cadaver at all. Even when his mother died many years before in a car crash, the casket was closed. He kind of liked that, because he felt he didn't have to say goodbye face to face.

Now seeing the deceased Mrs. Crassman, he felt a little nauseated. He turned to the right so that he didn't have to focus on that terrible crime. Then his gaze fell on the horrible sight of what happened to Mr. Crassman. Sheriff Conway's head began to spin and suddenly he vomited all over the floor. He began to lose his balance, fell backwards and banged his head on a dinner tray in the room. He hit it so hard he blacked out.

When he came to, his deputy was squatting next to him with a glass of water.

"You okay chief?" Jerry asked.

The sheriff's head was humming like a screen fan was inside it. It felt like he had a construction crew jack hammering between his ears.

"Chief. Chief." Jerry went on.

Conway could see Jerry's mouth moving but he didn't know what he was going on about. Finally, he came out of the fog.

"Can you hear me?" Jerry asked.

"Yes. Dammit, I'm okay." He remarked.

"Help me get up." He added.

Jerry helped Conway to the open bed, Mr. Crassman's former

sleeping place. The sheriff sat on the victim's former sleeping location and put his hands on his temples and began to massage the sides of his forehead.

"Oh man what a mess Jerry." The sheriff said more than a little woozy.

When he sat down, Jerry gave him the cool glass of water.

Conway noticed the smiling faces and whispering from the federal agents.

He felt humiliated. His face felt hot and he wanted to get out of this place and into the brisk autumn air.

"Chief. I asked the facilitator about any employees that seemed distracted or acting abnormal during the weekend." The deputy sheriff said.

"Well?" Conway inquired.

"She said she wasn't on yesterday, but…" he trailed off.

"Say it man." Conway demanded.

"She told me Thomas Morgan started yesterday. She went on to say he didn't punch out. He left his jacket behind too, like he just rushed off in a hurry. Nobody knows what time he left. Also, they can't locate the male nurse he was training under. Melissa Willing said Jez left when she did at five past seven."

"Thomas Morgan. Well, that explains the writing on the wall." Conway said.

"But why?" Jerry asked.

"Who knows why any one does this sort of thing?" Conway returned.

"Should we pick him up?" Jerry asked.

"Let's." Conway responded.

He was glad to be getting away from this sinful scene and didn't want to return. He would make sure someone was put away for this and he had every intention of bringing 'Thomas' to justice.

That morning Thomas and Mary spoke of their tummy aches after having ingested too much candy the night before. They slowly made their way to school.

They got to school finally and passed through the double doors of the high school only to find the students were being routed to the auditorium.

As they went down to the hall where the school rallies were held, Thomas noticed the chill of the outside autumn air. Several windows and doors were broken leaving the halls feeling brisk. Graffiti littered the walls. In red paint the vandalism read statements like: 'this school sucks, the teachers are scum sucking reptiles,' screw the establishment' and other graphic filth.

The students filed into the seats in the auditorium. They were all speculating about the cause for the destruction and who the culprits might be.

Principle Kilcrop ascended the stairs to the stage and approached the podium. The sound of his dress shoes echoed in the auditorium as he made his even heavy steps toward the speaking pedestal.

All the students were chatting and full of gossip. The principle held up his hand without speaking and the room fell silent.

"Do you think we'll have some time off from school. Who do you think did it? What do you think will happen?" Went the hushed banter behind Thomas.

First bell rang and all was quiet. Principle Kilcrop spoke.

"Students. A disgraceful and malevolent act has occurred in our house." The principle started. As he went on, his manner of speaking got more intense. He began soft, but stern. As he continued, he got louder and more passionate. He paused between phrascs as if gaining speed.

"Vandals have defaced and defiled our school. We believe that the person or persons responsible are in this room." He bellowed.

The teachers were present and stood along either side of the student body also listening to this speech. When Mr. Abrams heard that the perpetrators were in the building he was suspicious.

"Believe me young people, we will apprehend the perpetrators and they will be brought to justice. I have issued a locker search. It will begin immediately upon attendance check. Your homeroom teacher will escort each student to his or her locker. One by one we will eliminate the doubt of who is responsible." He went on.

"WE WILL HAVE JUSTICE!" He ended speech with a roar, and pounded his fist on the podium.

The students and teachers howled their approval.

Everyone was inspired except Mr. Abrams. He wasn't as gullible as most. The wool couldn't be pulled over his eyes so easily. He wondered how the Principle came upon the information that the suspects were in the school. Something was wrong, and he knew it.

After the teachers and students returned to their homerooms from the auditorium, the pupils went one by one with the teachers to their lockers from their classes.

Thomas' teacher, Mr. Foolhardy, was going through the motions of this task. Mr. Foolhardy was a weasel of a man. He was not very respected or liked by the students. He was a man of medium stature. His receding hair was speckled with gray. And because he didn't have a lot of hair, his giant ears stuck out. He had a moustache where the ends were twisted up. He had beady black eyes and one eyebrow that extended across his fore head. But his voice was what made him a creep. When he spoke it was like the words wouldn't let go of his mouth and he always under emphasized every word. His speech was very slow and methodical. The words that did manage to get away from him were followed by a squeak and a lisp. Since the beginning of the school year, Mr. Foolhardy sucked up to the new principle looking for praise.

When Thomas' teacher was progressing through the students, Thomas had a startling revelation. Anguish flowed through him. Slowly he turned his hand over.

Oh no.

"Thomas. Come on, it's your turn." Mr. Foolhardy said.

Thomas went hesitantly out to the hall and on to his locker. When Thomas got there he was worried about what he might see inside. He remembered the black magic marker incident and he hoped this wasn't part two of the conspiracy.

"Let's go Thomas. I haven't got all day." He commanded.

When he said this, Mr. Foolhardy noticed Thomas' hand because it was turned up and Thomas was looking from it to the locker.

"I hope Thomas that's not what I think it is." Rebuked Mr. Foolhardy sympathetically, even though he hoped it was.

"Me too." Thomas remarked.

Thomas turned the lock dial to the right three times past zero to thirty seven, left twice past zero to twenty nine and right past zero to one. Click. Slowly Thomas pulled the latch up and opened the locker door. Inside his cluttered locker were three empty cans of red paint. Mr. Foolhardy screamed out in joy. He had found the culprit. Thomas just stood and stared into his locker. What was happening? He thought. A feeling of helplessness fell over him like a shroud. Mr. Foolhardy skipped like a schoolboy to the intercom inside the classroom.

"I did it. I got him. I did it." Mr. Foolhardy sang while he pranced to his homeroom class.

"Paging Principle Kilcrop." He announced.

A few moments passed. All the while Mr. Foolhardy was doing an Indian Dance, back and forth.

"Yes." Came the voice over the loud speaker.

"I got him. It's Thomas Morgan." He publicized.

"Oh my. Okay. I'll be up to collect him directly." Mr. Kilcrop said with pleasure.

Thomas knew he was the object of deception but he didn't know why or by whom. He just stood there in disbelief.

Mr. Foolhardy jumped from one foot to the other like he was engaged in an Irish drinking song.

"I got him. I got him. Oh yes I did. I got him." Thomas' teacher sang praising himself for uncovering the schoolhouse caper.

Thomas didn't understand the reason for this ruse and neither did Mr. Abrams. Mr. Abrams witnessed Mr. Foolhardy's reaction when Thomas opened his locker. He observed Thomas gaping into the locker. He deduced Thomas was betrayed.

Mr. Kilcrops footfalls could be heard coming up to the second floor.

Mr. Foolhardy came to intercept him to receive whatever kind of reward was warranted for his part of discovery. Thomas' homeroom was on the second floor along with most freshmen and sophomore classes. Mr. Foolhardy watched Mr. Kilcrop pass right by him without so much as a word, like he hadn't even seen Thomas' teacher. Mr. Foolhardy turned around with his head bowed and returned to class, pouting like a brat who didn't get what he wanted for Christmas.

Mr. Abrams ambled up to Thomas as Mr. Kilcrop was marching towards them.

"Why is this happening to me?" Cried Thomas.

"I know you didn't do it Thomas. I don't know who did but I'm determined to find out." Mr. Abrams said.

Thomas peered up at Mr. Abrams with worry and disbelief in his eyes.

Principle Kilcrop had reached them with a look of utter contempt. He was perturbed because he didn't know what Mr. Abrams was whispering to Thomas about. He wanted to know what the secret discussion was all about but he didn't ask.

"Let's go young man you're in deep now." He declared.

Thomas glanced at Mr. Abrams and then started his shuffle down to the Principle's office.

"Keep your head up kid." Mr. Abrams hollered.

The look of disdain, that Mr. Kilcrop shot back, would kill, if looks could.

Now Abrams knew something was amiss. He was sure the Principle was involved. But how to prove it, that was the question.

As Thomas passed class after class, he felt the eyes of the other student's falling on him. He heard the gossip and hushed discussions, which were surely about him.

Principle Kilcrop didn't say a word all the long way to his office. When they got there, he closed the door behind him.

Sheriff Conway was sitting in a swivel chair adjacent to the principle's desk.

Principle Kilcrop parked himself behind Thomas and stood gleaming over him.

Sheriff Conway rose from his chair with his hands behind his back. He paced back and forth as if to choose his words carefully. Finally he spoke to Thomas.

"I don't know what you're about Mr. Morgan, but I'm afraid you've gone off the deep end." The sheriff announced.

Thomas just stood there listening to the accusations and rehearsed talk.

"Is there any abuse or violence at home? Are you neglected Thomas? Are you chastised or afraid there?" He asked these questions in a manner that suggested that he believed this to be the case.

"I know your father Thomas, known him a long time now. He was always one to find solace at the bottom of a bottle." He went on.

The board meeting in his mind was called to order and they were discussing the scenario before them. They were arguing on the best action to resolve this matter.

The lion inside Thomas was restless in sleep.

Thomas' temper sent the message to his blood to begin the boiling stage. The molecules in the pot were starting to move.

"Is that the problem kid, your father's a drunk? Does he come home and harass you and your mother?" Is he a wife beater? Does he smack her around?" He snickered.

Now the molecules were rising to the top of the water.

The lion inside Thomas' belly was waking up now. Someone had disturbed it. Someone had walked up to it while it was asleep in its den and kicked it right in the face. His vision was cloudy. He clenched his fists.

"Or what, does your mother, does she… touch you?" Sheriff Conway asked with a smile revealing pure satisfaction.

The board members just stood and stared because they knew what the chairman was about to do and not all the persuading in the world would stop him.

This disgusting fat repulsive man had just insulted the honor and integrity of his father and the mercy and dignity of his mother. And like the true man that Thomas was growing up to be, he protected both with a lions share. Now all Thomas saw was red. The lion was fully awake and it roared. The molecules were rolling to the top of the pot and he was at full boil.

The lion came forth.

It came forth in the form of flying fists.

He let out a lions roar and all his focus and energy came forward like a hurricane.

"AAAAAAAAAAAAHHHHHHHHHHH." Thomas roared.

Thomas drew back and delivered a haymaker. He unleashed his right fist on Conway's left eye fracturing the cheek- bone below it. His left plowed into the sheriff's sternum, knocking the wind clear out of him. Before he could bend over to pull in breath and hold his chest, Thomas brought his right knee into his groin catching his left testicle and severely bruising it. The sheriff bent down and let out a huge gasp.

"UUUUUGGGHHHHH." Was all the sheriff could let out.

Thomas wasn't finished. Principle Kilcrop grabbed Thomas' shoulder and Thomas flipped him over the principle's desk. Thomas turned back to Conway who was on his knees. Blood poured from the corner of his puffy eye. Thomas took three steps, put his hands behind the sheriff's head and drove his right knee into Conway's nose. The nosed smashed across his face like it would if you stepped on a sandwich. He broke the nose and almost fractured the right eye socket. Broken bone and cartilage were rolling around in Conway's face and he fell to the floor, clutching several parts of his body.

Now Mr. Kilcrop knew he should do something, but he felt a tiny touch of fear. No one had ever had the spiritual strength to toss him about. He had seen every kind of man too. Emperors, kings, judges, generals and soldiers alike. He had seen them all, but this boy just flung him across the room like a stuffed animal.

He had the first taste of doubt that he's had in a long time. So he did nothing.

Thomas opened the closed door to the Principle's office and it slammed against the wall putting a hole in the drywall where it met the doorknob. He bolted down the short hall passed the Guidance

Counselors office into the secretary's office and into the school foyer. He knocked over the huge potted plant in the process of escaping and shot through the double doors to the front of the school. He ran down the walkway at full speed toward the sheriff's squad car.

There were two cruiser's parked on the curb in front of the school. No one was in either one. Good Thomas thought.

At this time Mary was looking out the window. She expected to see Thomas being taken off in handcuffs because the gossip had reached her that he was the criminal behind the vandalism. She didn't believe it. What she saw now drove her mad.

"OH NO TOM. OH NO." She screamed beating on the window, "RUN, TOMMY! RUN! RUNNNNNNNNN!" She bawled banging both hands on the window.

The entire class ran to the window. They all gaped at what was happening.

Jerry Collin's had gone up the street on foot to get donuts and coffee. As he came out of the donut shop he saw Thomas jump in the sheriff's cruiser and screech off. The deputy sheriff dropped the bag of donuts and spilled the hot coffee all over him. He shrieked. The inside of his right thigh had sustained second-degree burns. He hobbled down to his car wailing in pain.

Crap.

The sheriff's going to kill me he whispered to himself.

Where is he anyway?

At this time Sheriff Conway stumbled out of the school and came wobbling down the walkway howling in pain. He was holding his crotch with one hand and his other was trying to hold blood out of his eye with a towel.

"You idiot, you let him drive off." Sheriff Conway screamed.

Jerry bellowed orders into the police radio.

"Calling all units we have a murder suspect on the loose, he has assaulted a police officer and stolen the sheriff's squad car. He is considered extremely dangerous. His name is Thomas Morgan." The deputy went on in describing Thomas and finished with a whimper. He was hopping on one leg. After it had cooled down a bit and he started up the squad car he spoke to Conway.

"What happened to you?" Jerry asked the beaten sheriff.

"Never mind." The sheriff whined as he gingerly got in the squad car.

The sheriff sat on his right butt cheek to alleviate the pain from his left testacle. Jerry turned on the siren and went into pursuit after the assailant.

Thomas had taken off down the street in the police car. The only problem was he couldn't drive. He never really had the opportunity to, so it wasn't as effortless as he thought it would be. He bounced off several of the cars lined up, down School St. He came to the stop -light at High St, where it met perpendicular to School St. It made a T-shape. Thomas slammed on the brakes and the car screeched to a halt. Smoke was rising up around the car. He didn't know what to do. Thomas could hear sirens coming from every direction. His hands were so tight around the steering wheel that his knuckles were white.

Suddenly the door flew open and Thomas was pulled out. When Thomas was clear of the car he cocked back his arm to let a fist fly. Jonas caught the punch.

"I'm here to help." Jonas preached.

Thomas just stood there with his eyes blazing of rage. He was consumed with wrath. This is beserker stage. The stage you get to when you've been pushed far enough and will not be confined to the corner or darkness anymore. When you care not for the constraints of society but only to your survival. And when survival is no longer possible, then you want to inflict as much damage to your foe as possible before the end.

Finally Thomas said softly. "You don't want to get involved in this, believe me." Thomas replied.

"I have to." Jonas said solemnly.

"Why?" Thomas asked.

"It's what I do." He responded. "Come on we have to split." He went on.

He grabbed Thomas by the shoulder and pulled him until Thomas started to run.

"Hoped we could have kept the law out of this, but I don't see how we can do that now." Jonas said while they took off.

They ran past the fire station, through the auto parts parking lot, behind the seafood restaurant and onto the train tracks. They ran over the Old Depot Bridge and down to the chain linked fence bordering the factory warehouse district. Jonas and Thomas hopped the fence, their feet landing on the track stone and broken bottles below. Thomas thought to himself that Jonas ran fast for an old man, because he had all he could do to keep up. Jonas pulled open the basement window to the Phone Factory Warehouse. Thomas slid through and then so too did Jonas. The window was painted black so no one could see in. It was only possible for one person to fit through at a time. The drop to the floor was about five feet.

They both had their hands on their knees huffing and puffing.

"What are we going to do?" Thomas asked winded.

"We'll stay here until nightfall and head off down the tracks to High Bridge. From there we'll make our way passed Vale St., passed the metal recycling plant and up on to Lancaster Rd. From there we'll follow the tracks to Forty Caves. We may be able to hold out there for a while." Jonas proclaimed.

"You seem to know a lot about a town I've never seen you in." Thomas declared.

"I told you I'm in the business of knowing what is…"Jonas said until Thomas broke him off.

"And should never be." Thomas finished.

Jonas just smiled.

Jonas started putting the weapons he had arrayed before them into two Army duffle bags.

Remember that last item that Jonas went off to get from town a while back, well that would come in handy now.

School had been let out for the rest of the week because of recent events. The schools condition, the office brawl and mostly because Kilcrop had some planning to do, for his final preparations. It was announced that school would be closed for a week or so, for repair.

Mary ran home all the way. She knew what she had to do and she had to do it quick.

Three police cars pulled up in front of the Morgan home.

Laura saw them and went to the door. Captain Briber exited his vehicle first and approached the house. Officer Betedown and Patrolman Gudgy followed behind. Captain Briber had his hat in his hand. He was looking at the ground on the way to the door.

"Yes Officers." Laura said frightened assuming something awful had happened.

"Sorry to tell you this mam' but we have a warrant for your sons arrest." He stated.

"For what!" She shouted in disbelief.

"Well he's wanted for vandalizing the school, assaulting a police officer, theft of municipal property, grand car theft. He's also wanted for questioning in a double murder." Stated Briber.

Laura's knees were knocking together.

"This can't be! You must be mistaken! Not my Thomas!" She yelled out.

"Mrs. Morgan it does me no great pleasure to do this." Officer Briber explained.

"It can't be." Laura cried.

Jasper heard Laura's tone and he heard her cry out. Jasper flew down the stairs, scuttled to the kitchen and let out a bark that shattered the front window.

The policemen drew back in fear.

"Easy boy, Easy Jasper." Laura said through tears.

They were all about her face.

Jasper was furious that someone made Thomas' keeper this way. He hunched down ready to pounce through the shattered window. He scrunched back on his hind legs to spring through the window and to tear into hamburger whoever had done this.

Laura said in a very soft tone. "Jasper, don't."

Jasper heard this tone and relented. He didn't want to, but she asked him to and so he would.

"Mrs. Morgan we need to come in and search the place." He began. "Is Thomas here?" Briber asked.

"No. I thought he was at school." She said worriedly.

"Do you mind putting the dog out Mrs. Morgan, we wouldn't want anything to happen to him." He explained.

"It's not him I'm worried about." She returned.

Laura took Jasper out the back door and attached him to his chain. Jasper let out a long whine. He tried to follow Laura when she was leaving.

"It'll be okay Jasper." Laura said as she patted him on the head.

Laura walked back to the house and let the officer's in.

Jasper pulled the four- foot sauna tube right out of the ground and pulled it to the back door. Jasper didn't bark. Jasper just stood there and waited. He would not alert the enemy he was coming if he had to fight. If he heard any nonsense going on, he'd be ready. No chain, no matter how big, was going to stop him either. He'd jump right through the back window with the cement tube and chain attached. No big deal.

Officer Briber told Mrs. Morgan what he knew and what they as a force surmised, most of it circumstantial. The other officers checked the house. Patrolman Gudgy searched downstairs and Betedown did the upper floor. Gudgy didn't find anything incriminating and went back to the living room where Laura and the Captain were.

Officer Betedown came down stairs with Thomas' backpack. He placed it on the coffee table and opened it.

They all looked in.

They all gasped.

CHAPTER TEN

The shootout minor

Now remember that item Jonas still needed to obtain a ways back, well, it would come in handy now, like I said.

He purchased the police scanner and battery pack at the Army-Navy store downtown. The store was filled with clothing and gear, but if you asked the right questions and showed the right color, green, then you were privy to, much more.

Jonas put ten one hundred dollar bills down on the desk of the man at the counter. This bigot of a man hadn't previously paid much attention to Jonas but now was all ears.

The man behind the counter was a Skinhead Nazi wannabe. He said he had been sent here to spread the word of the Aryan race. He claimed to have fought in Vietnam, but when Jonas asked what outfit and time he served, he quickly changed the subject.

Jonas knew about men like him. Men, who brag or often talk about war, have usually never seen battle. Those who keep the scars of the fight, hidden, are the ones who have witnessed the sobering effects of war.

Killing doesn't make one brave. It's protecting life and liberty that is heroic.

The man kept going on about how the immigrant's were slowly

stealing the jobs, and those who weren't, were on welfare and sucking on the tit of society.

"Damn nigger's and chink's, either selling drugs or out whoring." He boasted. "And the Jews, well the Jews own all the Media and Networks. They own most of the Tabloids and the ones they don't own they are affiliated with." He informed Jonas. "How many of them work in government agencies, like the FCC?" He asked Jonas. "You don't think there are going to confront 'their people' about the propaganda that they spew forth on their Network channels do you." He said in angst.

Jonas hated these accusations of libelous words and he gave the man a glimpse of his Desert Eagle in his right holster, with a wave of his overcoat. He hated the racial slurs the most. Slander and profiling were something he didn't like but bigots he disliked the most.

The man quickly got the hint. It's amusing how tough some men are, until confronted. When the castle is under siege, some people stay and some people run.

Usually the one's who profess to be the big shot's, are the one's hiding when the metal starts flying. Oftentimes it's the quiet farm boy or the poor mechanic who can't read or write, which rises to this occasion.

The man showed Jonas to the back room after he had put down the thousand dollars. The money came off the counter as fast as a crocodile snatches its prey.

Good thing I didn't leave my hand there Jonas thought or he would have put that in his pocket as well.

The amount of contraband and the uniqueness of the objects in the 'invite only' part of the shop were impressive to say the least. There were rockets, dynamite and blasting caps, a Fifty Caliber mounted machine gun and body armor. The back room was a mercenary's wet dream.

The man gave up the police scanner and battery pack without much argument. Jonas also purchased a gas mask; four smoke grenades, a helmet, and Kevlar chest armor. Jonas didn't stick around for the change and the man was all too cooperative to keep it.

Now back at the warehouse as they listened to the scanner, they heard the information pertaining to Thomas and the charges that were pending against him.

"This is an all points bulletin. Be on the look out for a tall, teen Caucasian male. Color hair brown, eyes brown, about one hundred seventy pounds, wearing black jeans, gray sweatshirt and black sneakers. He is probably armed and is considered extremely dangerous. Approach with extreme prejudice." The voice announced.

There was no mention of Jonas and no mention of State Police involvement, or their K-9 units yet either. Jonas knew though, it was just a matter of time before the right channels got involved.

The authorities were not the only ones seeking Thomas' whereabouts.

Aside from them, Mary and the Morgan's, there was another possessing the urgent want to find Thomas.

His name was Blake Crassman.

Blake Crassman was a wicked man, who rode with some men that aspired to be a mean motorcycle gang. Blake and his crew of brigands stationed themselves at Railway Bar and Grill. This was their favorite hang out and base of operations. Blake had an office downstairs in the fully furnished basement. This is where they kept their safe full of money, drugs and weapons.

The basement held poker games, five slot machines and lady companionship.

You had to be a member to frequent the underground 'Casino and House of Pleasure.' Membership came with a price too. And it wasn't in the form of money. No it was better than money. The price of admission was favors. If Blake expected a favor of you, there was no denying the request. If you did there were dire consequences. Your house might accidentally catch fire. Your daughter might go missing. Your wife might get raped or your car might blow up. If by chance, you should fall on a knife in an alley several times, it wouldn't even make the newspapers.

No one gave them any trouble because the key players in town were on the payroll. As with all men who desire high positions in society, they need contacts of control and information. Money has a way of opening up these doors of persuasion.

People will pay much for the right information, because information nowadays, is the key to any successful enterprise. There is always someone who bends to the allure of money. He had purchased some vital information via a stuffed envelope of fifty- dollar bills.

His inside contact gave him the identity of their prime suspect, the parent's names and identifications of that suspect and his parent's. He obtained the address of the assumed criminal and his girlfriend, who was probably involved, as well.

Blake was the only son to the elderly couple murdered in the nursing home.

He was a large man of about six feet and was well over three hundred pounds. He had long blond hair that he was losing up front. He was forty -two years old and could handle himself in a brawl.

Running drugs, guns and racketeering was his gang's modus operandi. Raping teenagers and bar room knock down drag outs, was his epitaph. Smashing beer bottles over patrons heads and tearing up the bar were his daily rituals.

When he had heard of the grizzly murder of his parent's, he

vowed to torture to death, the person or persons responsible. So he got his posse together, and the four- gang members, went about finding their bounty.

The four men stood hunched down in the swamp across from Mary's, waiting for her to go about finding her love. Blake knew if anyone would bring him to Thomas it would be her.

A police car pulled up to Mary's house and Brenda, Mary's mother, let the two officers who called, into her residence.

"Hi mam.' I'm Officer Balbrak and this Officer Troothgedder." Said the male officer.

The female officer, Troothgedder, offered her hand to Mary's mother to shake.

Brenda shook it and led the police officers into the living room.

Mary saw the cruiser pull up and opened her window while introductions were going on downstairs.

"I'm coming Tommy." She whispered to herself.

He was her rock and she was not to roll.

She would not let her best friend, her true love and companion, face this danger alone. He had always been there for her when she needed some one to lean on, and damned if she would forsake him now he was up against it.

She climbed out onto her oversized windowsill and descended the ivy trellis that was attached to the side of the house. She went down carefully so as not to bump against the house to alert the occupants and then jumped down the last four feet to the soft ground.

Blake saw her making her escape through his binoculars. She jumped down the last few feet and ran through the backyard into the pricker patch. They followed, out of the murky swamp they went and then they skirted the picker patch. They crossed the bridge at the west end of Cross' Cove and sprinted over Fry's cabbage patch.

Then they ran through the dogberry bushes and moved up behind the twin Dogwood trees.

They saw Mary taking Jasper off the leash that he had dragged up out of the ground and brought to the back door. She bent down next to him whispering something to him, all the time staying out of sight of the police cruiser, in the front yard of the Thomas residence.

Jasper was still concerned for Laura, but those 'men' had at least left the house, so he convinced himself that she would be all right. Besides he caught Mary's desperate tone and deduced there was trouble.

Officer Betedown was reading a golf magazine. He didn't notice Mary and Jasper traverse the backyard and go off by the old shooting range. They went behind the glue and linen factory and Jasper was sniffing all the while trying to pick up a scent. Mary brought him to where Thomas had left the squad car.

Jasper noticed the smell because he knew his masters smell color by heart and this was it. There was desperation in the scent left behind and he sensed Thomas was in trouble. He dashed after the scent. Mary followed.

Mary's mother had forbidden her to see Thomas anymore. So when she went upstairs to tell her the police wanted to question her and she was appalled to see she had snuck off. Yeah right, Mary thought, when her mother told her to stay clear of Thomas and the Morgan family.

There are few sure fire things in this world. One of them is, if you tell a girl who is in love, not to see the boy she cares about, it only drives her into his arms all the sooner. This here was no exception.

When Jasper and Mary had gotten to the train tracks, Mary spoke to Jasper who was sniffing around in circles trying to locate the best route to take to his master. Mary bent down to Jasper and rubbed his ears. She spoke in a very soft, sincere and desperate tone.

"Jasper. Thomas and I need you now, for we're in terrible trouble." She whispered.

Mary had told Jasper that Thomas was in trouble. Although he didn't understand the context of the words, he understood the mood and severity of the words spoken to him. Mary's tone and speech were desperate and Jasper recognized Thomas' name in her text. So he understood all he needed to. His master was in trouble and maybe Mary too. He brought forth all his power and tracking spirit and went in search of Thomas. It wasn't long before Jasper picked up the trail again. He dashed off again with Mary trying to keep up.

Blake and his cronies stayed back, just far enough, so Jasper wouldn't pick up their scent. They didn't want any trouble with the canine, not at least until they located Thomas.

Jasper took Mary on the path that Thomas and Jonas used when evading the law. Up onto the tracks they went and over the bridge. When they got to the fence, Jasper started looking for a place to cross to the other side. He went right under the bushes and along the fence to where it met the foundation of the bridge. There was a three-foot gap between the fence and the end of the bridge foundation. The elevation of the drop at this location was much lower than at the place where Thomas had jumped over the fence. Jasper went around the fence and jumped the two feet down onto track stone and went to the basement window. He started to scratch the basement window and bark.

At the time Jasper was trying to find another way down to the basement window to the phone factory, the police put out a request to pick up Mary. Mary was out there trying to aid the fugitive it went on to say.

Thomas heard this over the scanner. Now he was worried. The thought that something might happen to her made him panicky.

He heard Jasper at the window.

It scared Thomas at first then he heard Jasper bark.

Now Mary, she couldn't follow Jasper, because she would have had to get on her knees and the bushes were much too dense anyway. So she came back to where Thomas and Jonas had scaled the fence and began her ascent. Suddenly she was grabbed around the waist and a hand shot over her mouth. She tried to bite at the hand, but the person gripping her, squeezed her neck in a headlock. Mary tried to make sounds audible enough for a person to hear, but the man's hands were too large for her to emit much sound from her small mouth.

A person couldn't hear, but Jasper could. Jasper's mind went into panic and dread mode. He felt as if he were too caught up in trying to find Thomas he forgot his obligation to protect a girl in trouble. Nothing in this world is more upsetting to a dog than letting harm befall a woman or child. His love for Mary came forth and he grew into a rabid wolf. Blue energy exploded through his taut muscles and his teeth grew an inch longer and sharper. His nails became razor pointed knives. Then as he was transforming, a blue diamond burned into his forehead and onto his front paws. This energy pried his third eye open.

Mary.

Trouble.

Bite.

Tear.

Kill.

Now.

These were his only thoughts.

When he saw the man dragging Mary up the hill and her kicking and swinging he went into stealth mode. He bent his large frame to the ground and inched along it like a ferret. Then he crawled against the bridge foundation and jumped back up onto the ledge where it met the fence and disappeared into the bushes. He didn't make a sound the whole time.

When Blake got back to the apex of the tracks over looking the fence and basement window, he called out his demands to Thomas.

"Come on out you murderous scum. Thomas I got your pretty girlfriend. She's awfully cute. You know what, after I'm done making you suffer I'm going to have my way with her. In fact we all are, eh boys." The big man laughed.

The other's laughed as well. They savored the thoughts of the upcoming moments of sexual violence, which they would inflict upon this young girl.

Thomas looked at Jonas and they devised a quick plan. Thomas opened the basement window of the warehouse and climbed out.

"Okay I'm coming out." Thomas announced.

The other three members of the biker-gang started talking worriedly, amongst themselves.

"Where the hell did that horse of a dog go?" Asked the tall skinny one.

"I don't know but shoot it if you see it, I don't want it getting a hold on me." Went the small fat one.

Jonas climbed out the side window of the warehouse. Since no one was concerned about an accomplice for Thomas, they didn't notice him run underneath the bridge and up the embankment on the opposite side.

Thomas lifted himself up the five feet to the window, pushed it open and squeezed through. He climbed up the fence and hopped over. Thomas got to the top of the bank on the first rail of the tracks.

The whole time he had done this he kept his back hidden from the men who were opposed to him. In the back between his jeans and his sweatshirt was an ivory handle revolver. The handle was face up and the barrel was at a forty-five degree angle inside his jeans. The chamber was itching to explode.

"What's this all about mister?" Thomas asked unruffled.

Seeing the look on Mary's terrified face made him eerily calm.

Mary saw this and she was frightened. She had never seen this look in his face. A person who was facing incoming artillery was supposed to be frightened, but not the man who had nothing left to lose, he almost welcomed it.

She knew the shit was about to hit the fan.

She prayed.

She prayed for Thomas, not for herself, but for him Please Lord let my Tommy prevail and I will spend the rest of my days loving no other. The Lord heard her prayers and watched the confrontation unfold.

Blake drew out a Glock- 17- Semi Automatic Pistol. He let it dangle from his right hand. His left arm still held Mary tight.

"Don't act like you don't know. You killed my parent's and I'm here to kill you. First I'm going to kill you. Then I'm going to cut you into uniformed pieces and mail you to your folks. Then after they receive the package, I'm going to make them eat you. Then I'm going to take this sweet piece of ass and screw her until I get bored. After that, I'll kill her too. Not easy, like I'll kill you. No, she'll beg for death before I'm done with her." Blake finished with smile.

"I don't know what you're talking about, but if you let my girl go, I'll forget this ever happened." Thomas assured him.

"Did you hear that boys?" He asked with a laugh. "He's giving ultimatums. Gotta' love this kid. Too bad we gotta' kill him." The big man holding Mary said.

Blake leaned down and started sucking on Mary's neck.

"Mister I warned you to let her go. I'll give you one last chance

209

to go, and I'll even forget this trespass. If you don't, I'll kill you all." Thomas said this like he had ice running in his veins.

Blake picked up his head from Mary's neck and was about to say something when a Wolf's Howl came from somewhere in the bushes.

HOOOOOOOOWWWWWWWW!!!!

The hair on everyone's neck stood up.

Everyone's neck but Thomas'.

The sound was so close and terrifying that one of the men was caught by surprise and terror and he dropped his hand- gun. A large urine patch made itself evident in the crotch area of his jeans. His legs began to wobble. Then he shit himself.

At the instant the howl stopped and Blake turned his head back to Thomas, his life passed before his eyes.

Thomas had drawn the revolver. He squeezed the hair tight trigger and it kicked like a mule. A bullet screamed out to taste flesh and lodged into Blake's throat. The hot metal had found a new home.

Blake dropped his pistol and let go of Mary. She fell to the ground and out of the way. She watched as Thomas came forward fanning the gun so it would spit out metal all the sooner. Blake clutched at his throat. Blood ran threw his fingers and stained the track ties and stone.

Then Jasper burst threw the bushes and slammed into the short fat man holding a rifle. Jasper grabbed him by the throat and swung him back and forth like a rag doll. The rifle went flying aside. Jasper's fangs broke threw the man's neck skin and muscles very easily, like a person does biting through a hot dog. Veins and arteries snapped like fishing line under to much pressure. Blood and fatty tissue filled Jasper's mouth. Jasper broke his body on the train rail and track rock. His broken body was like a busted bag of dinnerware.

One of the other biker's, the youngest, turned and took aim at the dog.

Suddenly the roar of a shotgun filled the air. The eight-gauge scattergun tore the man taking aim at Jasper, in half. The scattering beads from the gun ripped the jean jacket he was wearing in two uneven pieces. About six inches of the jacket came apart with his lower body the rest with the top half.

The once prolific Deity From Hell emblem was blood red and scattered.

His body fell in two different places. The top half lay outside the rail, with his head at the bottom of the rock stone mound. The other lay inside the track. The feet to his lower body were twitching as if the nerves weren't receiving the information they requested from the top half before it went on permanent vacation. His top half was doing something too. Its mouth was trying to talk but only blood and chunks of stomach and lung were coming out. The eyes were looking for the other half of his body. His arms were trying to pick up this half and take it back to reunite with the other. It was not to be.

A shotgun blast rang out again and put an end to his suffering.

Three more bullet's slammed into Blake's person from the oncoming Thomas. Blake's body twisted back and forth with each incoming hit.

When the shoot out began Thomas was about fifteen feet from Blake. By the time all four bullets had overtaken Blake, Thomas, was standing over him. The second round hit him above the right nipple. This turned Blake around ninety-degrees. It tore through the upper part of his lung. It began to fill with blood. The third one that roared out from this widow maker, hit him just left of the navel. It pierced his intestines and stuck itself deep into his pelvis. The last one struck him in the left knee, shattering the kneecap. Bone and cartilage were showing this through his pant leg.

Blake fell and his head bounced off the train rail. He tried to lift himself up but he was too damaged. Blood ran through his jean jacket in two places. The blood from his knee was running down his leg and it showed through his faded jeans, all the way to his work boots. He positioned himself on one elbow and spit out a mouthful of blood. Then his strength gave out and he fell, face first, to the ground in the center of the track. He was dead.

The last man reached down for the gun he had dropped and a bullet tore through the back of his skull. The forehead of this man was no more. It sprayed the bushes where Jasper had leaped from with hair, brains and blood. The empty shell of a man fell to the earth.

His body lay across one of the rails. His head and chest were on the outside of the track and from his waist down he was on the inside. When he fell, his legs crossed and his right arm fell underneath his body. When he hit the rail his upper body bounced off the metal.

By this time Mary was sick with vomit. She puked several times and couldn't get to her feet. She swayed back and forth like she had just gotten off an amusement- park ride.

Thomas went to her and picked her up by the arm. She fell against him and he held her with one arm, still looking at the scene before him. Thomas wasn't frightened or sick. He felt tranquil. An inner peace had reached him. He was glad for this displaced aggression.

Jonas was yelling to Thomas to come help him get the gear.

Thomas told Mary to sit on the track and get her bearings.

Thomas called to Jasper who had been sniffing around at the fallen enemy to make certain there was no longer any threat. He too had reached a serene mood. His eyes blazed with blue fire.

His thought was on Mary. He couldn't help but think that he had left her in danger. He would never make that mistake again. His

212

body was fully flexed. It looked like his shoulder and back muscles were larger than, before the melee. They were.

He came to Mary in a jaunt and licked her face, as if to say, I'm so sorry. I am nothing. Please give me another chance. I won't fail you again.

Mary seized two handfuls of dog hair and pulled Jasper close. She began to bawl.

Jasper sensed her melancholy and began to whine. He felt so bad.

Mary looked up at Jasper and caught the brightness of his fiery eyes. It calmed her down, she knew he would protect her life and she felt safe.

Thomas jumped the fence and saw two Army duffle bags being pushed through the warehouse basement window.

Jonas didn't come out immediately. He went back to the workbench and moved it exposing the six-foot floor drain. He pulled up the drain cover with a rebar pole that was lying about the littered room. He pulled the green box to the drain hole and carefully laid it in. He put the Panzerschreck on top, and slid the heavy cover back over the rocket blaster. He took a weathered piece of cardboard from the floor and split the tape on both ends. He unfolded the cardboard, so it was elongated to its full length. He placed it over the floor drain and it covered the hole enough so at a quick glance one wouldn't know there was something hidden there.

He thought it unfortunate that he couldn't take his favorite toy, but it wasn't feasible. He pushed the workbench back over it, then went to the window, pulled himself up and slid through.

Thomas climbed the fence first. Jonas handed the heavy bags over one at a time after he had cleared the fence. Then Jonas climbed over.

They each carried a bag up the embankment to the track bed.

Mary and Jasper were waiting.

"Thomas, what are we going to do?" She asked terrified.

"First we have to hide these bags and then we need to get you home, Mary." Jonas said in haste. Thomas?" He started.

Thomas turned to Jonas.

"Is there anyone you can trust other than your parent's?" Jonas asked.

Thomas' mind was racing to find a solution, like a computer going through codes or coordinates.

"You can't go home." Jonas remarked. "They'll have your house under surveillance. Probably yours will be too, Mary." He went on.

"I'm not going anywhere without you Thomas." Mary stated emphatically.

"Don't worry Mary. Jonas knows what he's doing." Thomas responded, still trying to think of somewhere that he could hide out.

"I don't even know him Thomas." Mary remarked.

"Mary, he has saved my life already and yours too for that matter." Thomas stated.

Thomas saw the look of doubt in her eyes. He took her by the hand and talked softly and tenderly to her.

"Mary, Jasper will be with you. Nothing in this world will bring you to harm while he's with you. Please believe in me." Thomas said trying to comfort and steady her.

She looked deep into his eyes and through her teary ones, she nodded her head yes.

"Mr. Abrams!" Thomas shouted before she could answer. Thomas turned to Jonas.

"You can trust him?" Jonas asked.

"He was the only one who believed me to be innocent at school." Thomas told Jonas.

"Okay, we'll hide these bags on the back hill of the cemetery and we'll meet there at first whistle tomorrow.

First whistle referred to the time when a whistle sounded, alerting the apple pickers that the first work shift was under way. All it meant was, that it was eight o'clock.

They all climbed the hill to the cemetery, which was adjacent to the tracks.

The hill was steep and they struggled to get the armament up to the top. Finally they reached the summit and pulled the bags aside a big rock. The four of them stood there regaining their breath.

Jonas opened one of the bags and reached inside. He moved some of the weapons out of the way and retrieved a large manila envelope and the police scanner from the bottom.

He placed the envelope and scanner on a smaller rock and proceeded to camouflage the bags under the much larger one. The rock was large enough for a man to squat behind and be totally shielded from sight or assault. They wedged the bags under the rock as far as they could manage and covered what was exposed, with fallen dry leaves. After they had hidden their arsenal, Jonas turned to Thomas.

"Take these to Mr. Abrams." He said handing over the manila envelope and scanner.

"What do you want me to do?" Thomas asked.

"Do you think Mr. Abrams will let you stay the night?" Jonas questioned.

"I think so. I hope so… I'm sure of it." Thomas ended confidently after some thought.

"Keep the scanner on so you can stay ahead of the fuzz." Jonas explained.

"What about the envelope?" Thomas asked inquisitively.

"Maybe Mr. Abrams can bring its contents to the police. I don't know. I don't have all the answers, but it seems like the smartest thing to do." Jonas said assuredly.

"I'll take Mary home and Jasper can stay with her." Jonas went on.

"Where we he stay?" Thomas asked concernedly.

"I'll wait until my mother goes to bed and then I'll bring him in." Mary stated.

"There will probably be a police unit waiting for you, so be careful." Thomas responded.

"Thomas do you know a route that you can take without being discovered?" Jonas asked.

"Yes. I'll be okay. I'm more worried about Mary and Jasper." He said troubled.

"They'll be fine, I promise." Jonas assured Thomas.

"Jonas they're everything to me." Thomas remarked.

Mary felt a pinch of happiness. Even in this danger he's thinking of me, first.

"I love you Tommy." She said with all the love in her beating heart.

"Me too." Thomas replied. "Me too."

Thomas bent down and rubbed Jasper on the nose and spoke to him.

"Take care of Mary, boy." He said.

Jasper barked, as if to say, no doubt brother.

Jonas reloaded the six- shooter for Thomas. He took a box of shells from inside his overcoat and gave them to Thomas. Thomas put the box in the pouch of his hooded sweatshirt. He put the revolver in the back of his jeans, barrel down and pulled the gray sweatshirt over it.

Then they all broke for their destinations.

On the way to Mary's house, She and Jonas started coming up with a cover story to tell the authorities, about her disappearance.

CHAPTER ELEVEN

The crash

Laura and Henry Morgan were beside themselves in grief and worry. Henry paced back and forth running his hands through his salt and peppered hair. He couldn't concentrate at work, and his supervisor, being sympathetic to his situation, gave him a few days off with pay.

Henry was liked at the cereal factory and everyone respected him. They called him the silver fox, because of his hair. It was dark with silver streaks running through it.

Many of the ladies were fond of him too, but he paid no mind to them. He had eyes only for Laura. Even though the women were upset that he didn't take to their advances, they respected him all the more for being faithful to his wife.

Henry was a tall well-built man of six feet three inches. He had broad shoulders and the muscles on his chest and stomach were pronounced. Many times Laura would find herself running her fingers over his abdomen just for the pleasure of the knowledge that this brute was hers.

Henry grabbed his wrist flexor and squeezed it in and out. He often did this when he couldn't sit still and was excessively nervous. Normally Laura would tell him to sit down and relax, but she was in an awful state of dismay too.

She hadn't been sleeping well these past couple of weeks, because of the baby and because she knew something was wrong in Thomas' life. Thomas was quiet and modest and she knew he wouldn't open up and tell her his problems or his strife. He was an introvert, mostly keeping his feelings hidden and bottled up until it was too much to handle. She worried that one of these days he might snap and show the true colors of a quiet man repressed. These were not shortcomings in a man but she worried that, he was taking on too much, without letting off steam. She hoped that this is not what had happened. She hoped it wasn't because of the pressure she had forced on him to get a job. She was filled with remorse and guilt.

Dark circles were present underneath her hazel eyes. Wrinkles started to make themselves visible on her forehead when she frowned or was surprised. The lines, which started on one side of her forehead, stretched across to the other. On both sides the age creases began roughly one inch from her hair. When she smiled there were five distinct lines and when she frowned there were six. The sixth one wasn't a solid line like the others though. It started like the other five, but then about halfway to the other side, it then began a descent toward her right eye. It ended up stopping somewhere underneath her eyebrow. Her short Chestnut colored hair was starting to show signs of white. Laura was thirty-nine and she was proud of the fact that she didn't have any gray's. These recent events though had caused her hair to blotch with white spots in sporadic clumps on the right side of her head. They weren't big areas, about the size of a nickel, but all the same they were still noticeable. Laura was also getting comments from neighbors and folks who couldn't help but notice the signs of her showing under her stretched garments. Her belly could no longer be hidden under guise. She would have to tell the men of the house.

She had to at least tell Henry, but how and when? Thomas was sure to figure it out and if not he would surely hear it through the town gossip pyramid. Surely she couldn't tell Henry now that this peril was upon them. She was distressed. She was angry with herself for not telling Henry right away. She would have expected something as important as this, to be shared by him, if he were in her position.

"Henry I'm pregnant." She blurted out.

Oh god. I can't believe I just added weight to this unbearable situation. He's going to be cross with me. Go ahead Henry and let me have it.

"I know." He said softly.

She worked a short quick grin. How did she think that she could keep a secret as hefty as this, from the person who knew all of her secrets? She loved him.

She stood up and gave him a great big hug.

"It's going to be alright. Thomas is going to come out of this. I know it." Henry said with surety.

"I hope so." She shot back quickly.

Then the phone rang.

They both were startled and the couple jumped.

They looked at the phone vibrating on the hook and were afraid to answer it.

Laura went to the phone apprehensively. She picked it up and waited for a voice to reveal their identity and state their intentions.

"Hello." Came the hushed, barely audible voice.

"Hello." She said impatiently. "Who is this?" She demanded.

"Mrs. Morgan we have apprehended your son Thomas. We'd like for you to come to the station, so we can explain his charges and offer you counsel." The voice went on.

"Okay we'll be there, straight away." Laura said slamming

down the phone.

"What is it Laura?" Henry asked hurriedly.

"They have Thomas up at the police barracks and they want us to go up there." Laura explained.

"I know Thomas didn't do this." Henry said confidently.

"I do too." Laura agreed.

They got their jackets on and started out into the spitting rain. It was beginning to get chilly, and patches of sleet were falling, from the night sky. Henry opened the door for Laura and helped her into the car, then scuttled around the back and into the drivers seat.

The man in the big car, across the street, frowned and spit on the dashboard when he saw this gentlemanly act.

The Morgan's backed out of their driveway and pulled away in their red Honda Civic. The large car across the street with its lights out started out behind them.

They started down Moffet St. and turned onto Rigby Road. From there they crossed South Meadow Lane and turned right again on Route 62. They were driving parallel to Mudjets orchard. Henry was driving faster than usual, in haste of getting to Thomas.

In the rear view mirror the car behind them put on his high beams. The car came up behind them and was right on their rear end.

"Let them pass Henry." Laura commanded.

Henry let up on the accelerator and they began to reduce speed. The trailing automobile shot around them and moved quickly in front of their Honda. The rear bumper of the passing car tapped the front of the Morgan's car so they began to swerve and lose control. The slick surface on the road made it impossible to stop.

"Look out Henry, Turn. Oh Noooo!" cried Laura.

Thomas.

Laura's only thought.

They jumped the curb and slammed into a large twisted apple tree, on the perimeter of Mudjets orchard.

The black Town Car sped away.

Thomas scaled down the back hillside of the cemetery and came to the lower train track, which ran directly underneath the Old Depot Bridge. It continued onto the supermarket and shoe warehouse and other outlets on the other side of town.

This was a very important access way for businesses in the past. Before the world decided that Lee Iococca's idea of boxed truck was more suitable, this was the modus operandi. It certainly wasn't more profitable, at least not at first. But with all things, if you have enough money and resources to outlast your opponents, you can succeed.

This is the war of attrition. Take a little less from the consumer, show a small loss and see how long your competitor can hold out. Throw in some industrial espionage and political bias and you have yourself a victory. Now, I'm not suggesting that's what happened in the case of the railway, but that's what I'd do. Besides it's not like the railway was always innocent of wrongdoing or strong- arming. The things they did to citizens and workers alike, in the past, was nothing short of criminal and treason.

Karma.

Monopolies are like that, so beware of the super chain stores and large resource companies that constantly look to expand. For they all have the same appetite.

Take.

This will kill the Mom and Pop stores in the country. You know the place where you're greeted with a smile and great service. The store you go into and Mother Kennedy showers you with homemade chocolate cookies or candy. Soft and gooey even hours after they're made. The little shop that told the pregnant Mrs. Helperin that she could pay next month because the Kennedy's knew that her husband had suddenly passed away from cancer and she hadn't received any State Assistance yet. The money they never sought to collect. The heart's of these small business owners is what this country is all about.

When disaster strikes these folks give everything to make sure that the welfare of the people is secure. Some of these foreign business merchants see tragedy as a way to exploit prices in time of need of product. This is treason, and it cannot be tolerated. This country belongs to us, the people. We will not be bullied by outside threats or domestic ones at.

If the small businesses should be overrun by these super chain stores, then all is lost. If this happens we will be forced to buy from one place. You know what happens in a country that has no choices. They can charge you whatever they feel appropriate.

Communism.

Its starts that way anyhow, and then it becomes worse, an autocracy and finally a fascist state. We've seen it in the past. Italy, France and Russia have gone through this change several times each in the last few centuries.

Then to squeeze the profit margin even further, they start sending jobs over seas and then you can't even buy the stuff. All the jobs are elsewhere. When the next Great Depression hits it will make the previous one look like nothing. There are already great countries and empires of old claiming bankruptcy. What? A whole country has gone to pot. When the rest of the world has had enough starving and exploitation the last World War will begin.

Then as you look for work and find none, you turn to theft to feed and clothe your children. The corporate brass does not care that you can no longer survive. This is some of the reason for the worry of the confederate states before the Civil War. The people in those regions were worried that if it came to a large republic, that the citizens when distraught with corruption and betrayal, would not be able to just go down to the local pub to straighten it out. Where do we go to picket such crimes? Who will listen? Who is responsible? By the time we get there will the wrongdoers be privy to our revolt?

We profess to stand for liberty, justice and good will to all and yet corporations are allowed to send our employment to countries that support child labor and political slavery.

Disgusting.

Highly controversial stuff right, but all true. Just ask the Native Indians or the African Americans. Ask the Chinese or Mexicans. They will tell you nothing has changed except the names.

Anyway, let me turn back to Thomas.

Thomas was now on the lower track way, headed south, toward Coachlace Pond. He crossed over the twin track rails and climbed down the retaining stonewall, which stood behind the furniture factory. He sprinted behind the building until he got to its distribution center. From there, he crossed Main St. and made his way into the park at Franklin St. and Park St.

Thomas heard sirens in the distance and he thought he might have been spotted. He ran into a driveway on Park St. that ran at a slight pitch uphill and into the backyard behind the house.

If a car was parked there you could probably see the backend from the street. The front stairs were on metal beams and Thomas scurried underneath to try and hide in the shadows. The lights to the home were off and there were no cars in the driveway. He assessed that there was no one home. He hoped so at least.

The sirens didn't seem to be approaching to his location. On the contrary, they seemed to be getting slightly less audible, as if they were moving out toward the edge of town. Must be a fire or accident Thomas thought.

He cautiously continued his hike to Winter St. where his preordained destination was. He reached the house and stood in the darkness of shadow from a giant oak tree in the front of Mr. Abrams house five feet from the road.

He decided it best and most prudent to go around back. There were tall pines in the backyard, making it private to neighbors so it would provide ample cover. He ran along the inside wooden fence that was well taller than he was. The fence divided Mr. Abrams property with his neighbor to the left if you were facing the street.

Thomas got to the backdoor, and hesitated. If he were wrong about Mr. Abrams, it would get complicated. Finally he relented to his suspicious mind and knocked upon the glass in one of the framed windows in the backdoor. The door had a window in it where it was sectioned into six equal little windows.

There was a yellow curtain covering the small, sectioned window glass. The light to the kitchen popped on, and the soft glow was inviting to Thomas. He wanted to go home and feel the warmth and security of his folks. He had a touch of melancholy. This was not the time for guilt and depression. He shed the thoughts from his mind and tried to stay stoic.

Slowly, the curtain was drawn aside and a man wearing bifocals, peered out at him. Quickly the locked sounded and Mr. Abrams opened the door. He pulled Thomas through the door and slammed the door. He double bolted the locks.

"Thomas what has happened?" Mr. Abrams asked.

"Everything and nothing." Thomas replied.

"What?" Mr. Abrams asked dumbfounded.

"Someone has done everything they could, to do me in. I have done none of it." Thomas remarked defiantly.

Mr. Abram's pulled out a chair for Thomas to sit down on.

Mr. Abrams who had a book in his hand, which he was no doubt reading when the knock came on the back door, went to the fridge to retrieve ice tea for the two of them.

Thomas' back was exposed as he reached for the chair and Mr. Abrams caught sight of the revolver. When he was pouring a glass of tea, Thomas saw his look of apprehension. Thomas took the gun out and laid it on the table.

Mr. Abrams wasn't really worried about the gun. He had seen and handled many in the past. It is the intent of the person who carries the firearm that makes the weapons dangerous. Guns and weapons are a very important part to the survival of a free state. People shout about the ban of automatic weapons and I say they are necessary. What happens to a state that can no longer trust the people in power? What do we fight a super power with? Fireworks? Sticks and Stones? I think not. NRA forever.

"You're all over the news Thomas." He said.

"I'm sure." Thomas responded nonchalantly.

Thomas told him about the shootout at the Old Depot Bridge. He told him about what really happened in the principle's office and his flight from the school to the warehouse. Mr. Abrams poured them both a second cup of iced tea. Thomas had downed the first thirstily.

"Well, you've had a hell of a day to say the least." Mr. Abrams said breaking the silence.

Thomas pulled out the extension to the battery pack attached to the scanner, which he set on the table. Then he plugged the scanner adapter into the socket nearest the kitchen table.

Then he handed Mr. Abrams the manila envelope. Mr. Abrams peeled back the tape and turned it upside down. The contents fell to the table.

Both of them stared in awe at the contents.

Mary, Jonas and Jasper had made their way to the pricker patch and sat there a moment to rehearse her story. She was to say that she went off looking for Thomas but didn't locate him. Then she was to ask the police officers if they had any information about his whereabouts. If they were to say no, she was to start crying. This was to feign concern for her lost fugitive friend.

They approached her house through the back yard and came to the trellis.

Jonas began to help her up, when two cars pulled up, in front of the house. Mary came back down and she and Jonas went to see what the traffic was about.

Mr. Kilcrop got out of his Town Car that he had just parked in Mary's driveway. He shut the door, whistling a tune and approached the Camry on the street. Mary came up behind Jonas and peeked out around the corner. Jasper lay down listening. Mr. Kilcrop walked up to the open passenger side window.

"Well?" He asked the driver through the opposite window.

"Man a real mess, but everything is going according to plan. I didn't think you were going to kill anybody. This is getting out of control." The driver said.

Mary knew the voice but couldn't place it. She couldn't believe they were talking about murder.

"What about the Morgan's." Kilcrop said.

"They're both dead sir." The mysterious driver said.

The news rang like church bells in Mary's head. Her legs wouldn't work. They were losing their strength. She slumped against the house and slid down to sit on the ground.

The agony.

She began to weep.

Jonas put his index finger over his mouth to warn her to keep quiet.

"You know she was pregnant right." The driver explained.

A smile broke across Kilcrop's face, for he did know, but he wanted the gruesome details.

Tears rolled down Mary's face, she couldn't believe what she was hearing.

She was going to be sick. Her head was swimming and she felt like she couldn't breath, as if she were under water.

Poor Tommy.

Her poor Tommy.

How would he come back from the void, now that this terrible fate had befallen him?

"Damn thing lived, how I don't know. It's a miracle I suppose. A baby girl it was." The driver said.

Kilcrop roared out his anger and brought his fists down simultaneously on the hood of the Camry. He pounded away like a kid having a giant tantrum. The profanity that came next I will not repeat, for it was pure and utter filth.

A small seedling of hope sprouted in Mary's spirit.

"Get out of here Conway before you get spotted, and don't send any patrols back here. I need to think." Kilcrop demanded.

Conway.

The sheriff. Jonas thought.

Conway.

Mary thought.

Despicable.

"When am I going to get the video, Mr. Kilcrop?" Conway asked. "I think I've done enough." Conway claimed.

"When it's finished." Kilcrop returned perturbed.

"When will…" Conway was cut off by, the irate Kilcrop.

"Get out of here!" Kilcrop blasted.

Conway put the Camry in drive and sped away.

At that same moment Brenda, Mary's mother opened the door.

"Oh, Burn, I thought I heard someone out here from the bathroom." Brenda said.

"Oh just a person looking for directions." Responded Kilcrop.

Kilcrop quickly composed himself and greeted Brenda with a kiss on the cheek.

Mary was sick to her stomach. How terrible. That man's a monster, she thought. Mary didn't know the half of it.

Her tears stopped and she felt resentment starting to inject itself into her blood stream. Endorphins were doing the salsa dance in her mind.

"That disgusting liar, creep, bastard shit! He's seeing my mom. I'm going to kill him." Mary stated.

Mary started off toward the front door and Jasper got up, ready to help her carry the fight.

Jonas held them both up.

"Mary this isn't the way." Jonas explained.

Mary looked at him in frustration for stopping her.

"Only Thomas knows the way." Jonas went on.

"What am I to do then?" Mary asked.

"Just go on like everything is the way it has been." Jonas explained.

"I can't. I can't look at that devil and act like everything is okay." Mary cried.

"You have to Mary." Jonas responded.

"I can't." She whined.

Jonas looked at her with sincere and serene eyes and he spoke to her gently.

"Mary, Thomas needs you more than ever." He said.

She brought her focus back to Thomas and his newly born baby sister.

"You have to care for that child now." He informed her.

Mary started to realize that Jonas was right.

"Will you turn your back on Thomas in his most desperate hour?" He asked.

That small twinge of hope that Mary experienced just moments before grew into a beacon of light. She would have courage for Thomas' infant sister and for him. Mary thought of Thomas. She reminisced of how she thought he had slighted her at school and really it was a product of Kilcrop's doing. She remembered the flowers that he'd brought her and the way he made up to her, even though it wasn't even his fault. The look he gave her while holding those flowers when she flew into his arms. The look that says you're my everything. I'm broken without you. My wheels won't stop squeaking unless you grease them.

Mary clenched her jaw and fists.

She was with Thomas for better or worse. She was going all the way with him, wherever that may lead. They would face the fire together.

"I'll stand by Thomas and do my part!" Mary exclaimed.

"Good." Jonas said.

He helped Mary climb back up into her room via the trellis.

He told Jasper to stay put until Mary could come to him.

Watch out and listen for any trouble from the 'man.' Jonas told him.

Jasper knew. If anything went wrong in there he would break

the door down with his head. He wasn't the least bit afraid of the 'man.'

Jonas petted him under the collar and disappeared into the misty night.

Jasper sat and listened.

He waited.

As Deputy Sheriff Jerry Collins pulled up to the scene of the crash on Route 62 that Mary and Jonas had just been informed about, he saw a man lying on the road not far from the wrecked car. The apple tree was not far from the road and when the impact occurred the driver was ejected out onto the road. The man was not wearing his seatbelt or otherwise he may have lived. The man's face had slid across the pavement and his broken teeth were all about the ground around him. One of the man's arms was bent behind him, across his back. Blood leaked from his ears, nose and battered skull.

It was Henry Morgan.

My God.

What is happening to my quiet little town?

Jerry Collins had lived here all his life, except for the small stint he had performed with the National Guard. He had never witnessed a string of events quite like this not even in the Guard. There he just went to the barracks in Gardner and did drills, studied tactics and under went some physical and creative reckoning exercises. Although looking back there was one incident he remembers being close to this one. His unit had been called upon and dispatched into duty in order to stifle a civil disturbance in Philadelphia. It was quite more than a disturbance, really. A group of radicals had blown up a section of a federal building and they were sent in to thwart any more resistance or violence. It was very hush hush. Philadelphia was a nightmare. The crime and poverty he had witnessed in that corrupt city, was about all he could stand. He was glad to be done with his tour of duty.

Looking down on Henry Morgan lying in the street, he felt like his quaint calm town had ingested a cancer and it was spreading. It had reached its final phase and was about to threaten the whole body.

Henry had been thrown from the Honda Civic and was killed instantly on contact with the pavement. His battered body had slid five more feet across the asphalt after contact. He finally came to a stop on the double yellow lines along this patch of the no passing zone on Route 62.

Laura however, was not so fortunate. She had been fatally injured in the crash but was still alive. She was trying to hold on long enough for help to arrive. That help was her brother Bobby. His EMT team was the first to arrive at the scene.

Bobby had responded to the scene with his partner not knowing what he was about to stumble upon. Bobby and his partner were playing checkers when a 911 call came in. The call came in from a house sixty feet from the crash. The woman who called in said she heard a crash over at the orchards and to send help.

Bobby arrived to see Henry first.

Oh no.

Henry.

Oh no.

He jumped from the still moving ambulance and sped to Henry, who was face down on the road. He picked Henry up into his arms and turned him over. He put his right hand on his jugular to see if he still clung to life.

No pulse.

Nothing.

The rookie, who had been driving, knew this was Bobby's family and immediately ran to the car wrapped around the tree. He wanted to see if anyone else was in the automobile, hoping for a sign of good fortune and life to extend to his partner.

What he saw stopped him dead.

Laura was in the front seat.

She was trying to say something but only blood was spilling out. She coughed and blood splattered on the window.

The rookie, Jeremiah Helplos, turned his attention back to Booby in sorrow.

Bobby saw his look and bolted to the car.

Not Laura.

Please Lord.

Not Laura.

Jeremiah was trying to open the passenger door to no avail. Bobby got to the passenger side door and threw Jeremiah out of the way. Jeremiah flew several feet toward the road and landed on the hard dirt near a storm drain.

Laura reached out to Bobby and smiled.

Then she was gone.

A large branch from the twisted Macintosh Tree had come threw the window on impact. It pierced through her chest and drove right through her right lung and then though the passenger seat. It pinned her against it, so she couldn't break free.

A small fire was catching underneath the hood. Bobby heard yelling and people were running toward him.

Bobby had all these memories that were flooding back through his head. He remembered when Laura was in second grade and didn't get any valentine cards from the boys at school. So he went to the pharmacy downtown and bought some.

The store was closing and he had to convince the shopkeeper that a little girl's hope depended on it. The shopkeeper was a big softy. When he heard that this boy was trying to bring a small girl out of pain and sadness, back to the land of confidence and faith, he relented.

Laura was only seven years old then and was crying on the floor holding her teddy bear in her arms when he came into the room. He gave her a stamped envelope and said it came in the mail.

It was from a secret admirer. She was so thrilled. She was ecstatic. She danced around the room holding the valentines and kissing them. I wonder whom it could be she thought.

Later that evening when she was going to bed, she took up her envelope of valentines and upon closer inspection noticed that the stamp wasn't marked with a postage mark.

That meant...

She understood what her big brother had done for her. She got out of bed and went to his room. She tiptoed across the cold hall with her little bare-feet and looked at her brother in adoration from the doorway to his room. He was already asleep. She pulled back his blankets and got up into bed with him. She kissed him on the cheek and snuggled up next to him. She put her thumb in her mouth. She shivered from the cold night. He put his arm around her and they slept. Her brother was her hero and protector. She never felt better or safer.

Bobby's mind was shattering in madness and sorrow.

Now back at this awful accident, another EMT squad had arrived.

So many emotions were going through Bobby.

Chester Livery, a twenty-year veteran, put his hand on Bobby's shoulder.

Bobby knocked his hand away and was about to strike Chester, when he heard the sound.

From inside the car, a baby began to wail.

Everyone hushed.

Silence.

AAAAAAAAAAAAAAAAAAHHHHHHHHH!!!

Bobby's mind went into overdrive.

Then he had a visit from the adrenaline monster.

Bobby grabbed the piece of door metal at the top corner that was protruding out with his left hand. He punched a hole into the car door with his right and grabbed hold of the metal strip frame inside. He tore the door off the hinges and threw it over his shoulder like a playing card. Blood was all over his hands and pants. He was numb to this. He bent down to see a baby on the floor, with afterbirth and water all about it. Bobby took his jacket off and wrapped the baby in it. He clipped the almost severed umbilical cord with his Swiss-Army knife. Chester Livery tried to take the baby and get Bobby to clean and treat his wounds.

Bobby charged right over him with a stiff arm and ran toward the ambulance. Chester Livery took two size twelve's to the chin and right eyeball. Bobby made his way to the rear of the ambulance.

Jeremiah had already pulled onto the grass and opened the backdoor. Bobby climbed in and they raced off to the local hospital with both the siren and baby wailing away.

"Deputy Sheriff, you have a page over the police radio." Said Officer Betedown.

"Deputy sheriff, go ahead." Jerry announced.

"Jerry we have a call of a disturbance over at Depot Square." Sergeant Magett said.

"Can't it wait, Sergeant?" He asked annoyed. "I got my hands full here." He added.

"It appears to be gunshots." The voice came back.

"Great." Jerry said sarcastically.

"Officer Betedown, you're in charge here until the State Police show up. When you wrap up, file a report and leave it on my desk." Jerry said.

"Okay Jerry, will do." Betedown responded.

"And go off afterwards and see how the baby made out, okay." Jerry added.

Betedown nodded his approval.

As Jerry Collin's drove away he could only imagine what was in store for him next. What he found was beyond what he had imagined.

Figures that it would be.

Mr. Abrams arranged the material from the manila envelope across the table so that, he and Thomas could make out the information about it. On the table before them were pictures, newspaper clippings and articles.

First there was a photo from the 1970's, and in that photo were Mr. Kilcrop and Pol Pot. Pol Pot was the leader of the Khmer Rouge Party, the communist party in Cambodia who committed genocide on its population. One out of four people were annihilated. The next picture was from the 1950's, with Mr. Kilcrop and Joseph Stalin. Joseph Stalin was the paranoid Dictator of the Soviet Union. The man who was responsible for killing more people than the two Antichrists combined. Another photo was from the early 1940's. Kilcrop was standing next to a German Officer. Thomas being astute in history recognized the first two infamous and brutal men but not the latter.

"Who's this?" Thomas asked pointing to the other man in the third picture.

"Reinard Heydrich, a real fiend. They called him the Monarch of Death. He helped, with the most fervor, to establish the concentration camps and deportation of the 'less desirable' during the Third Reich. The project was called to order at the Wannsee Conference. I could go on in more detail but I won't. All you need to know is that these men were barbaric." Mr. Abrams finished.

Mr. Abrams got up and took down a bottle Chivas Regal from the cabinet over the fridge. He had been saving it for a much better and joyous occasion but this was overwhelming.

"This can't be. He hasn't aged a day " Mr. Abrams said refusing to believe the evidence in front of him. The photos must be doctored, that's it he thought.

Thomas read through the newspaper clippings and articles that were in the manila envelope as well.

The first was dated February 1902. It was about a mining company In Illinois before the turn of the century. Another pertained to the Civil War in Missouri, dated March 1864. The next was from Sept. 1803 and Napoleons conquest of Europe and parts of Asia. It spoke of France's involvement with Spain. It went into detail about Napoleon's brother, Joseph, and his short and brutal tenure as King of Spain. All of these passages and references referred to a man wearing strange spectacles, and having the ear of the said men in power.

The final article was a local one from the previous year. Thomas read it aloud. It contained the nasty details of a homicide-suicide, involving Dom Gladberry and his wife, in the presence of Penny Downtrodder. The article went on to say that a witness had seen a man wearing dark glasses at night, staking out the Gladberry Home.

That witness, was Mrs. Crassman.

"Oh my God." They said simultaneously.

Burn Kilcrop tried to keep his focus. His mind was all cluttered. He had spent so much time and energy on his project that he would not let it go to ruin. No he would not stop now he thought. I can bounce back from this. No great thing he kept telling himself. I can fix this.

You see dictators, tyrants and all men who desire power or dominance over others, need not destroy you. They need only to subdue and extinguish your will to carry on. What they truly desire is total concession or submission.

Where there is life, there is hope. Kilcrop must destroy this hope in order to prevail. Where there is hope there is freedom. The idea of living free is a very virulent seed. They will try to stomp out this seed before it germinates, cause once it takes root the outcome is inevitable. Its roots run deep and branch out to take hold in the body of earth and spirit. A seed, that once it takes root, cannot be unsown. It may take a long time to bear fruit, but the end result is always the same. Freedom is glorious and defeat while trying to gain it only makes victory taste that much sweeter.

Kilcrop knew that the child would bring hope back into Thomas' soul. Thomas would be devastated by his parent's death, no doubt, but he would carry on for the sake of his sibling.

This made Kilcrop furious. He hadn't counted on this. He would have to regroup. He would have to come up with a new strategy for his endgame. He needed new pieces to the puzzle now.

He heard the woman before him going on and on. He wanted to smash her skull with a thunderous handclap over the ears, and watch her smashed brains fall about. He would love to ice skate on her Grey Matter all around the kitchen.

This made him grin.

But he had to wait.

This temporarily postponed his ritual, but it by no means, thwarted his plans for the unveiling of his final act.

ANCIENT ARROWHEAD

He had to stay near his prize, his new queen that he would take with him. He would have her. Mary would be his. His mind was bent on it. She would be broken, and she would yield to his demands. She would sit beside him on his throne and together they would rule the Third Sphere Underworld.

"Will you excuse me Brenda?" Kilcrop asked holding his stomach.

He went into the bathroom and faked illness.

"Are you okay?" She asked at the bathroom door.

He washed his face and hands and opened the door.

"I'm afraid I don't feel well. I should be going." He stated.

"Okay then…" She trailed off upset that her quarry had escaped again.

"Sure you won't stay?" She said in hope that he might reconsider.

"I really should be off, I'll see you again soon." Kilcrop promised.

He put emphasis on 'soon.'

He gave her a kiss on the cheek and she noticed his lips were on fire.

"You seem to be burning up. You must have an awful temperature." She said concerned.

Never had he wanted to reveal himself more than he did now. He just wanted to see her face when he made his transformation. That would shut her up. He had never wanted to kill someone so violently than he did at this moment, looking at Miss Talkalot.

"Yes I suppose I am a little warm." He responded keeping his malicious thoughts hidden under his false tone.

They said their goodbyes and he retrieved his jacket in the foyer and put it on. He swore he heard someone upstairs spying in on him, but he wasn't sure. He also wasn't in any position to investigate.

He opened the door and was off into the night.

Mary came down stairs after her mother went off to bed. Brenda had come into lecture Mary about her wrongdoings but saw that she was sleeping. Brenda decided it was best to leave her until morning and then she would let Mary have it.

When her mother went off to her bedroom and closed the door, Mary got up from bed and she tiptoed down the hall, descended the stairs and crossed the living room through the kitchen and opened the backdoor.

She was about to call out to Jasper but he was at the top step waiting on her.

"Hey Jasper, come on in boy." She welcomed him and she petted him on the way by.

He jetted by her to shake off the cold moisture even though it didn't bother him much, just a bit uncomfortable. He would've stayed out there in a snowstorm for Mary if she asked. He wagged his tail and put his front paws up on her shoulders.

She rubbed his chest and behind his ears.

Oh it was worth it, it was worth it he thought to his simple and reliable self.

He licked her face and ears.

She giggled.

"Jasper!" She said laughing.

She needed a little humor to undo the emotional stress she had witnessed that day. Jasper was all too ready to comply. His great big pink tongue hung over the side of his jaws while she pet him.

She pushed him off playfully after a while and went to the refrigerator and pulled open the raw meat drawer. She pulled out a two- inch Porterhouse steak.

Man.

He loved Mary. His appreciation for her, swelled in his canine heart. He delved into the steak and ate it veraciously. After he crunched the bones into dust and grit, he licked the package and floor clean.

Mary took the package and stuffed it deep into the trash. She took out a bowl and filled it with water. Jasper lapped away at it until he had his fill. She washed the bowl after he was done and put it back in the cupboard.

Jasper and Mary went through the living room and retraced the steps that she had just made. Mary told him to be quiet as they made their way upstairs across the hall to her bedroom. When she got there she took out a large blanket from her closet and folded it. Then she placed it on the floor for Jasper to sleep on.

Then Mary got into bed, said goodnight to Jasper and closed her eyes to sleep.

Jasper lay down upon the blanket and kept watch.

Jonas had originally intended to go off and find another command post knowing that they would be unable to go back to the warehouse now that the shoot-out had occurred. He thought he would find somewhere similar in another part of town and then he would meet up with Thomas in the morning. Finding a command post was priority number two now.

It was half past the witching hour and he knew where he must go and what he must do. He realized that when Thomas learned about the death of his parent's that he would go there to the crash site. Thomas would be determined to see for himself the bane of his parent's. He would forgo their meeting in the cemetery.

Being public enemy number one and also the target, Jonas had to go where the compass told him. It was pointing to the car accident and Thomas would too. He went off to the orchards and to the scene of the accident.

He rested.

He waited.

At the moment Jonas arrived at a safe distance at the perimeter of the accident, The Deputy Sheriff, Jerry Collins, discovered the remains of the biker gang.

The former Deity From Hell members were not happened upon by chance.

Someone nearby had heard the gunfire and reported it to the police.

That someone was Morgana Digame. She was the town crier.

When the deputy pulled up she came running out of her house full of energy and gossip. It didn't matter that it was past midnight because she had to see what the commotion was all about.

"Jerry." She said.

"Mrs. Digame." Jerry returned.

Mr. Digame was standing at the door and now he was wearing a smile. He was thrilled that even though it may only be for a few minutes at least it was someone else's ears that would be rattling.

"I heard loud bangs that sounded like gun shots and called you right away. No doubt some pranksters lighting off firebombs. You can never be too careful though. Especially with all that has been going on. Right Jerry. Don't you agree?" She said this as one long phrase.

She talked, walked, chewed gum and twirled her already curly short black hair as they carried on down the tracks.

Before he could answer this onslaught of verbage, she went on.

"Well did you catch that boy, you know, that murdered those folks at the nursing home. Damn shame really. Thought he was a nice kid." She said this although she had never even heard of him till today.

He broke in before she could irritate his ears anymore.

"We don't know that he killed them Morgana, he's just a suspect." He explained.

"You don't think he's innocent. They caught him red handed. No pun intended." She laughed.

"Everyone is innocent until proven otherwise." He said rather annoyed.

"Hogwash." She spit.

She was about to pour on more conversation, when they stumbled upon the four disfigured corpses.

"My God." Mrs. Digame gasped.

"Now what?" Jerry asked of the heavens.

So here he was having discovered the four men and their remains. One body totally mutilated, a ruined mess. One shot through the back of the head. One body was lying in two pieces in separate places across the tracks.

Then he came upon the last of the deceased. He knew the others of course but he dismissed their deaths as the product of a gang rivalry.

That is, until he saw Blake Crassman.

"Shit." He muttered.

He was in for a long night.

So was Morgana.

He turned to her to tell her something, but before he could tell her to keep her lips sealed, she was gone. Great he thought, so much for damage control.

Her phone burned up late in to the morning, and the gossip spread.

Thomas had killed again.

Thomas and Mr. Abrams were listening to the scanner some hours later when they learned that police had discovered the bodies on the train tracks.

"I didn't want to kill those men but they made it necessary." Thomas recalled.

"No doubt, but the authorities might not swallow it so easy." Mr. Abrams stated.

"Why not?" He asked. "It's the truth." He responded.

"Unfortunately it's not always the truth that matters in Law but what can be proven in court." Mr. Abram's stated. "We live with the law but justice is often more difficult to find." He went on.

"That's not right." Replied Thomas.

"Certainly not, I know but that's the way the system works." Abrams stated.

"Besides you physically battered one of their own. That doesn't help." He remarked. Mr. Abrams took a deep breath and went on.

"I have a feeling Kilcrop is more than he seems. But in proving that, we will need more than pictures and newspaper articles from decades or centuries ago." He said.

Thomas had some suspicions of his own.

"I think that Conway is involved in this too. I don't know why and at what capacity, but I will find out." Thomas said.

"Heavy accusations Thomas to bring against an officer, a sheriff no less. You may be on to something, but without any proof, all you have is insinuation." He finished.

"I don't have evidence yet but I'll get some." Thomas assured him.

The scanner went on to say that Jez Imadder was listed as a missing person and possibly Thomas was involved in that as well.

"What the hell?" Thomas asked.

He began to tell Mr. Abrams who Jez was when suddenly…

There came the dreaded news, the news Mary and Jonas had come by a few hours before. News no person should learn second hand.

The sky came crashing down on Thomas. He sat there in disbelief.

Mr. Abrams wanted to say something reassuring but what could he say. Mr. Abrams knew what Thomas would do too. He had seen it before. When you push someone down and take away all he cares about, the retribution that follows was to be hostile and swift. No planning, just vengeance. Nothing is more dangerous than a man with nothing left to lose, especially when he 'knows' he's acting righteously.

Impossible, Thomas thought. It can't be. He wasn't sad. He was enraged with reprisal. The lion was hungry again, hungry for man meat.

He picked up his gun and stood up from the table. He quietly and calmly walked to the door.

"Thomas wait!" Shouted Mr. Abrams.

Thomas' mind was closed to the world. He heard nothing, he saw Kilcrop and he was determined to bring the Hammer of the Gods down on his head.

"If you want justice for your parents you'll think this through." He explained vainly.

Thomas, wasn't thinking justice though, he was thinking vengeance. Justice and Vengeance are brothers of another mother. And Justice wasn't invited to this party.

Thomas went through the back door of Mr. Abrams' house along the tall wooden fence and walked down the center of Winter St. with the ivory handled revolver hanging from his right hand. The sleet had started to collect and stick to the ground and Thomas' footprints were evident in the path that he took. The air was cold but Thomas was numb to the environment. He trudged onward.

Mr. Abrams wouldn't try and stop him, for he knew better.

The scanner had given Thomas the location of the car wreck. It did not however, reveal the survival of his newborn baby sister.

CHAPTER TWELVE

Lost reservation

7:30a.m.

The reason that Mr. Kilcrop didn't have a thousand zombie-like creatures under his trance and control is because all magic takes energy. The more magic you make the more energy it takes. You do not want to undergo a magic spell without the proper rest and preparation.

A great deal of Kilcrop's energy was being used to simply exist, on this plane.

If he used too much energy, he was bound to make a mistake. Mistakes in magic use are not an option, unless you want to spend the rest of eternity washing dishes, in the china town in hell. I'm being humorous now, the effects of errors in magic use are much worse.

Nearly the rest of Kilcrop's power and concentration was fixed on completing his plan. He had a significant problem though. He needed his fabric to be solid. It order to gain real substance to his aura, it was essential for him to have the spirit of a child. If he could become solid, he would gain more power and use this energy to cast domination over a larger horde. Like he had done so many times in the past. The reason for using a child's soul is because the spirit is just made. It hasn't been changed and it is flexible to exploitation. It exists in its original form. This makes it susceptible to manipulation and distortion. It also has the most energy, like a brand new battery I suppose.

He thought he would have this when Henry and Laura died, and he would take their child's spirit in forfeit.

He was mistaken.

He had the book, the dagger, and the chalice.

He needed a child.

So here he was with this fat, greasy boy-fucker Sheriff Conway. They were sitting idle in a rental car and watching an Elementary School fieldtrip. Conway had a pair of sunglasses on as well. The beating he had taken from Thomas was written all over his face. His upper lip was split and fat. His right eye was black and blue with stitches just below the eyebrow. His nose was taped down with a splint, and it hurt just to breath. When he talked it was very garbled and barely audible.

Kilcrop thought he was pathetic. These were the people easiest to bribe though, and so he always found himself surrounded by these dregs of society. Most times too it was the people that were least suspected by society that held the dirtiest secrets.

The young students were sitting on the dike of the reservoir behind the grammar school, eating lunch. Two of the children who had finished their lunch first, began a game of hide and seek. One of the boys turned toward the water and started counting to fifty, while the other ran toward the woods dividing the schoolyard and the dikes, to find a hiding spot.

"Go get him Conway you stupid pig." Kilcrop said annoyed.

Kilcrop's nature was getting frayed and exceedingly violent. His temper was lost easily. He was losing control of his emotions and the necessary expected social etiquette.

Conway took off his two-way radio, placed it on the dashboard and got out of the rental car. He crept up to the boy through the wooded area. Sheriff Conway savored this moment of taking a child against his will. This was his forte. Nothing was more satisfying than the fear in the victim's eyes when they realized they were helpless.

When he seized the boy, his heart was pounding and he had the first erection he's had in two months. He apprehended the boy with his left hand and put his right over the boy's small mouth. The boy was squirming and trying to get away. Sheriff Conway punched the boy in the stomach and it knocked the wind out of him, before he could scream.

He opened the back door to the four-door sedan and shoved the hostile boy in. When he put the boy in the back Kilcrop immediately pulled out a cloth and forced it over the squirming boy's mouth. The chloroform in the cloth worked quickly and soon the boy was unconscious.

Darkness took the boy.

4:15 a.m.

Thomas walked down Winter St. and crossed Main St. through Farmers cul de sac. He crossed over Duck Harbor Bridge onto Pine St. Extension. He then traversed around the State Projects, climbed over the wooden fence at the Coopers Barnyard and went up onto Moffet St. He walked along the right side of the road until he got to the Mudjets apple orchard property, then he ran up the small incline into the orchards.

The six-shooter was loose in his hand.

Thomas didn't care who saw him, because he decided he'd kill them too.

He passed rows and rows of orchard trees. He went down towards

Route 62, which ran parallel to Mudjet's Farm. He headed to where the car accident occurred and where the people he respected and cared for most in the world lost their lives.

"Thomas." Jonas whispered.

Thomas saw him sitting under a tree.

It was two hours before first light, still dark but Jonas wasn't taking any chances.

Farmer Mudjet was always suspicious because kids would raid his orchard often and he was weary of trespassers. He was always in the window surveying his land. He had a dog too. Jonas didn't want to arouse suspicion or make any disturbances. He hid under cover and rested against a small apple tree.

"Don't try and stop me Jonas." Thomas insisted.

"There's State Troopers down there, Thomas. They'll kill you." Jonas assured him.

"I don't care, I'll shoot them all. I have nothing left to live for." Thomas said distraught.

"Think about it Thomas. You're not doing anybody any good by going down there with the authorities present." Jonas stated.

By this time Jonas was following the very determined Thomas.

"I'm not concerned about doing the right thing anymore. I just want this to be over. I'm going down there and if anyone tries to stop me I'll kill them." Thomas said emphatically.

Finally Jonas stopped and said. "Thomas your mother was… pregnant." He finished.

Thomas stopped in his tracks. Tears started streaming down his face, and he fell to his knees.

"Why have you turned your back on me?" He said to the heavens." Why have you forsaken me?" He asked.

Jonas was about to say something and opted not to.

"I hate you, I believed in you and you took my Mom and Dad. I hate you." He cried to God.

Jonas stood silent and watched.

He let Thomas vent.

He let Thomas cry.

When Thomas' fits of sorrow had subsided a bit, he spoke to Thomas.

Thomas was more resolved than ever to destroy everyone. He got to his feet took a deep breath and just about started off to his doom when Jonas broke in.

"Thomas, the baby survived. You have a baby sister." He informed Thomas.

Then when Thomas thought that all hope was lost, that the Lord was no longer listening or cared about him, a glimmer of light entered his spirit.

He stopped.

He smiled.

He prayed.

6:30am.

Mr. Abrams was well into the bottle of Chivas now.

When people who have drank in the past, stop drinking, it's for a reason. Everybody has their reasons, and they're always personal. Some men, when they have a drink after having given it up for a spell become calm, not violent or excessively drunk. It helps these men focus. This seventeen-year old blended scotch whiskey was doing what Mr. Abrams expected of it, relaxing him.

He had stewed on Thomas' situation. He had thought long on Kilcrop's participation and what it might mean if he were to get involved. He had lived a long life, sometimes when he thought he might not. Especially when he was in the jungle, in the fighting Tiger Army. He wasn't afraid of death now like he was then. Then he felt like he had much more to see and do, but now that he looked back on his full life and the lessons he'd learned, he had no regrets.

He had probably forgotten more than most people would ever learn, and he was content to go into this ordeal knowing it might be his last. He was thinking clearly now and he decided on what he must do.

He finished the glass of scotch whiskey before him and set about his task.

7:15a.m.

Mary got dressed quickly in gray sweatpants and a blue sweatshirt. She put on her blue Saucony running shoes and tiptoed into the bathroom to brush her teeth. She put her hair up with several bobby pins because she didn't want her hair all about today. It was something she didn't want to worry about today because there were greater matters afoot. She brushed her teeth and when she finished in the bathroom, she returned to her room and collected Jasper.

Mary and Jasper crept down the hall and scuttled down the cherry wood finished staircase, stopping intermittently, while pausing they listened for sounds of their exposure. Mary went to the foyer and Jasper waited for her where the kitchen tile and living room carpet met.

She grabbed her red windbreaker from the coat rack and went into the kitchen. She opened the fridge and took three bottles of water from within. She placed them in her windbreaker pockets. Mary filled up a Tupper-Ware bowl with tap water and Jasper drank it veraciously. When he was finished she placed the empty bowl in the sink.

Mary opened the backdoor and they stole away into the brisk morning air.

Mary and Jasper made their way through the swamp across the street from the front side of her house. It was wet and slow going but it was the safest way to trek to the cemetery. They made it out of the swamp and cut through the back of the State Projects. She crisscrossed the path that Thomas had taken just under three hours before. They crossed Woodlawn St. and entered the cemetery from the west. They made their way to the hill in the rear of the cemetery. When they got there, Mary and Jasper sat on the smaller rock where Jonas had placed the envelope and scanner the day before.

And there they awaited Thomas and Jonas.

6:15

Thomas and Jonas watched as, one by one, the State and Local Police left the scene of the accident. One stayed behind while the flat bed towing company could load the wrecked vehicle. Then he too left following the tow truck.

Thomas slowly made his way down to the crash site.

Metal, glass and plastic were laying all about. He saw where the impact had been. The bark on the twisted apple tree was split up the trunk. He observed the long broken branch, which penetrated the window of his parent's car. There was still blood on it. Part of it had snapped when the tow truck driver was lifting the ruined auto. This part was on the ground.

First light was breaking and the sun was rising over the trees, left of where Thomas was standing, and east in the sky. The warm morning sun fell on Thomas and the earth before him. This helped him see the earth below his feet much more clearly. He scanned the ground for remnants of his parent's existence. The sun fell on the broken tree branch and Thomas noticed that the branch was twisted in a loose spiral like that of a screw but the grooves weren't so even or pronounced.

Thomas picked up the shard of branch and held it tight in his hand. The splintered apple branch was about three inches wide at one end and it tapered down to about three quarters of an inch at the other. It was about three feet long. He could see the blood on it. He didn't know which parent was mortally wounded by it but it didn't matter. It was the last thing that ever happened to his parents and he would keep this as a token of their lives.

Thomas looked about the littered ground for anything else that might be left of his parent's, but found nothing. Thomas would keep the curse of his mother to remind him of what he lost. He would keep it to remember the people he so cherished in his heart. He would save this piece of wood because it was the last thing that ever touched the life of his parent's.

Thomas and Jonas went back into the orchard and talked about what they should do next. Thomas was saying something when they heard a screen door slam. It sounded like the screen door was no longer attached to the air spring that retracts when the closing door comes back automatically. It was like the door was swinging free and the wind slammed it up against the house.

Whack!

Farmer Mudjet had let out his dog and they new it was only a matter of time before they were discovered.

They both realized that Mary was going to do something, but whether she stayed at her house and waited, or went to the cemetery they weren't sure. They decided to split up. Thomas would go to Mary's and see if he could reach her there. Jonas would go to their supposed meeting place on the hill behind the cemetery and try to locate her there.

Jonas told Thomas that he left Jasper with Mary. If there was no Jasper about, there was no Mary. If that were so, he was to rendezvous with them at the hill.

Farmer Mudjets dog was making his way down the orchard sniffing and searching through the rows of apple trees. He was closing in on the pair and he was barking now.

They both jetted to their objectives.

7:55

Kilcrop and Conway pulled up to the mausoleum in the rear of the cemetery and arrived to see an old Ford utility vehicle was already waiting.

It was five minutes before first whistle.

A giant of a man got out of the rusted green Ford Bronco.

Sol went around to the rear and opened the truck bed door. He reached in pulled out a large brown hemp potato sack, which was directly behind the Bronco's rear seats. It was a twenty-five pound potato sack and it was half full of something. There were dark red stains on the sack and the smell was atrocious. Some liquid, which had soaked through, dripped to the ground as he swung it over his shoulder. He waited for the two men to get out of the car. The thick red liquid was dripping onto the back of his shoes and running on to his gray T-shirt.

It was a little chilly out this morning but the big man was nearly impervious to cold. It bothered him very little, the cold and the blood seeping into his clothes. He wanted to be done with Kilcrop and his business. So he waited patiently and he would do this final task. Then he would go, whether Kilcrop was finished or not.

Kilcrop approached the mausoleum while Conway attended to lugging the unconscious boy. Conway went into the backseat and recovered the limp child. He slung him over his shoulder and made his way to the crypt.

Sol saw the boy and was touched by guilt and regret. He was sorry for having ever gone about the bidding of Kilcrop. This is the end of this madness. This is wrong. I will not do it anymore.

Kilcrop came to the door of the crypt and the latch lock clicked as he waved his hand over it, for no lock could hold him from trespass.

The three men entered the death temple and Conway set the boy down on the large sarcophagus in the center of the room.

He heard an animal snorting and moving around. He could hear hooves clicking off the granite floor. Conway was afraid.

"What the?" He asked.

The room reeked of urine and feces. It smelled like the armpit of a Cave Troll might. The humid stale air was ripe with animal sweat and rotting flesh.

Conway stepped on the decaying arm of a human. There were maggots eating away at the remaining tissue. Next to the arm was a human ear with studs all the way up the outer part, and the lobe had a huge ring in it.

Flies were buzzing around his head, many of them.

"What is this place Kilcrop? He asked. It's nauseating." Conway stated.

"Shut up fool." Kilcrop responded.

"I'm leaving this ghastly nightmare." Conway said walking towards the open door. "I should have left this madness long ago." Conway muttered.

Helyza, the disfigured boar beast, raced in pursuit of his flight and blocked his exit. The sick animal snorted and grunted. Saliva and putrid hot air emitted from her snout. She was inching her way toward the grotesque excuse for a man.

Conway receded to his former place against the wall, rethinking his decision about escape.

Easy Helyza. Kilcrop said in 'mindspeech' to his pet.

Easy. You can eat him after we are done.

This seemed to calm her down.

"We aren't going to have anymore problems are we sheriff?" Kilcrop inquired.

"No. N-No sir." The sheriff stammered.

Sol took his sack and threw it on the floor. It landed and slid against the back wall, behind the sheet music stand.

Helyza turned away from Conway and sniffed out the scent of flesh. Helyza sensed her feeding time was here and she dashed to the soaked bag on the granite floor. She ripped and tore at the hemp sack containing her food. She shook it about tearing the seams. With one of her back long legs she stepped on the corner of the bag and sunk her tusks into the sac. She pulled her head back while her jaws were clenched and her back hoof was still on the sack, tearing it. The sack tore enough to stick her head in and she went at the meat inside. She squeezed her head through and pulled out a dead rabbit.

Sol had gone to the pet store and purchased several domestic animals for Helyza to feed on. She preferred live quarry but her master hadn't fed her much of anything since her arrival, so she was famished. This would suffice until she could get her jaws on the sheriff.

The rabbit, which suffered a broken neck at the hands of the giant janitor, was being crunched away in Helyza's mouth. She didn't even break the rabbit down before she swallowed it, half digested. She went on tearing carcasses out of the bag while Kilcrop set about his ritual. There were rabbits, guinea pigs and kittens in the bag and all were dead and now being eaten.

Kilcrop took the ritual dagger and chalice and placed them upon the sarcophagus next to the boy's head. The chalice was pure silver with stars and moons engraved around the outside. They alternated back and forth around the rim of the cup. The dagger hilt was dark green and had gold trim. It had a large ruby in the center, which was evident on both sides. Two snakes twisted around one another and alternated from one side of the dagger to the other. Finally the snakes met with one facing the other on each side of the ruby. The snake's mouths were open on either side of the ruby as if ready to devour it before the other one could. The blade itself was pure silver and about five inches long.

"Conway, take this dagger and stand over the child. I'm going to read passages from this book here. When I'm finished I want you to drive the dagger through the boy's chest." Kilcrop explained impatiently. "Sol, when he does, pick the boy up and drain as much blood into the chalice as it will hold." He added cruelly.

Conway stood fixed and couldn't focus. He wasn't a saint, far from it in fact, but he was no murderer.

Kilcrop saw his reluctance to cooperate.

"Conway, need I remind you how deep you are into this. Your reputation is a sham. Quit the charade and do what I said." Kilcrop ordered.

Conway shook his head in resistance.

"When you take something by force from the innocent or less fortunate you murder some part of the world anyway, so what's the difference. You've killed innocence before, now it's time to do it once more." Kilcrop explained ruthlessly.

"I'm not doing it." Conway proclaimed in grief.

Kilcrop was upon him.

He was sweltering with wrath.

His glasses came off and the red sockets of lava colored radiance bore into Conway's mind.

"You will do as I command or else." Kilcrop grumbled exhausted.

Conway nodded his approval.

Burn Kilcrop's time to fill his reservation on this earth was running out.

At the same time this was going on, something unexpected happened.

Coincidence met luck and had a child, called fate. This fate would be the undoing of both Burn Kilcrop and Jonas Lightbringer.

You see Jonas' task was simple, and the rules of engagement for these assignments were too. Find the target and protect them until their destiny is revealed, then step out of the way and let the Sister's of Fortune do their work.

That's it. No more. No less.

Jonas had to pass the mausoleum from the path he had taken through the south gate on his way to the hill, where Mary may be waiting. He climbed through the wooded area in the direct path to the mausoleum and was passing by when he heard the commotion. Jonas heard the boy awaken and scream for mercy. He was pleading to be set free.

Sol had a hold of the boy and had pinned him down, but he was filled with contrition. He let up on the boy and began to protest his part in this situation.

The door to the crypt was still slightly ajar.

Just then a canister clinked on the ground.

Kilcrop looked down and saw what had disturbed his ceremony. His forked tongue shot from his mouth and he hissed.

On the ground was a grenade, a concussion grenade.

Kabaaaaaaaaaaaam!

A moment later the door shot open with a kick from Jonas.

Kilcrop went to apprehend Jonas and inflict pain on his enemy for no physical weapon could stay or harm the principle. He assailed Jonas and was about to overtake him when... The angels on Jonas' Bracers lit up. A purple glow started to emanate from the carvings in the gold bracelets. Just before Kilcrop grabbed Jonas from behind, he drew back as if zapped with static electricity.

Kilcrops fury was overtaking him now.

Conway and Sol were on the ground. Conway was semi conscious rolling about. Sol was holding his head and ears. Blood was leaking from his nose. The boy who had been on the grave was somewhat protected from the blast from the marble top. The child was still in the room and was certainly affected but the sarcophagus absorbed some of the blast. Because he was crying and screaming aloud his canals were open in his ears and throat so the blast didn't jar his head as bad as the others.

Jonas grabbed hold of the briefly disabled boy and threw him over his shoulder. Then he stepped over Sol and bolted through the open doorway of the crypt. He headed for the hill at the back of the cemetery where he hoped Mary and Jasper were not waiting. They were.

Jonas could kill scumbags. He could take a bullet without thinking twice, for the target. He could walk into a dire situation knowing he was going to his peril, but he would not turn away from children in need. Jonas could deal with most situations and ordeals and turn a blind eye, saying it was God's plan. When it came to children though, and people who hurt them, he could not stand idle.

This was no exception. When he heard the child's agony he broke the rules, but he was content and felt righteous for having done so. He wasn't sure the referee would feel the same though. He would cross that bridge when it came, probably sooner than later.

Protect the target and complete the objective, were the only rules. He stepped outside those parameters and the consequences would be swift. The punishment would be brutal. He was prepared to take his chances and so he did.

He didn't care.

He had done right because it was right.

8:05a.m.

Thomas heard the grenade blast from the east gate and he ran toward the resonance.

Oh no.

Mary.

Run. Thought Thomas.

Mary heard this explosion too. She and Jasper also ran toward where the sound came from.

Oh no.

Thomas.

Run. Thought Mary.

Jonas and Mary nearly collided when he rounded a large Maple tree. She was coming down hill at full speed and he couldn't see her because of the obstructing tree trunk.

"My God Jonas." She said frightened. "What's happening?" She asked.

"War." Jonas responded.

"Where's Thomas?" She asked concerned.

"My guess is that he's on his way, now that the whole world heard that blast." Jonas remarked.

"What do we do?" She questioned fretfully.

"Take the boy and wait here for Thomas." Jonas said. "Then go back to the pricker patch, while I deal with this." He finished.

She began to ask more questions but it was to Jonas' back as he ran back into the fray.

Jasper though did not stop to chat when Jonas and Mary nearly banged heads. He bolted past them, for his nemesis had come out looking for revenge on her master's behalf.

Helyza had recovered from the blast first. She got to her feet and jumped from the back of the mausoleum to the open door in one leap. She cleared a distance of ten feet, and she could've gone further. She had sought out the path that Jonas had taken with the boy over his shoulder, and she was gaining on him. She was in sight of her prey. Her jaws opened and she was salivating. White foam had collected around her gums and nose like she was a rabid animal.

A few more meters…

Smack!

Jasper crashed into Helyza's rib section with his forehead on her left side and broke three of them. She yelped out in agony.

They rolled upon the ground in a desperate grab and wrestle. Helyza bit Jasper on the chest. Her bottom jaw penetrated his white coat and skin. Blood covered his hair down to his belly. The broken tusk from her upper jaw sliced a four- inch gash in his nipple area. Jasper was desperately trying to get a hold of his foe, but Helyza kept using her long back legs to kick Jasper back off balance. After she did this he would charge back awkwardly and then she would sink her teeth in again. She did this time and time again. She bit him on the left foot half way up, on his right shoulder and on his rear end before his tail. Just when it looked like Helyza would prevail, Jasper backed off to take a new approach. Helyza stepped back as well. She put her back legs against a small rock embedded in the ground and shrunk down to pounce. Her hooves were about to unleash her in a spring- loaded attack but Jasper was quicker. He shot from his previous defensive posture and slammed into her. Her cloven hooves slid off the damp rock and Jasper put on his death grip. He gripped her by the neck and suffocated her. Blood filled her throat and lungs as she futilely tried to break his hold on her, but his jaws were locked. Black blood spilled out of her snout and fell upon the earth. Helyza coughed up her last breath.

She fell limp in his mouth. He made a final squeeze to be assured that the threat was finished and her neck snapped. Then he dropped her lifeless body to the muddy ground.

7:45 a.m. to 8:05a.m.

Thomas had gone by Mary's house to see if they were about. He left the orchards and retraced his steps back to Rigby Road and crossed into Goreman's field and came upon the pricker patch. He went through the pricker patch, which was now turning to brown now that fall had come to visit, and proceeded on to Mary's house cautiously. Thomas stayed as clear of her house as possible. He couldn't locate Jasper and his thought was that they had gone to the hill at the rear of the cemetery. He had considered throwing a pebble up to Mary's side window but decided against it. He didn't want to risk alerting Brenda, so he went in haste to the cemetery.

Thomas hiked through the swamp, the route that Mary and Jasper had tramped just under an hour ago. So it was when Thomas was coming through the east gate that he heard the grenade echo. Thomas began to run toward the fight.

Thomas was on his way to the rear of the cemetery when he heard Jasper in a dogfight. He heard Jasper yelping and another one snorting and grunting. Then he heard gunshots.

Oh no.

Jonas had returned to the mausoleum in time to see Conway stumble around the corner with his 44 Magnum drawn. Conway went to his car and acquired his two-way radio. He pressed the button to talk and radioed in for assistance.

"Calling all units. This is Sheriff Conway requesting backup in the cemetery near the mausoleum. Urgent need to respond to a kidnapping and heavy weapons detail, shots fired." Conway called out. Conway fired his gun in the air with the radio microphone held on open. The sound transmitted to all police units.

Sirens immediately started screaming out their approach.

Sol had also recovered by now but he was not in sight. Suddenly Sol came out of the passenger side of his utility vehicle with a loaded M1 1903 rifle. It had a five-bullet magazine protruding from the bottom side of the rifle. His uncle gave it to him after his tour of duty which was over sixty-years ago. His uncle Fred was a veteran of the Second World War. He had fought in El Alamein in July 1942. His uncle Fred had seen some of the nastiest and bitter fighting in the history of the world.

Sol aimed the durable old rifle at Jonas and squeezed off a round. A spent shell casing ejected from the chamber. Sol wasn't thinking clearly or he wouldn't have been in conflict with Jonas. The grenade blast shook him up and he was after revenge. Jonas did not know what Sol was about either. However, a bullet just flew by him and that was indication enough of his intentions.

It's not so easy to fire a weapon and hit the desired target especially one that's moving. The bullet missed Jonas by eight feet or so. The second shot missed his ear by inches and tore through the brush behind him.

Then Jonas was close enough to let his Eight-gauge loose. He swung his arm up over his head and grabbed the stock of the scattergun from its holster. He aimed and the barrel screamed out to take its abuse. The gun roared. Buckshot metal and fire spit out of the mouth of the hand cannon. Scattering metal ripped into Sol's upper body, but the giant man didn't flinch.

Sol let another bullet loose from his rifle and it struck Jonas in the upper shoulder and passed right through. Jonas turned from the bullet wound but didn't falter.

The shotgun coughed again and this time it took the left side of Sol's head off. The janitor tried to work his rifle for the next few seconds but he couldn't employ his faculties any longer. He dropped the rifle and fell face first into the dirt under a big oak tree.

A large dust cloud rose up when he made contact with the earth.

Jonas felt the sting of another round, which the scoundrel Conway set loose. He had hit him in the left hip area. The second bullet narrowly missed Jonas' head.

Jonas dropped the shotgun and swerved his body left. His overcoat swung open and he pulled the Desert eagle that was in his chest holster, in place of the revolver he had given Thomas, and started letting shells fly. The heavy-duty handgun made a monstrous racket. It was much louder and deadlier than the average handgun and it wanted to inflict damage.

Conway ducked in behind his car as the semi-automatic tasted steel. The heavy bullets bit into the engine block of the rental car. Fluid was dripping from the bottom of the car.

Conway was about to squeeze off more shells, when he fell against the front quarter panel on the passenger side of the rental car. Two bullets had slammed into his back. Thomas stood behind him with a smoking revolver.

Conway slid off the car, and blood streaked the white vehicle. He tried to keep himself upright against the car but he didn't have the wind or strength. As he lost his balance and grip on the hood he fell and landed on his left side on the graveled road.

Thomas approached him with his gun focused on Conway's head. When he got to Conway, the sheriff was trying to bring air into his lungs. He took a couple more quick deep breaths and then he let out a long sigh.

Conway was gone.

Good. Thomas thought.

Good.

By this time Kilcrop was transforming into what he really is. A Demon of Babrik, which is the highest kingdom in the Third Sphere Underworld. The thing that posed as Mr. Kilcrop was hissing like a snake and panicking. His fretful face had turned bile green and some of his face flesh had melted onto the floor. He was slowly reversing into his true horrid form. Claws burst from beneath his fingernails popping the nails off one by one. The claws were yellow at the hand but red as they came to a point. Two large humps burst through the white shirt and black suit coat he was wearing. His neck grew and his jaw jutted forward. The bottom jaw came out slightly further than the top, creating an under bite. Large jagged teeth broke through his jaw line and all the previous mans teeth fell to the floor, the teeth he didn't swallow that is. The ones he didn't started dissolving into a puss-like liquid on the floor. Where his eyeteeth were, fangs became present. Short green spikes ran down his spine. His feet burst out from his dress shoes and he welcomed the pain. A small yellow claw grew from his heel. Claws came forth from his toes like the fingernails. They popped like kettle corn from what used to be his man feet. He ripped the remaining clothes that hadn't been tore through and tossed them aside. Kilcrop knew his situation was hopeless and he sought to get away. This is like all men who have held position of dominance and had fallen on total defeat. When the state of affairs have made a turn for the worst, they become craven, which is what they really are. They seek to escape. And when that is no longer possible they will take the prize so no one else can have it. Kilcrop cleverly looked about to see about his get away. He put a hand on the outside of the mausoleum and peered out. His claws were gripping the metal frame in the doorway and Thomas could see his features. Thomas knew his real figure and he shrunk back in horror. He wasn't sure if his eyes were playing tricks on him because he was under so much duress.

Jonas was on the ground trying to get up his strength for the ensuing firefight. He couldn't believe he had been hit. He hadn't been in a long time. In fact he couldn't remember when. The bracelets were supposed to ward off all harm. It seems like the consequences for his actions were already taking effect. Oh well he thought. It is what it is. Jonas was trying to put a defense strategy together to secure Thomas' get away.

Then Kilcrop's head and upper body came slowly forward out of the shadows and Thomas saw his total true nature. He was mortified. He still couldn't register what his eyes were telling him and he couldn't speak. What is this ghastly creature? My eyes aren't succumbing to the pressures of my situation are they? Or is he really a ghoul after all.

Kilcrop looked at Thomas and was about to strike him, like a cobra does when its territory has been breached. Then he saw Jonas' bracelets begin to light up. Kilcrop had seen these relics before in Stalingrad sixty years ago. At this, Kilcrop shrunk back, hissed his annoyance and bolted off.

He ran like an ape does, using his front arms to pivot and move upon the ground. He pivoted with his arms then he swung his lower body forward. He did this over and over and disappeared from sight very quickly.

Kilcrop knew where he would go.

Thomas turned back to Jonas who was dripping blood about the ground from his hip and shoulder. At least they're not really bad wounds like a gut shot Jonas thought. Thomas tried to say something but couldn't find the words.

He clutched the bark from the apple tree in his left hand and his vision went fuzzy. What do I do? Where will Kilcrop go now? How do I fight him?

He just stared into nothingness.

The sirens were very close now.

8:05 a.m.

Mr. Abrams pulled up to the county ward for the mentally unfit in his Ford Focus with Barbara Downtrodder. He had a hard time convincing Barbara to let him see her daughter, Penny. He told her it was to help Penny out of her state of immobility. He thought that he had something that might break her silence. He hoped he was right but in the back of his mind knew it was probably futile. Needless to say, he would do something even if it were wrong. He was loath to stand inactive. Barbara still clung to hope that her daughter could be saved from the perpetual silence. So she let herself believe Mr. Abrams was the way to her salvation.

They entered the ward through the automatic doors and walked across the lobby to the information/registration desk. The ward was quiet this morning and not many visitors were about.

"Hi Mrs. Downtrodder." The young woman behind the desk said.

Her nametag said June. Just the first name was on it. This was the new administrators way of getting to know everyone on a first name basis. He felt that this would open up the doors of communication and it would allow the employees to share their trust in one another. So far it still hadn't produced much difference. People still seemed to want to keep their personal lives personal.

June gave Abrams and Barbara visitor nametags to stick on their chests before they went off to see Penny. Then she called for a nurse to assist them to Penny's room.

Donna, the nurse assigned to look after Penny, came through the computer locked double doors leading to the housing units. Donna accompanied them to Penny's room. When they got to Penny's room she called the main desk over her two-way radio attached to her shoulder and spoke into it. The two technicians running the doors could see the nurse through the video monitors next to each door.

"Open room 212 for visitation. Two visitors, one male and a female." The woman said.

"Opening room 212." One of the techs called back.

The door latch clicked and the nurse manually slid the now opened door the rest of the way along the metal runners.

"I'll be back in twenty minutes to check on you." The nurse informed them.

"Okay." Replied Barbara.

Mr. Abrams and Barbara Downtrodder went in and the nurse shut the sliding door behind them.

Penny was sitting upon her bed. She had tubes and wires attached to her.

There was a monitor for her heart and brain activity. She had two I.V. in her arms. One was for sustenance, the other for sedatives and psyche medication.

Penny's mother approached her slowly and sat in the chair next to the monitor. Barbara looked at the monitor and had a touch of sadness. She always did when she thought about what her daughter had become. A girl stripped of life's wonders and trials. It just wasn't fair. She blamed herself for this and often went home in a deep state of depression and anxiety. This is the reason for her hesitation for coming here today but Mr. Abrams was adamant that he had something she must see. Who knows?

Maybe just maybe…

"Hi honey, it's mommy." Barbara said.

No response.

Penny just went on staring into the void.

"Honey this is Mr. Abrams. He has some pictures he wants to show you, okay." Barbara finished.

She waited for a response, but none came, as she well knew.

She looked at Mr. Abrams as if to say it's no use, why bother.

"It's worth a try." He said in response to her look of dismay.

Barbara just shrugged her shoulders and got up from where she sat. She crossed the room and took another seat in a metal chair against the wall, which faced the sliding metal door that kept Penny.

"Penny, I have some pictures here. I want you to tell me if you recognize the man in the photos." He explained.

He took the clearest photo of Kilcrop, the one with He and Joseph Stalin, from his pocket and held it in front of Penny.

Nothing.

Penny continued to gaze out towards the wall into negation. She was totally catatonic. Abrams moved it around in front of her, to try to get it in line with her vision. Still she was mute and still.

Nothing.

He did this with the other pictures too and she still did not respond. He was about to give up with the last picture when suddenly she broke her silence. Mr. Abrams and Barbara were startled with her unexpected return from the void. She grabbed the photo from his hand and jumped up on the bed. She ripped the wires and I.V. out of her arms. She began to jump back and forth like an irate baboon.

"He's a bad man. He's a bad man. He's a bad man. He's a bad man." She said over and over.

She tossed the photo like one does a baseball card when playing knock down keep 'ems. Then she reached down and picked up her pillow. She was bouncing up and down on her bed now. She had the pillow over her head and continued shouting.

"He's a bad man. He's a bad man." She went on.

She brought the pillow to her mouth and bit into it. She pulled and ripped back with her clenched teeth, tearing through the pillowcase cover and into the fluff in the pillows interior. Feathers and down went all about, snowing down on the floor.

"It's raining it's snowing the old man is blowing... Blowing? Blowing his brains out." Penny sang jumping up and down.

Barbara tried to get Penny down from the bed but Penny just smacked her mother's hand away.

"He's a bad man." She continued. "He's a bad man."

Barbara finally grabbed Penny and pulled her down from her perch on the bed. Penny stood on the cold floor with bare feet and finally began to feel the environment around her. She shivered. Then Penny started to freak out.

She began hitting her mother, Barbara, with her fists on the chest. Barbara put her arms around her and hugged her daughter tight.

"SHHHH. SHHHH. It's okay Penny. It's okay." Barbara cooed.

Penny lost her energy quickly and fell against her mother. She began to cry.

Barbara looked at Mr. Abrams and was overjoyed. She couldn't tell him in words what he had done for her. She had the beginnings of the conspiracy to which Burn Kilcrop was responsible but now wasn't the time for her to be thinking about that. She was just happy to have her Penny back and hell would frost over before she put anything before Penny as a priority again.

The first part of Abrams planned had worked. He was about to find out if the second part would evolve in time enough to spare his town from chaos.

8:10a.m.

"Thomas you must take Mary and get somewhere safe." Jonas commanded.

"I'm going to stay with you and fight." Thomas argued.

Thomas' mind was set on loosing his frustration, he wasn't thinking of the big picture. He wanted to inflict pain on those that would come to hurt his friends.

Maturity and experience help you grasp a broader view of circumstances.

That is not to say that young peoples ideals and intentions aren't decent or righteous, because they certainly are. It's just that when we age we become wiser and more tactful. We're not as rash and crass as we once were, and certainly we're not as invincible. Although confidence in thinking one is invincible can be both a positive and negative attribute in a person. A person who has no fear can prove to be a formidable ally. It can also be their downfall.

Jonas would be proud to make his stand next to Thomas if the conditions were different. If he was on the battlefield with nowhere left to run he would clasp Thomas' hand and they would go over the wall together.

Here was this tenderfoot who had lost everything, and instead of run, he stands tall and challenges the oncoming danger. Jonas considered this a real commendable feat. He had seen this before. Boys, who were just off their mother's tit, were willing to give everything to help the rest of the family prevail. They held the door when the 'Death Storm' came. They stood tall under God in front of their loved one's and took the brunt of attack, so that their dearest could go free. He was first witness to greenhorns standing in the face of fire, just to give their families enough time to escape.

This was the most noble of sacrifices.

Nonetheless Thomas was the target and he must escape to defeat the enemy.

"Thomas you must escape in order to save Mary and destroy Kilcrop." Jonas insisted.

"How? How do I kill him? How do I kill that… thing?" He asked.

"Only you know, Thomas." Jonas said.

"But I…" Thomas started.

ANCIENT ARROWHEAD

The sirens were howling now.

Jonas pulled the Bracer's of Defense from his arms and made a silent gesture to Thomas to take them.

Thomas looked at the bracelets and had the first inkling that he may never see his friend again. He had a hunch that Jonas was about to give his life for him. This filled Thomas with an overwhelming sense of grief.

"I can't Jonas. I can't. You'll die. We can all get away." Thomas cried out.

Jonas felt a warm rush of pride. He told himself many years and too many season's ago he would never allow himself to become entangled in human emotions and fondness for another. He was mistaken. He had grown partial to Thomas and now it was time to say farewell. Jonas was not keen on long goodbyes.

He shoved the bracelets into the large holding pocket in the front belly pocket of Thomas' hooded sweatshirt.

"Go!" Jonas yelled.

Thomas was taken back by his blunt reprisal.

Jonas saw this and knew that he had to make Thomas understand very quickly that he must seek safe passage. Soon the hornets would be upon them and if he didn't get away all would be lost.

"Thomas the shit storm that is headed this way will destroy any chance of you saving Mary and probably her mother. Under different circumstances I would be proud to make a stand with you but this is not the way to victory this day. You must confront Kilcrop and overthrow him. Goodbye my friend." Jonas said holding out his hand in friendship.

Thomas held out his hand and Jonas grabbed it elbow deep. He took his other hand and laid it over the other.

"Thomas. The Russian's have a saying that I have over time come to appreciate. They say hold a friend with two hands." Jonas spoke these words with a garbled voice for he was getting choked up as well.

"God be with you Jonas." Thomas said, placing a hand on his shoulder with a tear-laden face.

"I think God's going to sit this one out kid." Jonas replied.

Thomas' face was starting to twist into a bawling fit and he turned away from Jonas before he was stricken with more heartache. He took off toward where Jonas said Mary was hiding. As he ran he heard the sirens getting very close. They will be upon him soon he thought. What will he do?

Jonas made his way to Sol's Bronco.

"Good the keys are still in it." Jonas said aloud.

Jonas got in and started it up. He put it in gear and drove about ten feet and angled it so it that the vehicle blocked any other's from coming in from this side. The road was narrow and there was a huge island of earth obstructing any vehicles from coming straight in at him. There were only two ways around the circle of the wooded area to the mausoleum courtyard for vehicles to approach. A force could come on foot through the pines and oaks but they would be without much cover and be directly in his firing line. They could not bring police squad cars through here so it would be an obstacle for his adversaries. The way Conway, Kilcrop and Thomas had arrived from the east side and the way Sol had approached in his old Bronco from the west were the only ways to approach by vehicle. Jonas had come in from the south through the wooded area and remembered thinking this would be a good place to bottleneck an opposing force. He opened the glove compartment and found Sol had extra magazine clips for the M1. Good. He took these and put them in his overcoat pockets. He threw the keys in his pocket as well.

Then he hopped out and heard the sirens were wailing now. They were probably already in the cemetery. He had but moments before he would have to engage them. He crawled underneath the front of the Bronco and pulled a grenade from his overcoat. He removed the tape. He wedged the fragmentation grenade between the engine block and the water hose from the antifreeze and water overflow reservoir. Then he carefully pulled the pin making damn sure the trigger gauge didn't pop. He crawled out from underneath Sol's former vehicle and ran to where Sol had fallen. He picked up the M1 and ran over to Conway's former rental. He threw the M1 in on the front seat and hopped in. He knew Conway would have left his keys in the ignition. For who would risk the theft of a sheriff's car, rental or not? People of authority and position always feel like they're exempt from the mischief of others. Jonas pulled the white Crown Victoria into a position mimicking Sol's Bronco. Unfortunately he did not have time to arm it with an explosive. They would momentarily be present and be itching for a fight. He grabbed the M1 and the keys from the ignition and bolted to his battle station.

Thomas spotted Mary holding a boy by the hand near a large Maple tree. The young lad was crying fitfully and holding his ears.

Jasper limped behind him. Mary saw Jasper and screamed. Jasper hobbled up to her and he let out a whine. Thomas cried out, because he had not seen Jasper until now.

"Jasper. Oh Jasper." Mary cried.

Thomas put his arm around him and squeezed the dog hard.

"Come on." Thomas said.

"Where?" Mary asked.

"To kill Kilcrop. That's where." Thomas claimed positively.

The group of them split off from the trail leading to the hill in the rear of the cemetery. They made a new path towards the east side of the cemetery. From there they would go back to Woodland St.

and make their way through the swamp and onto the pricker patch. It wasn't as fast going as Thomas would have liked but Jasper was hurt and he didn't even consider leaving him behind. With any luck Jonas would keep the authorities busy.

Jonas trudged on to his hidden munitions.

Let them come.

Jonas thought about what his mother had told him about death and the great change. He wondered if he would be allowed to make that journey now that he had broken his covenant. He shook off the worry and set his mind for combat.

CHAPTER THIRTEEN

The shootout major

Jonas arrived at the spot where Mary and Jasper were waiting, when this fiasco started. He tried to steel himself against the lingering pain. He had lost a considerable amount of blood but so was the way of the warrior.

He began taking out his arsenal of weapons and he laid them about for easy access. The 'Authority Brass' had no idea the brawl they were about to engage in. He was about to show this quaint little town, what an army of one, was really all about. Nothing is more dangerous than a wounded animal. Put that animal in a corner or make it believe that there is no escape and you have ferocity squared.

Jonas had served in two Civil Wars, on two different continents. He had worn the uniforms of three nations in the two World Wars. He fought in Korea, Cambodia, Laos, and Somalia. Several other nations have memories of him in song and praise also, but I won't bore you with the details.

He had seen it all. He had the distinct advantage of knowing battle tactics. And because he would, no doubt be greatly outnumbered, he needed this advantage.

He knew he could not win this fight, but that was not important.

He needed only to give Thomas the means of escape and time to solve the riddle of destroying Kilcrop. Like in most battles of war, oftentimes men must sacrifice themselves so that the main force can rearm and regroup. Time enough to make a bonified rebound, lest all be lost. That the main body survives is the key element to any conflict.

Things happen in war that no one plans for and it is the split-second decisions made by those in the trenches that determine the outcome. Sometimes making the wrong decision is better than not making one at all. The troops serving under a man who is terrible under pressure will not follow him into death's fray. A man who is calm and focused will get the unit's full approval, and they will never second-guess him, even unto their demise.

Three quarters of a mile away Thomas, Mary, Jasper and the little boy sat huddled together on the wet ground in the pricker patch. It was no easy means to get here unnoticed but Thomas figured that the calling all cars request the former sheriff put in had the troops full attention.

The boy was sniffling and Mary was trying to comfort him.

"There, there. It's okay. Everything is going to be all right." Mary said softly.

Mary said these word's of encouragement but she only half believed them.

Jasper was licking the wounds he had sustained in the bout with Helyza, the boar bitch. He was hurt bad but he didn't display much discomfort. He knew there was still trouble and he tried to concentrate on healing.

Thomas looked down at his shaking hands. One was holding the ivory handled revolver and the other the bane of his mother's existence.

The walls started closing in around him.

Hard to breath.

Can't concentrate.

Panic.

The feeling a person gets when they are trapped in a compartment of a capsized boat.

Desperation.

Dread.

And then… a glimmer of light and hope enters the back of the mind.

An idea was taking shape in Thomas' consciousness.

A seed had taken hold and began to borough down into the soft spring soil of his mind. It started to germinate. Deeper and deeper it dug into the fertile ground, sprouting in all directions. The roots were branching out and taking a firm hold in his being.

The grand design came to him.

He knew what he must do.

He whispered to Mary and ran off.

Mr. Abrams rang the desk from Penny's room and then began banging on the door.

The female nurse came running to the door to identify the problem. She was accompanied by, two male assistants. When she arrived at room 212 she radioed to have it opened and she rushed in.

The woman had mustard smeared across the side of her face, as if she had been in the middle of a ham sandwich, when she heard the alarm.

"What's the …" She started and then saw Penny crying against her mother.

Mr. Abrams went out to the lobby and asked the woman behind the check out desk to use the phone. This desk was opposite the information/registration desk that June was previously at but that station was empty. Mr. Abrams figured she was out for break and approached this station instead.

"I'm sorry sir this phone is for emergencies and ward business only." The woman said.

The woman went back to her conversation like Mr. Abrams didn't even exist.

"Well I told Maurice if he kept up with that ho' I'd throw his ass out." She huffed to her friend over the phone.

Mr. Abrams grabbed the phone from her and spoke to the person on the line.

"She'll have to call you back." Mr. Abrams hollered in the receiver and then slammed the phone down. He picked it back up and put it to his ear.

"You can't use that phone I said." The irate woman complained.

"I'm not asking." He said flat.

"Well I never." She shot back.

"You can call Shanequa back when I'm finish with real business." He shot back.

"Oh no you didn't." The woman responded waving her finger back and forth in front of his face.

"Young lady if you don't cool it I'm going shove this phone up your nose." He said passionately.

"I'm calling security." She replied.

She was about to call the administrator and security when she heard his intentions.

"Yes operator, I would like FBI dispatch in Boston." Mr. Abrams stated.

The woman sat back in her chair and listened intently.

"FBI dispatch, how can I help you?" The voice came back.

"Please direct me to Special Agent Donald Savor." Mr. Abrams said.

"One moment please." The operator responded.

It seemed like a lifetime ago that Abrams and Savor had last conversed.

They had last met twelve years ago in a small tavern in Lodi, New Jersey. They talked about the 'unit' and their time served in the jungle. Abrams thought about those times often, and still had the nightmares to go along with those memories.

He recalled the fear and desperation in the tropical forest.

Jungle fever.

Always hungry, always scared, always wet and forever tired.

He had seen his mates, who were just boys then, arms blown off, eyes torn out, and their minds destroyed. Only to come back home, after giving everything, to find a country non grata. These were hard times to reflect on for Abrams and for all the men who came back from that 'conflict.'

The only thing Abrams was sure of nowadays was, only the men who carried the scars of war had the right to speak of the necessity for it. For they alone know what a person has to give. They know the immorality of warfare, and they will not needlessly send youngsters into the fray without just cause.

Abrams had saved Savor's life at least once, in the Tiger Army. He thought back about it while waiting for his old friend to connect. Their ten-man company had walked into an ambush. The man taking point, two positions away from Savor, had tripped a wire booby trap. He was blown into pieces. The next man was mortally wounded. Savor had taken shrapnel in the face and shoulder. Then he had taken a bullet in the thigh and lower leg from enemy positions. Abrams picked him up and threw him over his shoulders. Abrams, Savor, a young man named Boyer and a kid named Cesar, were the only ones to make it back to base. The others were listed as M.I.A. They never made it back to the Red, White and Blue. Their names still hold a place on the Memorial wall. Abrams carried Savor two miles through the dense rain forest, and back to safety. Boyer and Cesar had to keep stopping to hold off the enemy long enough, so they could safely maneuver. Stick and move, stick and move all the back to command post. The only reason they were not overrun was for the rain. It came down in buckets upon their retreat. This ultimately saved their lives.

So now, all these years later, Abrams felt like Savor would find it prudent to help him.

"Special Agent Savor speaking." Came the voice through the receiver.

"Savor, It's Abrams." He said.

"I don't suppose this is a social call." Savor responded.

"No. I need your help." Abrams called back.

Burn Kilcrop had gone through stage one and two of defeat since the debacle at the mausoleum.

Stage one is denial. Like all men who have held dominion over others they are reluctant to give up that post. They are the last to admit defeat. Stage two is to save their selves, and run like the cowards they are. Stage three is the place where, through desperation, if they can't have it, no one can.

Kilcrop knew his time on this plane was up, but he would salvage his right to the girl. He would not leave without her. He was determined to take her as his partner. If he couldn't, he would make sure Thomas wouldn't have her either. He would destroy her or the purity within her causing Thomas to turn away in disgust. If he couldn't take her he would make certain Thomas never wanted her again. This thought made Kilcrop grin.

That's what he would do. He would violate her so that, Thomas, would be repulsed by the sight of her.

He would go to the place that would cause them to come to him.

Mary and Brenda's house it would be.

When Jerry Collins heard the desperate dispatch from Sheriff Conway he pulled out all the stops.

He didn't know about Conway's involvement in this farce. If he had known of Conway's deceit, then the hostile situation that was about to unfold would never have been. The combative reality of this circumstance was evolving into something now that could not be avoided.

And Jonas was about to bring that reality to bear right down on Jerry's head.

Jerry called the State Police, who sent a S.W.A.T. team and several units with K-9 squads attached. The State Police referred the call onto the State Department. That in turn dispatched a team of U.S. Marshals who were fully equipped with helicopters, Armored Cars and Buses. The U.S. Marshals then turned the response over to the military, which initiated an Army Reserve unit.

Special Agent Savor arrived to greet Abrams by helicopter.

Abrams told Savor about as much as Abrams thought he could handle. He told Savor about Kilcrop's involvement with the Gladberry homicides and the nursing home murders. He also told him about the Morgan's mysterious deaths and maybe the involvement of Sheriff Conway.

Savor showed up with many agents under his command and began reiterating his orders. He had already told them about the phases that they were going to undertake on the way over but Savors was a guy that would second and third check everything. Let's get it right, was his attitude. He broke the agents up into two teams. One was deployed to secure Penny in witness protection, and the other larger team was to go with Savor to try and prevent WWIII.

Savor, Abrams and the larger second team of agents raced off to the little powder keg that had spent too much time in the sun.

They were too late.

The fight for the right to Cemetery Hill was underway.

Jonas had dug out the Army duffel bags and was diligently preparing for the Little Big Battle for Central Massachusetts.

He laid out his armament in a fashion that suited easy handling and fast reaction time. He removed his overcoat and placed it back in the duffle bag. He placed the shotgun holster over his Kevlar vest. He took the 'Bible' and put it in the front of his pants. He arranged the grenades to the left and to the right of his kneeling person. He had three or four still attached to his chest. The electrical tape was removed from them. His shotgun was loaded and he placed it back in the holster on his back. The Ak74's were loaded and ready to go. He placed one in the position behind him on the backside of the hill to thwart a flank maneuver, which he knew was inevitable. Next to it he placed one of the loaded Desert Eagles. The other was fully loaded and in his hip holster. Against a tree to the left of his position at the large rock he leaned the M1. He put the extra clips from Sol's glove compartment next to the rifle. He had a gas mask around his neck.

The Local and State Police units were pulling up one by one. Two Fire engines and EMT teams had also arrived. The rescue teams tried to aid the fallen men, Conway and Sol, but they were too late. One team of EMT personnel, body bagged the dead men and made off to the coroner's. Jonas would not fire at aid workers or medics so he allowed them ample time to escape the scene.

The K-9 units were out searching for the trail of the wrongdoers. They came to the location where Jonas and the others parted ways. They were confused. One team wanted to go one way, the other team of dog and officer, pulled to go the other.

This is when Jonas unleashed the pain.

He pulled his black leather gloves tight over his blistered and often broken fingers.

He had the assault rifles on three burst increments.

Tat! Tat! Tat!

Bullets screamed out to take their abuse.

Tat! Tat! Tat!

Both dogs went down. The officer holding the lead dog took a round in the lower part of the chest and one in the groin. The other officer in charge of the K-9 was not so lucky. He took a bullet through the left eye socket. He was killed on contact. His body fell lifeless to the ground.

Tat! Tat! Tat!

Officers went scurrying for cover, some behind their vehicles, others behind trees or culverts. Not before two more were killed and another injured.

Jonas was all too accurate, and the three bullet bursts hit home more than not. Bullets were coming his way now, although not with much accuracy. He kept returning fire to keep them pinned down.

Then the S.W.A.T. team showed up. The SWAT leader approached and asked an officer who was in charge. The officer pointed to Jerry, the Deputy Sheriff, and Bill, a State Police Lieutenant.

"I'm Lieutenant Censnot. What we got here?" The SWAT leader asked.

"We have at least one nut with automatic weapons and possibly some explosives." Jerry yelled over the gunfire.

"Whose vehicles are these blocking us out back here? Why aren't they out of the way?" The SWAT leader asked.

"Because he knows what he's doing Lieutenant. This man is ex military, a rogue and/or a mercenary. Either way he had a plan of attack before we arrived." State Police Lieutenant Bill replied.

"Well, they need to be removed." The SWAT Leader announced.

He called in to the local police dispatch on Jerry's radio and told them to dispatch a tow truck detail to the scene.

"You sure that's wise?" Jerry asked.

"I know what I'm doing Sheriff." The SWAT leader responded arrogantly.

"Okay." Jerry answered unsure of this approach.

Jonas released a smoke grenade and the battlefield grew dense with smoke, making visibility impossible. Shots became sporadic from the law enforcement side because they were not used to this kind of operation. Soon the smoke began to clear and all hell came loose.

Jonas whipped a fragmentation grenade and it exploded a few feet from a local policeman blowing his left arm off and throwing shrapnel into his rib section and shoulder.

Jonas started in now with the M1. He had crawled over to the huge oak tree when the smoke was dense and readied himself from his new position ten feet away from the old. Jonas started picking off Officers one by one. He hadn't used the sturdy M1 in many years but remembered why he liked it so much. He felt then and still did today that it was the most reliable and accurate weapon ever produced. One officer took a round in the chest and another through the cheek. One by one the positions were falling back or dead.

The SWAT leader decided it was time they broke into teams.

"I disagree Lieutenant. I think we should pull our men back and come up with a plan of attack now that we know what we're up against." Bill, the State Trooper commented.

"Nonsense. We attack now simultaneously from different angles and we overrun him." The SWAT leader fired back.

Jerry and Bill looked at one another and knew it was foolish.

"Hey your in charge." Bill said.

The SWAT leader took his men and told them the strategy. The officers already deployed were to remain in their positions. As soon as both SWAT teams were 'GO" they would all open fire keeping the man or men pinned down.

They split into two teams. One engaged Jonas straight- forward, the other went in a flanking maneuver down onto the train tracks.

Jonas saw this flanking move and crawled from the tree to the large rock. From there he crawled to the edge of the hill over looking the train tracks. He saw the men trying to get a foothold on the hill and make a rush attempt at his position. He dropped two grenades right on top of them. The front two men were totally annihilated, blown into bits smaller than a half dollar. One man behind them lost a leg and shrapnel took the sight of his left eye. Two more were injured in the blasts and it had the desired effect. They pulled the wounded back and retreated. The team that had come forward to engage him was less than twenty feet from his location.

Jonas put up his gas mask and threw out two smoke grenades closer this time to his position so it required the mask. The S.W.A.T. team was not prepared for this tactic and they stopped dead. Bullets screamed through the smoke hitting one man in the chin and another in the chest through the right lung. The bullets were passing through the armored vests the paramilitary force was wearing. This is because Jonas had made each bullet by hand using a special alloy of metals.

The others returned fire into the black smoke without any results.

Jonas tossed another grenade and it fell amongst three men huddled behind a large oak. The blast tore a medium size birch tree from the earth and it fell over on top of another man ten feet away. He was momentarily pinned. Under the conditions he elected to stay put as if seriously wounded. The three men using the oak tree as cover were obliterated.

A tow truck had pulled up during this melee that the SWAT leader had dispatched to remove the vehicles that were bottle necking their means of an all out assault.

The SWAT leader told the man to hurry and briefly explained the scenario to him. The tow truck pulled up to Sol's Bronco, turned around and backed the front end of the tow bars under his utility vehicle. As he began to raise it up the law enforcement concertedly opened fire on Jonas giving covering fire to the tow truck and its driver.

Three.

Two.

One.

KAAAABAAAAAAAAAAAAAAAANNNNNNNNG!!!!!!

The fragmentation grenade had fallen from its place between the engine and the hose and clinked on the ground. No one heard it under the massive onslaught of gunfire.

KAAAAAAABOOOOOOOOOOOMMMMMMM!!!!!!

The tow truck exploded seconds after the grenade. The tow truck driver had just gassed up before being routed to the cemetery. He was bringing back some gasoline in a five- gallon container for the snow blower he had just got running at his shop. He was preparing for the long hard winter Farmer's Almanac had predicted for this upcoming season. This gasoline just added to the blast. Several police vehicles were now ablaze.

KAAAAAAABOOOOOOOOOOOMMMMMMM!!!!!!

Another car came several feet off the ground exploding. The original detonation had proven more effective than Jonas had hoped.

Hot metal and shrapnel flew in all directions from these discharges. The amount of cadavers and wounded in these blasts is often speculated. Every time the number increases, but the way I heard it from a eye witnessed account was that, the SWAT leader, the State Police Lieutenant and two Berlin Policemen all lost their lives. A Sterling Officer and Four Local Police from town were seriously injured. One of these men a few days later would die of his injuries.

More sirens were present in the background. Fire Engines and more EMTS were racing to the fight. Jonas diverted his attention away from those sounds and listened carefully.

Helicopters.

Jonas thought he heard helicopters.

The U.S. Marshall's pulled up to see these explosions and pure chaos about the ranks of law enforcement.

Acting Sheriff Jerry Collins was shell-shocked. The only reason he wasn't killed is because he had gone and pulled a wounded man from a culvert fifteen feet from the explosions. When the detonations occurred he was in sort of a gully so the blast fragments and metal shot over his head. He stayed down for a time and then pulled the officer back beyond the smoking vehicles. Luckily for Jerry, Jonas doesn't shoot the wounded or soldiers in the back, which are retreating.

This had better be brought under control thought the Lieutenant of U.S. Marshall team, and soon because this untenable situation was turning into a nightmare.

This team leader for the U.S. Marshall's had just walked into a major cluster fuck. He tried to get some semblance of order but it was very difficult. It looked like when he was in Lebanon in 1982, when his and two other unofficial SF groups helped aid Israel occupy the country. The civil war fighting in that country was bitter.

He looked around him and grabbed Jerry and proceeded to inquire about the situation they were in and asked for some input on what they might be facing for opposition. He needed to gather enough information to make a necessary strategy to overcome this fight.

"There's only one guy?" He said in response to Jerry's paranoid speech.

"Yes." Jerry replied in extreme concern.

Some State police had taken a route around the mausoleum to flank Jonas on the left. He tossed a grenade as far as he could toward their group. It didn't hit target but it was enough to warn them to back off.

While all this was going on, the youngest member of the SWAT team, a real Boy Scout trying terribly hard to make his bones, crawled up to the rock Jonas was using as a barrier.

He popped up and put two slugs in Jonas. One hit Jonas just below the kidney on his right hip and the other in the right shoulder.

Before the rookie could gloat, Jonas spun on him with the Desert Eagle and took the left side of his head off. His brains were hanging into his jaw area when he fell to the ground.

Sensing Jonas was mortally wounded the members of the police forces began closing in from all directions.

He fired wildly into their clustered groups, hitting only one and they returned heavy fire.

Jonas had to escape.

The Apache Helicopter was overhead now and Jonas reached down and grabbed the Ak74 he had left at the back of the hill in case of a flank maneuver or need to retreat.

He lit off the last smoke grenade and made for the train tracks. He had to reach the cover of the warehouse if he were to continue this fight.

He fired at the Apache and put holes in the side from the fuselage all the way to the open cabin wounding the sniper who was about to finish Jonas off. The helicopter veered off to get out of harm's way. The pilot would come around for another approach. The pilot realizing that a team member was wounded called in the injury report and was ordered to bring the injured man to Umass hospital. He was informed that another helicopter was already nearby and would join the battle in his stead.

Jonas had one thought. He needed get to the cover of the warehouse building. There he would regroup. There, he would unleash the Panzerschreck. Then they would know what real pain was.

He slid on his butt down the steep embankment; he stumbled over the train tracks and slid down the rail rock down to the fence dividing the tracks from the warehouse district. His vision was blurry and his balance was off.

Bullets were whipping by him now. He struggled up the fence and fell over the other side. A bullet found him on the calf.

He limped to the basement window and slid through, all the while bullets were ricocheting off the brick walls to the warehouse, and fence behind him.

PING! PING! PANG!

Jonas opened the basement window with his left hand and fell to his knees. He crawled through and tried to spin his body around to leverage himself and then jump the five feet to the floor without getting shot in the back. He slipped off the narrow ledge and fell. Jonas fell to the cement floor with a thud, landing on his shoulder. Pain seared through his body. He had separated his left shoulder and broke his left wrist in two places. He cried out in agony. The pain was overtaking his ability to concentrate. He slowly got to his feet and moved the workbench that was hiding his baby. His vision was almost gone and he couldn't remember what he was doing. Then he recalled his time in Tibet.

Concentrate.

Empty your mind.

There is no pain you are receding.

TEN. NINE. EIGHT. SEVEN. SIX. FIVE. FOUR. THREE. TWO. ONE.

A calm ocean.

A blue sky.

You are Jonas Lightbringer.

He opened his eyes and he contemplated his situation. He took in his surroundings. It was clear again. He knew he must go on, just a little while longer. I will defy. He kept a fire inside burning so he could unfold his final heroic act. He would deliver as many of his adversaries into the abyss as he could. Keep their focus on you, Jonas thought. Thomas must have time to achieve the desired outcome.

He pulled the floor drain up with the rebar in his right hand and tossed it aside. He grabbed the rocket launcher and put it aside. He opened the green box beneath it. He did all this with his right hand. His left was almost useless. He took three rockets from it. He took the rockets and grenade gun and went to the dilapidated stairwell near the front entrance. He carried the rockets in his right hand and against his body. The rocket launcher he held underneath his left armpit and he crossed his right arm over his stomach and rested the end of the rocket launcher on his right wrist.

PAIN.

It pulled on his shoulder muscles, but he steeled himself against the hurt. Before he ascended the stairs he remembered his book. He turned around and put the rocket launcher down. He pulled the 'Bible' from his pants and placed it in the floor drain and slid it in under the cement so it could not be seen. Hopefully he thought the right person would find it. Besides who could read it anyway?

He picked up the Panzerschreck once more through stark pain and ascended the stairs cautiously to the second floor and then the third. As he was about to get to third floor the old staircase started to creak and groan. He jumped the last two steps to safety. The stairs fell down with a crash three floors below.

"Well at least no one will follow me up here." Jonas said aloud with a short sarcastic laugh.

Jonas went to the broken window facing his enemy.

He leaned each rocket against the wall and loaded the grenade launcher. Then he fell against the wall and slid down on his butt to take a much-needed breather. He spit up blood on the dirty floor between his legs.

He had wounds all over his body now and he knew that his end was near. This is it he thought. All those scuffles and brawls he had been in before and now he would die in this little town in the boondocks.

He knew why too. He had broken the covenant. He wasn't supposed to get involved with the boy in the mausoleum. No matter he thought. What's done is done, and he would do it again.

Bullets had ceased now, and he knew it was time to finish it.

A quarter of a mile away, two sniper teams had taken up positions in desperate search for the culprit. One two-man team was located on the top of the D.P.W. building southwest of Jonas. The other was southeast atop the Supernaut Wire building.

Both were seeking out his whereabouts. They had a secret wager. Whichever team killed the terrorist, the others owed them two hundred quid. Both teams were anxious to find and terminate him.

Jonas stood up and leaned against the wall for support. He spit up blood. He bent over and vomited, mostly blood but some bile as well. Then he steadied himself.

He slid the Panzershreck through the busted window.

A group of officers were slowly making the descent down the dirt hill to the train-tracks. It would be their last effort in this life. When they got to the bottom of the hill they fell about the liquid mess that was the SWAT team before they were annihilated. They saw Jonas' footmarks in the gooey mess. One officer puked and another just walked off in a daze. Two more kept on the path to the warehouse. They would not make it.

SWISHHHHHHHKABOOOOOOM!

Fragments of person and metal flew all about. There was a giant hole at the bottom of the hill. Dirt and other soil debris were littered about the mess the rocket made of the men.

He reloaded, aimed and fired.

SWISHHHHHHHKABOOOOOOM!

Two police cars in the rear of the cemetery spit metal and burst into fire.

Just then a helicopter flew overhead.

Reload. Aim. Fire.

Jonas put the helicopter in sight and let the Panzershreck feast again.

SWISHHHHHHHKABOOOOOOM!

He hit the rotor and the metal bird fell from the sky like a boulder.

Before Jonas could witness the impact of the falling copter, a bullet rang out from the D.P.W. rooftop. It hit Jonas between the eyes. Jonas slumped to the floor.

Confusion.

Quiet.

Rest.

The Lord looked down on Jonas and saw his plight. He wasn't angry with him like Jonas believed, but the contrary. He was content. He saw Jonas sacrifice himself for the good of an innocent, and nothing pleased the Lord more. The Lord may be strict with discipline but He is also kind and forgiving. He puts these rules in place to test men and their convictions. Jonas had passed this test.

As Jonas lay upon the ground awaiting Judgment, gold stardust started to fall from the sky. These supernova gold trails passed through the warehouse ceiling and fell all about Jonas.

Jonas felt as though he were sunning himself on the beach. A soft tickle was running through his body. He was transformed. His spirit left this place to begin a new journey.

Metamorphosis.

Change.

Rebirth.

Now because of the firefight on the other side of town, all units had been dispatched to the cemetery. Including the unit sent for surveillance of the Morgan home.

Thomas saw that there were no patrol cars present and went around the back of his house. Thomas had heard the 'War for Cemetery Hill' from his location at Mary's and the resonance followed him to his abode too. He worried for his friend Jonas and prayed that he would be safe. He had no idea the casualties that were piling up in the cemetery. He had no idea that his comrade was entering his finest and final hour. He pulled his mind back to the task at hand.

He took the key from under the dead potted plant on the back porch and opened the door. He went to his room and set about his project. He picked up the bow and quiver. He went into his old fishing tackle box and retrieved the arrowhead he had found many moons ago. He took out his old work boots and removed the thin strap lace from one of them. He took the hawk feather from the windowsill.

He left his room and walked down the narrow hall to his parent's room. He opened his father's drawer and moved the socks aside to find the pocket- knife his father used for fishing. He found it, picked it up and began his task. He put the bow and quiver down. He took the apple branch he'd been carrying from the wreck site and began carving at it. He went about this carefully. Slowly and meticulously he shaved at the wood. When he got it down to the right thickness, he went downstairs to the renovated pantry to find some sandpaper. He sanded it down to a proper finish. The stick was still in a small spiral but it was only about a half inch in diameter. The stick was still almost three feet long. He notched a little rut in the end for the Hawk's feather. He then went to the den to seek out the cement glue that he and his father used for their model collection. He located the glue and opened the small can. He dipped the end of the arrow stem in the quick drying cement. He closed up the cement can.

He looked about the room and surveyed the many projects that he and his father had accomplished. He looked at the P51 mustang that was half done and he had a moment of regret. He wished he had spent more time with his parent's, but he knew that feeling this now was futile. His mind was between remorse and vengeance.

"I will avenge you, I will avenge you both." He said all choked up.

He put the end recently dipped in cement glue, which was shaved into a tip, and inserted it in the little space at the end of arrowhead. Then he wrapped the bootstrap around it forming an 'X' around the arrowhead and stem branch for extra support. He put his homemade arrow in the quiver and set out to bring justice down on Kilcrop. He didn't have long to let the cement set and he hoped it would be long enough.

Now he would seek him out.

He set out to Mary's house, to collect her and find Kilcrop.

He was prepared to do battle,

"Oh Brenda. Brenda darling where are you?" Came the distorted voice from the foyer.

Brenda descended the stairs in a rush.

Kilcrop had called and said he was on his way, and that he had a surprise for her. He had a desperate voice, like that of a hungry animal, and she couldn't wait to see what he had in store.

She got all done up in makeup and put up her hair in a weave. She had skimpy underwear on and wore a green satin gown. She heard him in the foyer and thought. "Well he didn't even ring the bell, he must be after something sweet."

And she had the 'box of chocolates' for him.

Little did she know that he was after something salty instead.

She got to the corner of the foyer and froze. The terror she felt was so much that she peed herself.

Now today for autumn it was unusually warm. Especially where it was sleeting last night and the morning was quite cool. But because it was unseasonably warm now most windows in Mary's house were open. It seemed that the temperature had increased some twenty degrees in the past two hours.

Brenda screamed.

"AAAAAAAAAAAAAAHHHHHHHHHH!" She cried.

Mary who was in the pricker patch heard her mother's alarm.

Mary darted out of the pricker patch in route to her house. The boy, not wanting to be left behind, went after her. Jasper sensing trouble limped after her as well. As Mary approached the stairs on a run, Thomas saw her because he was coming up to her house from the street, like he did so many school days before.

Thomas saw Mary going into her house, and he saw Kilcrop's Town Car across the lawn.

"Mary stop!" Thomas screamed to no avail.

Mary ran into the house anyway through the two doors and into the foyer and on to the living room.

There in the center of the living area was the creature Kilcrop.

Mary was not afraid.

"I'm not afraid of you." She said.

"You will be." He hissed.

Mary's mother was hanging upside down from the chandelier. One leg was straight up towards the ceiling and the other was tied above the knee and attached to the ankle. Both of her arms were tied behind her back. Another rope went around her arms and waist, so she couldn't struggle. The gown she was wearing was down over her purple face. Kilcrop had pulled her gown down over her head before he tied her so that her naked body was exposed.

Kilcrop took his right hand and put his index claw over Brenda's belly and started an incision. He went about two inches and stopped.

Brenda didn't feel this at first because of the heat coming from Kilcrop's body. It was really the heat that made the incision not the nail. A burning heat was emanating from Kilcrop's person. His fury and want were becoming of him.

Brenda finally cried out in pain.

"AHHHHHHHHHHHHH!" Brenda screamed again.

The heat was intense enough to keep the wound from bleeding, like the incision started clotting soon after the opening was forced. Still her nerve endings were on fire and she let it be known.

"Mom!" Mary yelled.

"If you don't do as I say, I'll spill her bowels all over the floor." Kilcrop assured her.

When Brenda and Mary cried out Jasper went into instinct mode. He brought forth his second wind and all the energy he could muster and reacted. He climbed the eight stairs of Mary's porch in two leaps and crashed through the porch window. He was upon Kilcrop in two more. He dove into him without hesitation for he did not fear the sight of this foul creature.

Kilcrop screamed and emitted a frighteningly horrible sound. A sound, that would make a grizzly bear go impotent.

"RAAAAAAAAAAAAAAAAAAAAAAAAAAAAAAAAAR RRRRRRRR!!!" He howled.

Jasper grasped Kilcrop's left arm and wouldn't let go. Pain and distrust tried to overtake the dog through Kilcrop but he would not be swayed. Fire burned into Jaspers lips and gums and still he would not yield. All about the room you could smell burning dog flesh. Back and forth Kilcrop swung the dog but his bite was not to be undone. Finally after an exhausting tussle and desperate struggle Kilcrop managed to free his arm. Kilcrop swiped at Jaspers side and a deep gash opened up and this was enough to break the giant dog's hold on him. Kilcrop swung the dog and Jasper flew into the china cabinet with a smash, he fell limp to the floor. Broken dishes, glass and splintered wood fell with him about the floor. Jasper lay lifeless on the floor. He had given everything to give his master time to arrive and save Mary.

"So much for your fierce protector, Mary." He said. "Now where were we?" He asked.

"Let my mother and Jasper go and I'll do whatever you want." She said defeated.

"Doesn't look like Jasper is about to go anywhere." He said and kicked the spent dog. Kilcrop let out a ghastly chuckle and returned his attention to his new candidate for bride of the Third Sphere Underworld.

Without warning the bottom panel to the screen door came crashing in. Thomas kicked the door a second and third time. Then he ripped the door from its place, which was hanging about one fastener on the hinge after being brutalized by Thomas. The hanging door went flying behind Thomas as he strode through the door. Thomas walked through the foyer and stood at the entrance to the living room quarters. Never had Thomas' resolve been so strong. He looked at Kilcrop with a cold stare and spoke his mind.

"You're not going anywhere with my girl." Thomas announced.

Mary turned toward Thomas and Kilcrop seized the opportunity. He grabbed Mary and pulled her back to his place in the living room. Kilcrop was wearing a grin now and he told Thomas he was just too small a person to do anything about it. Mary was going with him and there was nothing to be done to the contrary.

"She's mine little boy. If you leave now and say goodbye to your ex girlfriend I'll spare your life. In fact I'll throw in Brenda too. How's that? Can't say I haven't been a good sport, eh Thomas." He said. Then began a laugh taunting Thomas.

He was trying to goad him into acceptance. Even though Kilcrop wanted to see this young man dead and buried he still felt an ounce of doubt. Thomas had marched right up to him and demanded he let his girl go. Kilcrop can't remember a time when someone had challenged him so. He put on like all was right and he had the upper hand but he wasn't as completely certain as he had been just days before.

"Well what say you boy?" Kilcrop demanded.

"Let her go, you foul beast. Let her go and I'll consider not killing you." Thomas commanded.

Kilcrop let out a long devilish laugh.

"Haaaaaa Haaaaaa Haaaaaa. Ha!" He went.

Thomas pulled the Bracer's of Defense out from his sweatshirt belly pocket and put them on. Immediately the Angel's started to emit that purple energy light.

Kilcrop hissed. He was so angry and frightened now that hot froth fell from his mouth and fell to the living room floor. When it landed there it sizzled like acid when it comes in contact with something tasty to devour. Mary pulled her legs out of the way at the last minute to avoid a most serious burn. Kilcrop's eyes turned a dark red like 'Black Death." He tried in vain to convince his rival to relent.

"You've lost this fight Thomas Morgan. I'm going to do things to her you never even thought one ever could." Kilcrop shouted.

Thomas' resolve could not be won over.

"I said be gone, creature from the netherworld. I cast thee down from this place, never to return. You are banished forth with from this planet and you may never return to the earth. Ever!" Thomas said defiantly and with the outmost authority.

This broke Kilcrop's patience. His face was a contorted twisted menace.

"You have no power over me!" Kilcrop grunted.

He belched out an awful stink like that of a dead stunk. This was his last gasp.

"Be gone." Thomas shouted.

"I'm taking her." Kilcrop said.

Kilcrop began speaking in a language of tongue not of this world.

Thomas took the arrow from his quiver and notched it in the bow. He let it fly.

"Be gone." Thomas barked again.

Kilcrop's face lit up as he saw the coup de grace being dealt. His body was suddenly visceral and the layers of his face were transparent. You could see the hollowness of his being. Underneath he was nothing but fluff and hot air. The red lava like color that was Kilcrop's life force flickered. A second before the arrow pierced his chest all the energy around his body imploded into him. Then as quickly as it sucked in, it burst out like a star does upon dying.

"NOOOOOOOOOOOOOOOOOOOO!" Kilcrop shouted in a far away voice.

Orange energy burst from Kilcrop's form and he was gone. When his form returned to its place of origin so too did the corpse of the boar bitch Helyza. Their union would be elsewhere and that's all that mattered.

Mary ran to Thomas and cried upon his shoulder.

Thomas did no crying.

He never would again.

CHAPTER FOURTEEN
Picking up the pieces

Picking up the pieces after a war is always the same, slow and tedious.

Oftentimes leaving more questions than answers. The sleepy town went about its business sweeping and rebuilding all that was destroyed and all that was brought to bear on it. Gossip in this politically driven town of favoritism and social bigotry was prevalent now more than ever.

Thomas buried his parent's in the local cemetery and many came to the funeral. Thomas buried the arrow and bow with his mother so she could have them to use as tools, which might protect her in the afterlife. He buried the P51D mustang fighter model with his father. He had spent a whole night finishing it with Mary.

Mr. Kilcrop was gone but the authorities had many questions to which Thomas could not answer. If he did the information was so outlandish as to be mistaken for fiction. If they did ask him to explain and he went on about the 'Principle from Hell' and 'Jonas' the military genius from another time they would get frustrated and tell him he was mistaken. Isn't it true that you belong to a cult and this man "Jonas' was your leader? Isn't that what happened? He refused to be taken alive and when confronted with the kidnapping of the boy for a bizarre ritual he killed Sheriff Conway. Right

Thomas? Thomas would just shake his head undeterred and tell them to ask Mr. Abrams or the young boy. When they collaborated his story the States Detectives just got more resolved and claimed that they were hypnotized under the spell of some mind control technique or drug. You expect us to believe that Kilcrop was a Demon and you sent him packing. What did you do you with him? I killed him Thomas would say. Where did you bury his remains? You murdered him Thomas didn't you. Back and forth they went until finally some men with more clearance came to rescue him from prosecution and ridicule.

Finally men in black sedans and eight hundred dollar suits arrived at the State Police Barracks. They forced their way into the detaining and interrogation rooms. You have no authority here said the State investigators. This is a Homicide investigation. Not anymore the men wearing suits and sunglasses returned. As far as you're concerned this never happened and showed their badges. Chairs and tables went flying about but needless to say Thomas was never questioned about it again.

NSA.

Or a division therein but I'll call them 'Secret Service' men for ease of conversation.

Thomas never thought he'd be so glad to hear three letters strung together as he was now.

They returned Thomas and Mary to the Morgan home. Bobby, Thomas' uncle had taken custody of the young man. He was surprised to see three black SUV's pull up in front of the house.

These 'Secret Service' men assured Thomas that he had allowed Kilcrop to escape and that he was now on the most wanted fugitive list. He was to say that Kilcrop was responsible for the 'hostilities' in the cemetery. Thomas feigned ignorance to the cemetery battle, even though they were sure he knew something.

Jonas' body was seized by these men and was taken to some hole in North Dakota that doesn't exist to be the subject of experiment and scientific scrutiny.

These men made it so that all charges against Thomas disappeared, so that no local authorities had any recourse. All formal charges from the nursing home murders, the train track shoot out and the Gladberry homicides were laid against Kilcrop. The 'Secret Service' men assured him, that if he were to go to the tabloids with this ridiculous story, they would make life very unpleasant for him and his uncle. Thomas didn't care. He was glad it was over, for he didn't want anymore to do with this. He just wanted it behind him.

So that was that. Thomas didn't really care for attention or fame anyway and he avoided talking to the press or nosy people every chance he could. When they did corner him, he would just play dumb. They didn't really have anywhere to go because he didn't give them anything to pursue. So they made up their own wild stories.

Anyway, Penny Downtrodder integrated back into society, slowly, but eventually she put the nightmare behind her one day at a time. Barbara Downtrodder called on Mr. Abrams often and this made him happy.

Mr. Abrams became the new principle and Thomas, the class president.

Jasper, through much time and rest, healed from his wounds. You didn't think he was dead did you? No sir. He was as vibrant and springy as always. He was really hurt but he recovered just fine. He still walked with a bit of a limp and wasn't as fast as he used to be but he was still the biggest dog you ever would see. He was battle tested too so most dogs and people for that matter stayed clear of him. He was no less defensive of Mary or Thomas, however, because this danger was past. He was still highly protective of both. Soon he would be most defensive of Little Laura. That's right Thomas' baby sister. Little Laura she was called and fitting I think. He would sleep by her crib every night until she got big enough for a bed. Then he would sleep at the foot of her bed. Sometimes though, she would let him jump up and sleep next to her. He liked that, often licking her face with his rough tongue, driving her into a fit of giggles. She would put her small arm over him and he would keep her warm through the cold winter nights. Jasper was always on guard; nothing would get at Little Laura. Nothing. Little Laura was Jasper's new favorite, and it pleased Thomas very much.

Mary and Brenda became very close and her mother grew to except Thomas as Mary's true love. Thomas was often invited to stay over or have dinner with Mary and Brenda. This made Thomas very happy indeed. Brenda needed no more proof that Thomas was right for Mary. In fact she wished she would find someone just like him. Enter Bobby. Bobby and Brenda hit it off and they began a long and fruitful relationship. Brenda had lots of money and was content to let Bobby just work around the house to earn his keep. If he didn't earn it during the day he surely did in the quiet whisperings of the night. So all was well at the home front.

Jerry Collins became sheriff and was very well respected. He also purchased the Railway Pub and turned it into a pizza house.

As time wore on and the moons passed through the sky, the little town in Central Massachusetts got back to its normal routine.

The first whistle was finished for the year and the other seasonal businesses closed up for the winter also.

Everything was pretty much, back to normal, well as close as can be expected after such a happening.

Let me tell you how Little Laura came into the picture and eventually home with the Morgan's. When Bobby, Thomas and Mary went to the hospital to take their first looks at a healthy six-pound baby girl, Thomas was awfully nervous. He didn't know how he was supposed to act around a new baby, let alone his new sister. He would have to raise her as if he was her father now and this caused him to be apprehensive in seeing her. If not a father then a very protective 'Biggest Brother.'

After all he had been through, this was the feat that made him most tense.

When they arrived at the hospital, Bobby spoke to the nurse on duty. She knew Bobby, and also had a crush on him, so she showed Thomas and Mary his baby sister in the maternity ward right away. Bobby had to agree to a date with Stacy, but it didn't take much convincing. She was young and very attractive and with a slight twist of the arm he relented. She didn't enter the ward because she wanted to flirt with Bobby who was waiting back at her desk in the main hall. Bobby would forgo this date though in honor of his relationship with Brenda. See so things had changed. Even Bobby was becoming responsible and mature, if not faithful too.

Thomas and Mary went into the baby quarters and saw that all the infants were crying. Thomas' sister was whaling the hardest. Thomas went to her and put his pinky finger in her tiny hand, but she continued on with her screaming. Mary instinctively picked the tiny prize up and rocked her in her arms. Thomas' sister immediately stopped her crying. Mary opened up her blouse and let the baby suckle on her breast. She didn't have much in the way of milk but the baby was content to have the motherly touch, and her warmth. Lots of times a baby just needs to know someone is there. The other babies stopped their crying as well.

Thomas was moved in adoration for Mary. He knew at that very moment that he would spend the rest of his life serving her every wish. Actually it just reconfirmed it for he knew a long time ago that his life partner was Mary.

They took Little Laura home that day and she grew bigger and wiser every day. She liked to ride Jasper as though he were a horse. She had a cute little laugh and Mary loved to feed her and dress her up. Thomas named her before they arrived home from the hospital and he only thought it appropriate to name her Laura.

A few nights after Little Laura had been brought home and settled in to her new home Mary came calling and had a surprise for Thomas.

Bobby went out on a date with Brenda to the local theater and she dropped Mary off at the Morgan home and she called on Thomas.

Mary fed little Laura, and put her off to bed.

Thomas jumped in the shower and cleaned himself up.

Mary came back to Thomas' room as he was getting dressed into sweats and a T-shirt. She stood in the doorway with only a bra and panties. The black lingerie was a nice contrast to her light skin and strawberry blonde hair, which she had in twin pigtails.

Thomas' jaw dropped wide open.

Mary slowly paced her way to Thomas who stood fast against his bed. He dropped the T-shirt that he was about to put on before being struck immobile.

She came right up to him and he bent down to kiss her. She pretended to want to kiss him too, but at the last moment, she pushed him back on the bed. He lay there with eyes wide open. She climbed up on the bed and stood over him. He could see the moist crease in her panties and he started to get excited. He pitched a tent in his sweatpants and she giggled.

"What's this Tommy? Didn't get all the starch out of your clothes?" She asked playfully.

He blushed.

She kneeled on the bed and dragged her fingertips over the sweat material.

It cried for want to be released. She pulled his pants down and looked at it in the light.

"It looks hungry." Mary said with a laugh.

She bent her head down to it and kissed the tip.

It jumped.

She giggled again.

Then she put him in her mouth and Thomas groaned with delight. Ten seconds more and he loosed his semen and it shot down her throat. She swallowed all of it.

"MMMMM. Tastes salty and sweet." Mary proclaimed. "Love it." She added.

He was still fully erect, actually more than he was moments before. She removed her panties and straddled him. She was squatting over him and she let herself down easy on him.

A hint of pain went through her face, and Thomas was alarmed.

"Am I hurting you?" He asked in fright.

"Yes, but I wouldn't have it any other way." Mary responded. He put his hands up on her solid breasts and she rode them both into climax. Mary fell off him and rolled over on the bed.

Jasper came to the door and saw what they were about. Jasper turned his body around to face down the hall. He would guard his masters against any evil, now and until his death.

Thomas rolled over on top of Mary and she felt his hardness between her thighs again.

"Again?" She asked. "How many more times?" She added.

"Many." He assured her.

June 12 around 4 a.m.

At Umass hospital a woman in the delivery room was giving birth.

"UUUHHHH!" Went the pregnant woman.

"Breath, Breath!" The nurse came back.

"UUUHHHH!" "SWOOO WOOO SWOOO." She breathed.

"AWOO, AWOO, AWOO." That's it encouraged the nurse.

"Here it comes. Almost there." The nurse shouted.

"OOOOOOOHHHHHH!" Cried the expecting mother.

"One more push." The nurse encouraged.

"Push, Dana, Push."

Would you like to see your manuscript become a book?

If you are interested in becoming a PublishAmerica author, please submit your manuscript for possible publication to us at:

acquisitions@publishamerica.com

You may also mail in your manuscript to:

**PublishAmerica
PO Box 151
Frederick, MD 21705**

www.publishamerica.com

CPSIA information can be obtained at www.ICGtesting.com
Printed in the USA
244563LV00002B/29/P

9 781462 613564